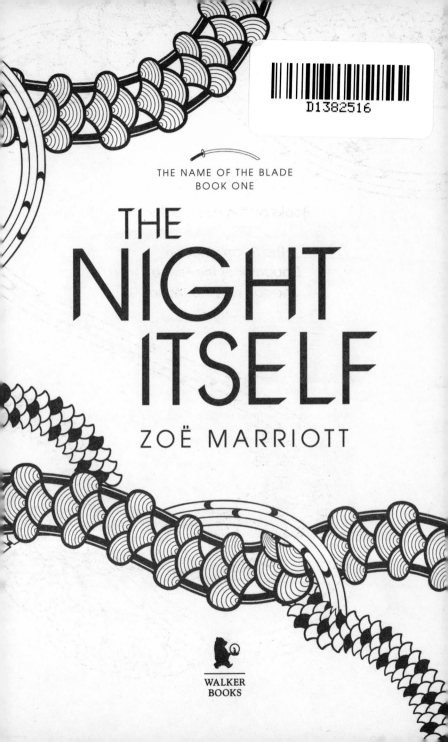

THE NAME OF THE BLADE
BOOK ONE

THE
NIGHT
ITSELF

ZOË MARRIOTT

WALKER
BOOKS

First published 2013 by Walker Books Ltd
87 Vauxhall Walk, London SE11 5HJ

2 4 6 8 10 9 7 5 3 1

Text © 2013 Zoë Marriott
Cover illustration © 2013 Andrew Archer at début art

The right of Zoë Marriott to be identified as author of this work has been asserted by her in accordance with the Copyright, Designs and Patents Act 1988

This book has been typeset in Berkeley

Printed and bound in Great Britain by Clays Ltd, St Ives plc

British Library Cataloguing in Publication Data:
a catalogue record for this book is available from the British Library

ISBN 978-1-4063-4238-3

www.walker.co.uk

PRAISE FOR

THE NIGHT ITSELF

"Japanese mythology meets urban awesomeness (and a swoon-worthy romance!). *The Night Itself* captivated me."
L. A. Weatherly, *author of the Angel trilogy*

"Mio is a wonderful heroine who reminded me of some of my favourite superhero characters, and her connection with Shinobu is touching and believable. The Japanese mythology was refreshing, and I absolutely cannot wait for the next book in the series!"
Karen Mahoney, *author of The Iron Witch Trilogy* and Falling to Ash

"A beautiful, awe-inspiring ride through an iconic London landscape harbouring extremely dangerous secrets. *The Night Itself* is a fantastic blend of Japanese folk tale and twenty-first-century thriller, populated by characters you will be rooting for at every breathless step."
Katy Moran, *author of* Hidden Among Us

"I fell in love with sassy, courageous, wise-cracking Mio from page one."
Ruth Warburton, *author of The Winter Trilogy*

Books by the same author

For Tina Rath and Rachel Carthy,
who provided the spark and the kindling that lit
the flame of inspiration that became this book

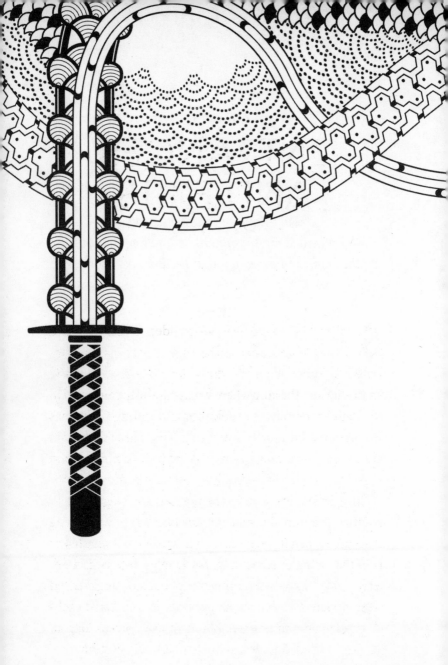

CHAPTER 1

ENTRANCES AND EXITS

Stealing the sword was a bad idea. I can't pretend I didn't realize that at the time. I wasn't even supposed to know about the thing, let alone sneak up and snaffle it from the attic where it was carefully concealed in the dark, under layers of cobwebs and rotting Christmas decorations. I was fully aware that if my father found out about the sword or about me taking it, he'd pop a blood vessel from sheer fury and kill me. Or die. Maybe both.

If your family's priceless heirloom is some ugly vase or painting, like on the *Antiques Roadshow*, the worst thing that can happen if you mess with it is that you'll smash it or ruin the patina or something. My family's antique is a different story. Sixty-two centimetres of curved, single-edged steel, designed with a single purpose: to kill. You'd probably call it a samurai sword. But its proper name is katana.

And I needed it for my Christmas party costume.

Since it was the first day after school broke up for the Christmas holidays, Jack had persuaded me out to the shops to help her get a few final bits and pieces that she needed for her fancy-dress outfit. We should have known better. Wailing hordes of desperate, last-minute holiday shoppers had clogged the public transport system like too many bacon cheeseburgers in an artery. Considering that I'd got about half an hour's sleep the night before, I was not in the mood to fight my way through them. But I didn't have any choice. I couldn't be late. When I crashed through my front door, my gaze shot straight to the foot of the staircase and I sagged with relief when I saw that the pile of luggage was still there.

"We seriously needed to run all the way from the station?" Jack asked as she elbowed past me. She dropped her bags on the chequer-pattern tiles and staggered dramatically into the hall to collapse in one of the chairs that sat either side of the phone stand, undoing the buttons on her coat as she went. "Didn't you give your mum a hug before you left this morning?"

"Look, I need to reinforce their mission statement, OK?" I said, kicking Jack's shoulder bag out of the way and then dropping mine on top of it. "They're going to be in *Paris* on my birthday, Jack. Paris. Opportunities for those kinds of presents don't fall in my lap every day."

"Yeah, right." Jack gave me a knowing look as she leaned her head against the yellow wall, but didn't say any more. That's one of the reasons why Jack is my best friend. She nearly always knows what I'm thinking, but she doesn't always have to prove it. Plus, anyone who wears their hair in a two-inch-long, bleached-white pixie cut with hot pink and purple streaks in the front is someone with serious guts, and I respect guts. I needed them, growing up in this house.

"Mio!"

I turned round just in time to steady myself on the banister as I received a hug that would otherwise have knocked me flat on my back.

"You managed to get home in time," Mum said. "I thought I was going to have to leave without saying goodbye properly."

She squeezed me until my ribs creaked. Mum might be a puny five-foot tall – three inches shorter than me – but she is strong. Probably from heaving teeth out of people's jaws all day long. Yep, she's a dentist. Looking at her, with her sweet, young face and her soft waves of black hair, you'd never imagine that she was capable of inflicting pain on people for profit. I suppose it's because she doesn't see it that way; she just wants to help people and make them feel better, and she does. It's her thing.

I leaned into her, breathing in her special mum-smell

as I hugged her back. Just for an eye-blink the words hovered on my lips: *Don't go without me. I don't want to be alone on my birthday...*

"If Mio would just answer her mobile once in a while you wouldn't have had to be in such a panic," a voice said acidly from the top of the stairs.

I sucked the pleading words back down my throat as I straightened up away from Mum. "Hi, Dad."

My father is definitely the dentist type. Either that or a traffic warden. Some profession where you can take pleasure in making other people miserable anyway.

"Hello, Mr Yamato," Jack chimed in cheerfully. "Sorry we didn't phone. The bus was packed, so we went on the Tube, and once we got off it didn't seem worth it."

"It doesn't matter," my mum said, letting me go as Dad stalked down the stairs. "You got home—"

"With a generous three minutes to spare," Dad interrupted. "Perhaps I should mark it on my calendar."

"Takashi, would you stop?" Mum chided.

He sighed, leaning on the newel post. "Fine, go on."

Mum turned back to me. "You're home, which means I can ask you if you're really sure you don't mind being alone on your birthday. Because I've got your passport. We could try to get you a last-minute ticket."

Yes, please! But there was no chance in hell of me saying it. Not with my dad standing right there, broadcasting doom at me. I knew exactly how much he didn't want me around. *Who cares? I don't want to be around him either.*

"Um, no offence?" I said. "But trailing behind while your parents make with the kissy-kissy in the world's most romantic city is not a teenage daughter's dream, you know."

"Besides, Mimi's not going to be alone," Jack broke in. "Me and Rachel will make sure she has a great birthday, Mrs Yamato. Promise."

Mum still didn't look convinced. Her scrunched-up expression reminded me of the gerbil we used to look after in nursery school. I know most fifteen-year-old girls fight with their mothers nonstop, but my mum is just too nice to fight with. Seriously, even my father can't manage it. And none of this was her fault. It was all my dad's idea.

I plastered on my best happy face. "Stop this crazy talk, Mum. It's your second honeymoon – the whole point is to be alone with each other. But don't think I'm letting you off easy. You have to buy me amazing presents. Boots. Hats. Coats. Everything. And then we can open them together on Christmas Day and it will be the best ever, all right?"

My dad cracked an actual smile at that. Well, he was getting his own way, wasn't he? I caught his eye and defiantly raked back the short length of my hair. The smile instantly transformed into his usual scowl. He'd barely stopped frowning since I'd gone out two weeks before – the same day he broke the news about his wonderful second-honeymoon plan – and got my hair, which had been nearly as long as Mum's, cut into a sleek, graduated bob that just skimmed my chin.

It's not that he's one of those guys who think women need to be able to sit on their hair. Trust me when I say that my father is *not* traditional. We don't celebrate any Japanese holidays or even eat Japanese food, and the only Japanese words I know come from kendo and watching anime. Dad's lack of interest in our heritage used to drive Ojiichan – my grandfather – up the wall, and is probably why Ojiichan was so determined to enrol me in kendo. No, what bothers my dad is that I cut my hair *without asking permission*. He's dead keen on that. Like making me beg for his blessing before I'm allowed to breathe is going to ensure I ask permission before I run off and get pregnant or something.

"Aiko, we really need to leave now," Dad said brusquely, heaving up a couple of bags. "The taxi's here. We're going to be late."

"Nag." Mum's smile was teasing. "Give your daughter a hug and a kiss first. We're not going to see her for a whole week, you know."

Dad heaved a deep sigh, then put the bags down as if the effort was exhausting and walked back towards me. He put one arm around my shoulder and tugged me against him in a quick, hard hug. Dad-smell, a blend of whiskers and aftershave and wool – entirely different from Mum's, but somehow still comforting even though my dad isn't – wrapped around me. His lips brushed the top of my head. "Take care, Midget Gem."

"Not a midget," I muttered. But next to him I was, and probably always would be. Dad's tall for an Asian guy, nearly six feet.

Before I could even decide if I was going to hug him back, the taxi's horn honked outside. Dad let go and hustled my mother towards the door, scooping up the bags as he went. Mum dragged the wheelie suitcase with her.

"Emergency numbers in your mobile, spare money in the tin in the kitchen, no loud music, no parties, no late nights, do your homework," Dad chanted as Jack and I followed them to where the taxi was waiting. "Rachel's making you dinner upstairs."

"Bye!" my mum managed to get out before Dad climbed in after her and slammed the car door shut.

Jack and I waved as the taxi pulled out from the kerb, brake lights winking, and then disappeared round the corner. I blew out a long breath, running my hand through my hair. The shorter length still felt strange, and the back of my neck was cold. *Really couldn't wait to get away, could he?*

Jack let me have a minute and then punched me in the shoulder. "Come on. It's cold out here and we've got a party to get ready for."

I went up the steps to our house, grabbed our bags, snapped off the lights, and then came back outside again, slamming the front door behind me so that the dead-bolt snapped home. Then we headed round the side of the building to the entrance of Jack's flat. Jack, her older sister, Rachel, and their mother, Beatrice, live on the top floor of the building that my parents own. It's a three-storey Georgian townhouse, and from the outside it looks like a posh doctor's, solicitor's or dentist's – which it is. A dentist's, I mean. The basement floor is my parents' joint practice, which has a separate entrance round the side with a little brass plate next to it. The two middle floors are where we live. The separate flat that used to be my grandfather's now belongs to Jack and her family. It has its own entrance, leading to the old servants' staircase.

Ojiichan bought the building when he came to London in the mid-seventies to set up his revolutionary hygienic dental surgery. He was actually kind of a celebrity dentist, back in the day. He did a filling for Laurence Olivier once, and that red-headed chick who was in *The King and I*. When Ojiichan died six years ago, Beatrice Luci, who is my parents' head dental nurse and practice manager, was divorcing Rachel and Jack's dad, and was struggling to find somewhere to live. So my parents offered her the top-floor flat at a cheap rate. That way they didn't need to worry about renting it to strangers, or losing their best employee. And somehow I gained a best friend in the process.

Not that Jack and me weren't friendly before that. We'd always gone to the same dojo, which was cool. But once she moved in, we went to the same school, too – though not in the same class – and we started hanging out all the time. I suppose, in a weird way, Jack filled the hole that Ojiichan left. Until I gave kendo up a year ago she even used to come to my matches and cheer me on, like Ojiichan did.

"When your parents get back, I'm seriously going to start petitioning for a lift," Jack panted, wrestling with her shopping bags as she went up the stairs ahead of me.

"Stop being a drama queen," I said. I was panting for real, but I knew Jack was putting it on. She still goes to karate twice a week and she has muscles on her muscles. "You run up and down these stairs all the time for training. You like being the fittest girl in school."

Jack wiggled her backside, in its purple denim miniskirt, in my face. "Why, thank you, cutie."

"In your dreams, Luci," I said.

Jack laughed like I knew she would. I'm not her type.

We got to the top of the stairs and Jack pushed open the door to her flat. Immediately the smell of tomato, garlic and melting cheese rushed out and made my mouth water.

"Hmm. Lasagne…" I said. I shoved my bag into the little cupboard next to the door, then toed my trainers off and put them in too. Both Rachel and her mum are neat freaks and you don't just drop your stuff wherever in their place.

Unless you're Jack. She flung her shoulder bag and shopping bags across the room onto the sofa, kicked off her ankle boots in opposite directions and pointed one of her short, black-polished fingernails at me. "Don't even think about it, Mimi. You are not coming out with me if you have garlic breath."

"But I haven't eaten anything since breakfast. I could brush my teeth twice," I offered.

"No. We don't have time. You haven't even finished your costume yet. We're in and out, OK? Maybe Rachel'll put some in the fridge for you."

"You're heartless."

"Like that's news to anyone. Stop whining."

Rachel poked her head out of the kitchen, a baguette in her hand. She pointed it at Jack. Pointing is a Luci-family thing. Beatrice does it too, only she's usually holding a sharp dental instrument, so it's considerably scarier.

"Are you bullying Mio again?" Rachel demanded. The warm light from the kitchen made her pale brown skin glow, and her long, toffee-coloured hair – the same colour as Jack's before she bleached it – gleam. Jack and Rachel's grandmother was from Barbados, which means they both have an amazing all-year-round golden tan. Unlike me. According to the manga I read, if I lived in Japan, my naturally pale skin would be totally sexy. Shame it only counts as pasty in the UK.

"No," Jack said.

"Yes." I did my pitiful expression. "She won't let me have any dinner."

Behind trendy square glasses, Rachel narrowed her eyes at her sister. "If you're thinking of developing an eating disorder, you'd better know right now that I will intervention your ass off, Jacqueline." Rachel is a graduate psychology student. She likes to work that into the conversation as often as she can.

"Oh, save it," Jack said, yawning for effect. "We're just in a rush, that's all. We've got a party to go to."

Rachel's eyes narrowed even more. "Mr and Mrs Yamato didn't say anything about a party."

"It's all right," I said, playing good cop. "They do know about it. It's an end-of-term, fancy-dress disco thing. And, to be fair, there'll probably be stuff to eat there anyway."

Rachel's suspicious look eased in the face of my smile. I do a very good innocent smile. Beatrice and Rachel love it. They think I'm a Sweet Normal Girl and a Positive Influence on Goth Rebel Jack. Poor naïve ladies.

"But I cooked," Rachel said, gesturing with the bread again.

"I'm so sorry. I didn't realize," I said. The distress in my voice was real. Rachel's lasagne is not to be sacrificed lightly. "Could we warm it up later? I'd hate it to go to waste."

"We—eell … all right." Rachel shot Jack a sharp look. "But your curfew is still in effect, and if you're even five minutes late, I *will* call Mother."

Jack gulped. Beatrice was taking advantage of my parents' trip to enjoy a relaxing week off herself, in a pampering spa in Cornwall. She'd left that morning. If she had to surface from her hot mud bath to deal with Jack, there would be consequences. The kind that made dental treatment look like jolly good fun.

"I'll make sure we're home before eleven," I said, lying through my teeth.

Rachel was squashing in a part-time job around her studies and Jack had told me that her sister had been up at five-thirty the past three mornings. She would be dead to the world by ten; a nuclear bomb-blast would just make her mutter and pull a pillow over her head.

"Good." Rachel started to go into the kitchen, then turned back. "Hey, what are you going as?"

"I'm a Fairy Gothmother," Jack said, striking a pose.

"Somehow I guessed that one," Rachel drawled. "I meant Mio."

"Oh, I'm going as an anime character," I said. "Rukia from *Bleach*. I'm going to wear my old kendo uniform."

Rachel frowned. "Doesn't that character wear a sword?"

"I've got my wooden practice one," I said calmly.

It was true. I did have it.

I just wasn't going to wear it to the party that night.

CHAPTER 2

ONE WHO
IS HIDDEN

I've been having the Dream for a long, long time. Since I was a kid. It wasn't often in the beginning: once a year, maybe twice. It wasn't my favourite thing, but it wasn't – I didn't let it be – a big deal. Not until this last year. That's when the Dream got really bad.

In the six weeks before my sixteenth birthday I was lucky if I could get through a single night without starting upright in the bed, flinging my duvet and pillows away as if they were on fire – fighting to get up, get away, go, go—

Where?

I'd make it out of the bed, my feet would touch the bedroom carpet – and just like that everything would be gone. Gone, like it had never been in my head to begin with. All I had left to show I'd dreamed at all was a face covered in drying tears and this terrible feeling that someone needed me. Someone needed me to find them, hold onto them, hold on tight—

Who?

I never knew, and that was driving me crazy. *I couldn't remember.*

Sleep deprivation does funny things to a person. After nearly two months of this, night after night after night, I was getting desperate to understand why the Dream kept coming back and what it was about. I was sure that if I could just figure out what I was dreaming, if I just knew who I was supposed to find or where I was supposed to go, the Dream would have to leave me in peace. Right?

But the more I thought, the more I picked at it, the more I *needed* to remember … the more I was plagued with another memory. That day with my grandfather. That last day.

I was nearly ten years old, and it was summer. I was dressed in shorts and a T-shirt, and my hair – it was long and unruly then – was tied back tightly so it wouldn't fall in my face. The greyish grass in our little postage stamp of a garden crunched and shredded under my bare feet, tickling my nose with that perfect-school holiday smell as I glided forward into the *okuri-ashi*, the most basic kendo movement. The shadow of the big old mulberry bush next to the garage wall fell over me as I shifted across the grass, but the chill was nothing compared to the weight of Ojiichan's eyes. He wouldn't miss anything. He never did.

I concentrated on keeping the line of my shinai – a light wooden practice sword – perfectly straight as I repeated the graceful, slow movement again, again, again… The last one had to be as perfect as the first, even if Ojiichan made me do it twenty times, a hundred times. That was the whole point.

"*Yame!*" my grandfather said. It meant "Stop."

I lowered the shinai and brought my feet back together, turning to look at him anxiously. He tapped his chin with one finger – he was thinking. "Good. Light on your feet, controlled, graceful… Better than your father was at your age."

I wrinkled my nose. I was pretty sure Winnie-the-Pooh would be better at kendo than my dad. Ojiichan saw my expression and his laughter spilled over, rich and golden and sweet, like the honey that my mum drizzled in porridge on cold days. His eyes crinkled at the corners, their darkness bright with smiling light. He leapt forward in a lightning-fast pounce – not like other granddads, with bent backs and wobbly knees – careful to fold the shinai out of the way so that it didn't hurt either of us as he lifted me up and hugged me.

"Good girl," he whispered into my hair.

"There you are, Mio!" My father's deep voice broke into the moment. "I've been looking all over the place for you."

I felt the sigh heave through Ojiichan's chest as he let

me slide back down to the ground. Tension rumbled in the air above my head, like low thunderclouds waiting to burst.

Don't fight. Please don't fight.

Before I could say anything, Ojiichan answered. "She woke up early, so I made her breakfast and brought her out for a little practice. You had only to look through the window to find us."

"It's nine o'clock on a Saturday morning. Most kids would be watching cartoons or, I don't know, spending time with their parents." My dad's voice had that funny, rough note it only got when he was talking to my grandfather. Like one of the boys from school trying to sound all grown-up.

"Daddy, you were still in bed. I wanted to practise." I meant my voice to come out strong and calm, like Ojiichan's, but instead it was small and wobbly.

My father sighed. "Wouldn't you like a day off once in a while? What if we go to see Auntie Fumi today, how about that?"

Auntie Fumi made cakes and let me lick the spoon, and she had a silly, fluffy dog that loved to chase sticks in her big garden. Guilt squirmed in my belly. "But I promised Ojiichan."

"Father…" That rough, angry note in Daddy's voice was back, louder than before.

"What?" My grandfather cut him off, a little too

sharply, a little too loudly. It was starting again.

I wanted to put both hands over my ears. Instead I stood still and squeezed my eyes shut, wishing I had the shinai back in my hands. If I had my practice blade I would chop and slash at the air, slicing up imaginary monsters until I felt tired and calm and peaceful inside.

Why are they always fighting? What am I doing wrong? Why do I make them both so angry all the time?

Stop fighting! Stop! STOP IT!

"She is my daughter, not yours," my father growled. "If you keep pushing, we'll leave. Then you won't see Mio at all. Think about that."

The kitchen door slamming made me jump. My father was gone and Ojiichan's head was bent as if he was upset, but his eyes were burning. He looked the way I'd felt when I scored my first kendo hit – as if he didn't know whether to yell or laugh or maybe even cry. He lifted the shinai and tossed it to me.

My hand shot up to catch it.

"Zenshin Kotai Okuri-Ashi!"

I responded automatically to the command, my body melting into the forms I had practised every day since Ojiichan had signed me up for kendo when I was five.

A while later we heard the garage door go up on the other side of the garden wall and then the deep roar of the car's engine. I waited for the next instruction to come from Ojiichan, but he stood perfectly still, his head held

24

slightly to one side as if he was listening. I tried to hear what he could, but all I could make out were the normal, dull London sounds and Mum and Dad's car getting quieter and quieter.

When the sound of the engine had faded completely, Ojiichan sprang to life. "Quickly, Mio. Come with me."

As I tagged along faithfully behind him, my grandfather nipped into the empty garage, taking a metal prybar out of the box of tools there. Then we went back into the house and climbed the stairs to the attic.

I'd never been in there before, because Dad said it was dangerous. It didn't look dangerous. But it was dark, and cobwebby, and unpleasantly cold after the bright sunshine outside. Ojiichan left me by the door while he waded through piles of boxes and broken furniture. I stood very still, worried about what creepy-crawlies might be on the floorboards – I was still barefoot – and rubbed goose-pimply arms.

"Got it!" he whispered.

He'd found a tatty old metal box, covered in peeling white paint. The paint was streaked with dark, bubbling marks, like burns. Long and thin, probably taller than me if it was stood on its end, the box had been shoved out of the way in the space under the sloping attic window.

That? That's what we came all the way up here for?

Ojiichan heaved it out, sending up clouds of dust that made him cough and sputter, but didn't stop him from using the pry-bar to bust off the massive padlock holding the box closed. The shriek of metal seemed to echo around the dim space for hours as he bent to open the lid. His tall, lean body went utterly still again for a moment. This was a different kind of stillness. I couldn't say how I knew that. I just did.

Finally Ojiichan let out a long sigh. He folded himself down in front of the box and turned his head and beckoned to me. All the tension – tension I hadn't even really noticed before – was gone out of his face. Lines smoothed away. Eyes lit up not with laughter but something else that I didn't know the name for. He looked completely relaxed. Happy.

"Mio, come here, love. Come and see this."

I gingerly picked my way towards him, trying to squash a disloyal feeling that playing in Auntie Fumi's garden with Benjy would have been way more fun than this. I peered over his shoulder. All I could see were layers and layers of thin, brittle-looking fabric starting to go yellow with age and covered in faded embroidery. The embroidered words were Japanese, I thought, although I couldn't read them. What was it? A dress, maybe? Why would Ojiichan care about that?

"What is it?" My voice, bouncing off the low ceiling, sounded too loud.

He reached into the box and folded back the material.

And everything changed.

Drifting dust turned to gold in the shafts of sun coming through the dirty skylight. The air around me – the *insides* of me – filled with a high, musical singing that made my hair stand on end and my bones hum and my veins tingle. I knew exactly what I was looking at. A Japanese long sword.

Katana…

"Do you like him?" Ojiichan asked.

I nodded wordlessly, my heart stuttering so fast it was hard to breathe.

"Would you like to hold him?"

I nodded again.

Ojiichan lifted the glittering black-and-gold shape out of the box. He carefully eased the curving black sheath, covered with golden flowers, from the blade. "Careful now, Mio. He's heavy. That's right, both hands together."

The sword should have been cold, but it wasn't. The black silk hilt wrappings were warm against my chilled palms. Warm as a living thing.

"Oh," I sighed. "It's so… It's … beautiful." Beautiful wasn't the right word. But I didn't have the right word for what it was.

The singing inside me reached out, and I could feel the sword respond to it. The metal started to sing too, throwing the feeling back to me until my whole body resounded with it. Energy pulsed where my hands gripped the hilt – pulsed with the same rhythm as my heart.

"He is yours, Mio," Ojiichan said.

Mine?

It felt like the time I'd pushed the roundabout too fast and gone flying off, only this time instead of landing with a hard, painful bump and skinning my elbows and knees, I carried on flying. Ojiichan put a steadying arm around my shoulders, telling me it was all right, it was all right, it would pass in a minute, just breathe...

"This sword has been in the Yamato family for five hundred years," he said. His voice was barely a whisper, even though there was no one to overhear us. "He has been passed from one Yamato heir to the next on their sixteenth birthday, without fail, for nearly ten generations. This sword is the greatest treasure and the greatest burden of our family."

Treasure? Mum and Dad had taken me to see the Crown Jewels once. I would have swapped every pretty, glittery jewel in those glass cases for what I held in my hands now. But what was so amazing was that I didn't have to. Because this was ours. It belonged to us. To *me*.

Mine.

Even with Ojiichan holding me and the tip of the blade resting against the edge of the metal box, my arms were already trembling. My muscles burned. But I could not – would not – let go.

Ojiichan was speaking again: "We don't know everything about the sword, but we do have some stories that were passed down along with him. I will tell you those soon. For now, know that he is very powerful. There are others – bad people, bad things – who search for him. They must never, never find him. It is our honour to keep him safe. Our purpose. That is very important. He is the *One who remembers*. The *One who endures*. The *One who is hidden*. He must always be hidden. You are your father's only child; the Hidden One will be yours when you are sixteen years old. Yours to guard and protect."

Mine!

"You mustn't tell anyone about the sword," Ojiichan was saying. "And you must never, never touch him – not even look at him – unless I am here. Not until you're sixteen. Not for any reason. Do you understand? Mio? Look at me. Look at me!"

I turned wide, blurry eyes up to him. "I—"

"Promise me on my life, on your mother's life, on your own life." He cupped my cheek in one of his warm, papery cool hands. "Swear to me that you will keep the sword hidden, no matter what. You will not come back here for him without me. You will never speak of this to your father. If you can keep those promises, the sword will be yours when you are sixteen."

He wouldn't make me swear unless it was important. If it was important, then I had to do what he said. "I–I promise."

Ojiichan never did get to tell me his stories. He never got to take me back into the attic again.

And I had the Dream for the first time that night.

There were times when I nearly forgot about that day. Bad stuff happened afterwards, memories that I wanted to forget. It would have been easier to lump it all together and just let it fade away. But every time I was in danger of forgetting my grandfather's promise to me, every time the memory of our family's secret treasure was beginning to blur and distort with time...

The Dream would come back.

In these last two months before my sixteenth birthday, the Dream had tormented and teased me until I felt like I was going crazy. The more I struggled to remember, the more easily it slipped away. But the Dream made me remember those other things so clearly. My grandfather. His promise to me. The sword...

Even though I'd not touched it since the day my grandfather first showed it to me – not even dared to enter the attic on my own, let alone open the box – I still wanted it.

The closer I got to my birthday the stronger that wanting became.

I knew it didn't make sense. I was scared of how irrational and how powerful my feelings were. It was just some dusty old heirloom. Ojiichan was dead and no one else knew about it, or cared. I shouldn't care. What if

I marched up there right now? So what? No one would notice. I'd look at it for five minutes, then close the box and walk away again. It was a sword. Just an old sword. Why couldn't I stop thinking about it?

Why couldn't I stop remembering that I was nearly sixteen and *it was supposed to be mine*?

When you wanted something that badly, all the cogs in the back of your brain started working together to convince you that it was OK – sensible, even logical – to take it. Then we got invited to Natalie Depaul's Christmas thing and in the middle of arguing with Jack about costumes, suddenly there it was. The perfect costume, and the excuse I needed to do the stupid thing I knew, deep down, I really shouldn't do.

So that was why, half an hour after leaving Rachel in her mum's kitchen, Jack and I were both in our costumes, hair done, make-up on – sneaking upstairs to the attic.

"You don't have to come with me," I said, casting a look at Jack's outfit. It wasn't exactly designed for cat-burglary. She was wearing a black bustier with fluffy, black wings strapped over her shoulders, a pink, puffball skirt, pink-and-black stripy tights and black biker boots. Jack never did anything halfway. But at least it meant no one was going to be staring at me in my kendogi. Kendogi are pretty low-key because they're designed for ease of movement and comfort and basically consist of a pair of ultra-wide-legged, pleated trousers – black, in my case – and a short, kimono-style top, also black. I'd tied a white, silk scarf around my waist, and I had my red shinai carrier looped over my shoulder. I thought I looked pretty good, even if my hair was a little too short to be a classic Rukia. Although it was annoying to realize that the old uniform still fitted me perfectly. Why couldn't my chest have expanded a bit in the last year?

"Don't worry, Maverick. I got your back."

"Oh my God. Jack, *Top Gun* quotes are not cool, OK?"

"Sez you," Jack shot back as we reached the top of the stairs. "You're the one who's going out dressed as an anime character."

"Touché. Now will you please stay out here? I can brush pretty much anything off my costume, but if you get dust and gloopy cobwebs on yours you're going to look less Fairy Gothmother and more Emo Girl."

"Perish the thought." Jack leaned against the wall and crossed her arms as I eased the squeaky attic door open. "Hey, if you've still got your shinai, why are you stealing this old sword from the attic? You know no one at the party is going to care if you've got a real sword or not, right?"

I hesitated. Jack didn't know about the Dream. No one did. It was too weird. Too … *personal.* Anyway, nothing she said was going to make a difference. Not now.

"First off, it's not stealing. Ojiichan gave me the sword, totally fair and square. Second, it's beautiful and it's going to make my costume look amazing. And third, I just…" My voice trailed off.

"Just what?"

"I want it, OK? It's *mine*." I snapped my mouth shut.

Jack's dark eyebrows went up. "Whoa. Getting a little intense there, Mimi."

Since I couldn't really defend myself, I settled for sticking my tongue out at her. Then I walked into the attic, snapping on the single, bare overhead bulb. "Fourth of all, shut up and keep watch. I don't want Rachel snooping around me."

The heavy door groaned shut behind me.

I'd been up in the attic a few times since Ojiichan brought me here, helping Mum fetch down decorations or bits of furniture. It wasn't spooky, even if it was dusty. I knew what everything was; that twisty shape on the left was a hat rack that used to be in the waiting room in the basement, the grey jumble under the window was my crib, filled with old toys that I'd grown out of early. I edged between the cobwebby leftovers of Yamato family life, drawn unerringly to what looked like an empty space in the corner under the window, where the roof sloped down.

Cautiously – because despite what I'd said to Jack, I didn't want to spend twenty minutes getting dust off me – I crouched and reached out into the shadows, my fingers searching, searching…

There.

Cold metal, peeling paint. A dangling padlock on a jagged, broken latch.

"Got it," I whispered as I pulled the box out.

Excitement and guilt warred inside me. I took a couple of deep breaths, aware that my hands were trembling. *One who remembers. One who endures. One who is hidden.* Ojiichan's voice rang in my head. *Promise me. Your father must never know...*

Dad's on the Eurostar by now, I told myself firmly, forcing my shaking fingers to curve around the top of the box. *You aren't breaking any promises. He won't ever know. It's fine.*

I'm practically sixteen.

I've waited six years.

The sword is mine.

I flung the lid back, ignoring the rattle as the broken padlock fell to the floor. A tingling, ringing sensation thrilled through my body. I plunged my hands inside the box, scrabbling back the layers of stiffly embroidered silk. My fingers closed over smooth, lacquered wood.

"Mine..." The word sighed out of me.

His saya – the blade sheath – was black lacquer inlaid with delicate golden cherry blossoms that drifted across the surface as if they'd been scattered there in a spring breeze. The grip was black too. Golden handle ornaments – menuki – in the shape of cherry blossoms, peeked through the intricately folded silk wrappings on the hilt. The guard was circular, pierced with the shapes of cherry blossoms, as was the hilt cap.

He – Ojiichan had called the sword "He" – was beautiful. So beautiful. So beautiful. *Mine.*

For a long, breathless moment I held him between my hands, as shivers of excitement tightened my skin. Then, shaky and tense, I drew the saya from the blade.

The cutting edge was shining silver, almost too bright to look at. Long, flame-shaped ripples marked the many folds in the metal, shading up to deep black on the mune, or blunt edge. Both sides of the katana were marked by a long groove. People called it the blood-letting groove, but its purpose was to make the sword both light and strong. When a warrior struck with perfect precision, he would hear three whistles from the blade. One from the cutting edge slicing through the air and two from the air moving along the grooves.

I gently laid the saya down and took the katana in a proper grip, grasping the hilt in both hands. Under my fingers the sword seemed to breathe in at the same time I did: a gentle shudder of life. Just as before, I could feel the sword responding to me, reaching out to me with its own singing. The grip heated against my skin until it was the same temperature as my hands.

Mine. Mine from now on. No matter what.

Mine.

The singing notes intertwined. Every particle of my body seemed to be vibrating – resounding at some perfect pitch that made me light up, made the air around me shift and glow like a heat haze shimmering off the pavement on a hot day. The sword was almost buzzing in my grasp now. Something broke, rushing and surging around me – a wave of energy that blew my hair into my face, tugged at my clothes. I gasped for breath.

The light bulb overhead shattered with a shrill tinkle of falling glass, plunging the room into darkness.

CHAPTER 3

SHADOWS AND DREAMS

On the landing outside, Jack yelped.

I blinked sluggish eyelids. As my sight adjusted to the dim, orangey streetlight that filtered in through the window, the darkness resolved itself into something I could make sense of. I realized I had slumped down onto the floor, curling almost into a ball. The sword hilt was still clutched in my hands and my hands were jammed between my knees. The tip of the blade had come down on the edge of the old, peeling box and … cut straight through it. There was a gaping gash in the front of the battered metal.

"Mio! Hello?" Jack called out. "The light out here keeps flickering, and I don't want to take the stairs in the dark. Didn't you find it yet?"

I cleared my throat. "It – it's all right. Just … hang on a second. Wait a second."

What happened? Did I pass out? I unpeeled the fingers of one hand from around the katana's grip and rubbed my breastbone. The singing feeling was still there, muted but … I could definitely sense it. It was like it had sunk down under my ribs and become a permanent part of me.

Using touch alone, I carefully eased the shining-edged blade back into the saya and then slid the katana over my shoulder into my shinai bag. The weight of him resting against my back was like nothing I'd ever felt before, and at the same time, it was as familiar – and right – as my mother's hug.

He's mine. Mine. Mine.

"Fiiiinally," Jack drawled as I appeared in the door-way of the attic. "Where's the ultra-cool sword then? I aided and abetted. I ought to get first peek."

My spine snapped as straight as if someone had rammed a hockey stick down the back of my kendogi. I only just resisted the urge to back away into the attic to protect the katana from Jack's curious gaze. *Mine.* "Er, aren't we late?"

Jack checked her watch and yelped. "Holy crap! Come on!"

She clattered down the stairs and I breathed a sigh of relief. I wasn't up to showing my sword off just yet. I'd only just got him.

After I won a brief tussle with Jack about whether we needed to take our coats – she said it would be sacrilegious to cover up "all of this", I pointed out that it was December and goose pimples were not sexy – we made our escape. The walk to the Tube station was only ten minutes, but frost sparkled everywhere, and by the time we boarded the District Line, I was seriously glad I had won that particular fight. I wished I'd thought to get a scarf and gloves too.

Even with most of what we were wearing hidden, our costumes got a couple of funny looks and some not-so-funny comments on the Tube. Jack's inherited ability to viciously stab people with her eyes soon discouraged the unwanted attention. It didn't really bother us; we were both buzzing.

Just in case it wasn't obvious before, we *weren't* heading to an end-of-term school "disco". Which, by the way, *euw*. It was a party that I seriously doubted our parents would have allowed us to attend, if they'd known about it. Natalie Depaul's mum and dad, like mine and Jack's, were away for a few days before Christmas. Unlike our parents, however, Mr and Mrs Depaul had trusted Natalie to be alone in the house without supervision.

Yeah, that was kind of a mistake there – but thanks, Mr and Mrs Depaul, for donating the contents of your booze cabinet to the cause of your daughter's popularity.

"Shannon Goldsmith is supposed to be going as a sexy nurse," Jack whispered to me. "I cannot wait to see. I'm totally going to sneak a picture."

"You're kind of a perv, do you realize that?"

"Hey, it's not like I'm going to put it online or anything."

I shook my head and *tsk*ed in mock disappointment. "Letting the side down, Jack. You know that objectifying your fellow woman makes you a traitor to Feminism."

She nudged me, grinning. "But objectifying guys doesn't count? I can tell you're holding out on me, you know, and I'm hurt. Who are you all excited about seeing? Spill."

I laughed. "Like I could keep secrets from you. If I fancied anyone, you would know."

"In that case, petty larceny seriously agrees with you. You're all glowy. You're going to get your prop out once we get there, right?"

"Maybe," I said, feeling a shade of irritation darken my mood. "And what the hell is 'larceny' anyway? I told you, my grandfather gave him to me."

"Him?" Jack's eyes flickered across my shoulder to where the red shinai carrier poked out of the collar of my coat.

Don't. Don't look at him. He's mine.

The fine hairs on my skin raked up in a fizzle of static electricity and the overhead lights began to flicker wildly. The Tube seemed to shudder around us. A deep, grating noise filled the air, blocking out the regular clatter of the wheels.

A woman stood by the doors let out a squeak of alarm

as she stumbled, catching herself on one of the Plexiglas dividers.

"What the—?" Jack began.

The Tube ground to a halt. The lights snapped back on and the announcement for "Kew Gardens" echoed over the intercom. Jack and I both jumped to our feet and piled out of the doors.

"Jesus, that was scary," Jack said, glancing back at the Tube as it coasted away. "You OK?"

"Yeah, f–fine." I was shaking with relief, partly because we'd got to the station all right – but also partly, I realized, because I'd managed to dodge Jack's questions. I didn't want to talk to her about the katana. And I didn't want to analyze why.

One who is hidden…

But only from my dad, right? I frowned as I tried to remember Ojiichan's exact words.

Natalie's house was down a wide street, lined on both sides by trees and cars. The music booming out of Number Five would have given the party's location away, even if we hadn't known the address. It was so loud that my body started to move in time to the beat. The house's beige-coloured brick was aglow with the light spilling out of all the windows. Natalie stood in the white porch, letting in someone dressed in a pirate costume.

"Zoh my God," Jack said, her voice going high with

41

suppressed laughter. "Seriously? She's seriously dressed up as Bella at the prom?"

"Be nice," I said out of the corner of my mouth, as we approached the door.

"Can't. You'll have to do the talking." Jack hastily rearranged her expression, although I could still see the laughter in her eyes.

"Hey, Natalie," I said. "I love your dress. The blue really suits you." Which wasn't a lie. It did suit her. The massive dark wig that looked like something Cher would wear? Not so much. But there was no need to bring that up.

"Thanks," Natalie chirped back. "You look really different dressed like that, sort of *Crouching Tiger*-ish." Her eyes slid towards Jack and she blinked. "Er ... nice wings."

"Nice leg cast," Jack said, straight-faced, as she shrugged off her coat.

"Uh, right. You can just throw your coats anywhere in the dining room, here. There're drinks and stuff in the kitchen. People are dancing in the living room," Natalie said, backing down the narrow magnolia hall to give us room. There was a crash from the back of the house as the final word left her mouth, and she flinched. "Um, see you later."

She zipped off to see how much trouble she was going to be in when her parents got back. As I pulled my coat off, my shinai carrier bumped gently against my back.

42

The light in the hall flickered, and for a second Natalie's rapidly fleeing back seemed to flicker too. There was a dark, wet stain spreading across the back of the dress, between her shoulder blades. She was falling...

Natalie disappeared into what was probably the living room. The light flicked back on.

"What is up with all the power blips tonight?" Jack threw her coat on the pile on the dining-room table.

"Power blips. Yeah." My blood sugar must be dropping or something. And I was tired. The Dream had stopped me from sleeping properly for weeks. I should eat. I should definitely eat. "Let's go to the kitchen."

"Good idea. Elbow me if you spot Shannon, right?"

"Right," I said, glad that the music was masking the strangled note in my voice.

We headed into the kitchen and each snagged a glass of unidentified stuff with fruit juice in it, then stood around for a few minutes talking to some girls we were friendly with while I tried to stuff as many Pringles and dry-roasted peanuts into my mouth as I could without choking. By the time Shannon made an appearance – in a sexy nurse outfit, including red fishnets, which I thought would give Jack heart failure right there – and Jack managed to orchestrate a "group" picture, which I knew would only have Shannon and her long legs in it, I was feeling much better.

Everything was fine. Nothing weird going on but the

fact that I'd skipped lunch and dinner, and was having too many of those stupid dreams.

"Mission accomplished," Jack said, clicking away on her phone and sending a copy of her treasure to her email account.

"Then let's go dance," I said, putting down my empty glass. They were playing a Ladyhawke track with a fast, driving beat – perfect. I grabbed Jack's hand and dragged her into the living room. The furniture had been shoved back against the walls and the overhead light was off, so the only illumination came from a couple of lamps on the windowsill. I was dancing before I even hit the middle of the room and I heard Jack whoop as I let the music stream through my body, taking control. My arms went up and I spun, clearing a little space around me. A couple of people shouted my name but I just grinned and kept dancing. It was like flying. The only other feeling that came close was making a perfect hit in kendo.

I shoved that memory away hastily.

I danced through three songs, sometimes meeting up with Jack – whose idea of dancing was a hilariously awkward Vogue thing – sometimes dancing in a small group with other people. A couple of guys tried to put their hands places they shouldn't and got their feet stomped on, but I was used to that.

When I finally collapsed in a chair by the window, I was covered in sweat, hair plastered to my face and neck, heart pumping. I felt amazing. Jack came over and sat on the arm of the chair, her hair sticking straight up in white, pink and purple spikes. Some kids from my tutor group and a couple of people that Jack knew from hers crowded around. One of the boys handed out a bunch more drinks. Jack told an exaggerated version of the Tube journey and made everyone laugh till they nearly cried. It amazed me how she could take something so ordinary and give it a twist and suddenly it was hilarious. Or maybe that was the fizzy fruit stuff talking.

Kylar Grant, wearing pale-blue scrubs that he probably stole from his father, who worked at a hospital, pulled another chair over next to me and handed me my second – third? – drink.

"I never realized you could dance like that," he said. "I'm going to be remembering that whenever I look at you now. You know that, right?"

I leaned my head back and blinked up into his chocolate-brown eyes. "Maybe you shouldn't look at me, then."

"Oh, I'll be looking," he said, voice getting deeper.

I didn't giggle, but I wanted to. *Whoops. Now I'm the traitor to Feminism.*

The tip of the katana's sheath dug into my back. I tried to wriggle into a more comfy position but couldn't. Now the guard was digging into my shoulder. No matter what I did, he ended up gouging a hole in me somewhere, like he didn't want me to forget about him or something. I put my drink on the floor and leaned forward, clumsily pulling the red shinai carrier under my arm and round to my front.

"What's that?" Kylar asked.

"Part of my costume," I said shortly.

"It's her mega-ultra samurai sword!" Jack said, doing jazz hands. "I can't believe I forgot. It's, like, a thousand-year-old family heirloom."

"Five hundred years," I corrected sharply.

"A real samurai sword? Oh my God, I have to see this," said one of the other girls.

"Come on, get it out!"

"I—I can't," I stammered. "It's dangerous."

Mine!

"She's right. If you want to see it, you need to get back and give her some room," Jack said.

I knew she thought she was being helpful, but honestly... I could have brained her with the katana just then. Everyone scrambled back and the next thing I knew there were twice as many people staring at us, all trying to figure out what was going on. Someone snapped on the overhead light, making us all blink.

Just flash them the sword and get it over with. What's the big deal?

Sick, irrational panic churned in my stomach, but I forced myself to get up and pull the sheathed katana out of the shinai carrier. The living-room light flashed over the brilliant shine of the black lacquer and golden flowers. The music was too loud for me to hear the *Ooooh*, but I could sense it.

A sneaking pride helped to soothe my uneasiness. *That's right. He's gorgeous, and he's all mine.* Slowly I drew the blade from the saya. Light flashed along the curved surface like the sharp, white smile of the crescent moon.

"Holy crap," someone said.

"You are so hot right now," Kylar said, moving a little closer. *"Angelina Jolie* hot."

Jack snorted. "Dude, that's not a compliment."

"Anyway," a boy called Simon interrupted, "she looks more like the girl from that vampire film – you know the one who had the leather pants."

"That was Angelina Jolie," Kylar said, annoyed.

Sarah from my tutor group shook her head. "No, it wasn't. He's talking about the one who was in the lipstick adverts. She's Bulgarian, I think."

"No, she's, like, Russian!" someone else chimed in.

Huh. OK, well, that was a lot less dramatic than I'd been bracing myself for. I slid the katana back into his saya and the saya back into the shinai carrier, then settled him onto his place on my shoulder again. By the time I looked up, everyone was so busy trying to work out the name of the girl from the lipstick ads that they all seemed to have forgotten me completely. I was relieved and then irritated at myself for being relieved. Why was I being so freakish tonight?

I turned to Jack to suggest more drinks – and saw the shadow coming out of the wall.

A dark stain unfurled against the bright terracotta wallpaper, tendrils whipping from the centre and hardening into claws as it dragged itself through the bricks, into the room. I gagged on the stink of it: wet animal, greasy fur, and something long dead and rotting.

The seething mass dilated like the pupil of an eye, spreading up onto the ceiling. It clawed across the plaster, leaving black streaks wherever it touched. Thick, glistening globs of liquid, like half-congealed blood, dripped down onto the people below, staining their hair and clothes and spreading across their skin. No one seemed to notice.

The thing twisted, and suddenly – horribly – I could see a face in the black. A face that might have been human, except for the eyes. Yellow, cat eyes, with vertical pupils. The thing blinked slowly, searching. Its gaze fixed on me.

It surged across the ceiling towards me.

I tried to scream but all that came out was a choked gasp that was lost in the voices and music. I staggered back, grabbing Jack by the shoulder to try and push her out of the way. But the room was too crowded. Jack and I both bounced off the people standing next to us and

I nearly went down. Jack caught me before I hit the floor.

"Jesus, you look like you saw Sadako," she said as she hauled me up. "What's wrong?"

"Did she drink too much?" Sarah asked. "Mio, are you going to be sick?"

Kylar and several others immediately leapt back out of range and Natalie appeared beside us like a frizzy haired genie. "Not on the carpet! Get her into the bathroom!"

"I'm not – there was – I saw…"

I looked up at the ceiling.

The thing was gone.

My eyes darted to the place on the wall where the shadow had emerged. Nothing. I looked back at the circle of people gathered around me. The glistening stains were gone from their skin. Half had their phones out so if I heaved on the carpet they could post it on YouTube.

"Mimi, you seriously don't look good." Jack patted me on the back.

"I–I think…"

Ojiichan's voice darted through my head again. *One who remembers. One who endures. One who is hidden.*

He must always be hidden…

Always? What had Ojiichan said exactly?

"I need to sit down," I managed to mumble.

"You can take her into the sunroom," Natalie suggested uneasily, clearly still watching for signs I was about to ralph on her precious shag pile. "It's quieter in there."

She pushed through the gawping people to the far end of the room, shoved a coffee table out of the way and opened a set of French doors that I hadn't noticed earlier.

"OK with you?" Jack asked me, putting her arm around my shoulders.

I nodded and followed Natalie into the other room. Predictably, it had a tiled floor and was mostly made up of windows, with more doors leading outside. The glass might as well have been brick now; with the lights on, the windows were dark and opaque, solid shadows. I shuddered. Jack guided me over to a wicker sofa. The saya dug into my side again as I sat down and I shifted, readjusting him. I could feel Jack's concerned gaze on my face, but I couldn't look at her.

"Uh, I'll just … leave you be then, OK?" Natalie said, already halfway back out of the door. "Like, call me if you need anything."

The door shut and immediately the noise of the party surged up again on the other side, muffled and distorted by the glass doors.

"Can you put the light off?" I asked, rubbing my forehead. My head hurt, and the darkness gave me an excuse to avoid meeting Jack's eyes. As the overhead light went out, the windows turned from black to deep blue. I could see walls and grass outside, and no one could see in here. I relaxed a little.

"Sorry," I said after a minute.

"Don't be stupid. This is my fault, isn't it? I should have let you eat the fricking lasagne. I didn't realize you were *this* starved."

"It's not that." I hesitated for a second, then admitted, "Something's wrong. I'm seeing weird things. Like hallucinations."

Jack went on the alert, her body tensing up like a bloodhound catching a scent. "Shit. Did anyone give you a drink other than me?"

"Um … yeah, Kylar did, but—"

"Shit! I can't believe this! He spiked your drink. I'm going to rip off his—"

"Kylar didn't spike my drink," I broke in. "I've been feeling off all night. Since…" *Since I stole the sword.*

And all of a sudden it did feel like stealing. Because all this weird stuff, these feelings, the flickering lights, had started then. Right after I got him out of the box, out of all those layers of embroidered cloth. Maybe I ought to have spent less time trying to remember my dreams and more time trying to remember my grandfather's exact words about this katana that my family had been looking after for five hundred years.

Hiding for five hundred years…

I think I did something really stupid.

"Mimi, if you're seeing things, it's the only explanation. The stuff they put in drinks can play tricks with your memory and—"

"Just leave it, Jack," I said, my voice coming out sharper than I meant it to. I took a deep breath. "I–I'm going to go home. You can stay if you want."

She shot me one of her stabbing looks. "Right, I'm going to let my drugged, seeing-things friend stagger home, alone, in the dark because I'm just that awesome. Shut up and let me call a taxi."

"That'll be way too expensive. Look, I feel better now, OK? Let's catch the Tube back. It's faster anyway. The walk and the fresh air will probably help."

Jack hesitated. "If you start feeling funny again you need to tell me straight away."

"I will. I will!" I said, jumping up and going to the doors that led outside into Natalie's garden. When I didn't wobble or collapse, I could tell that went a long way to reassuring Jack. She put her phone away.

But it didn't reassure me. I already knew I hadn't been drugged.

One who is hidden. Always hidden…

Ojiichan hadn't been messing about that day. And he hadn't just been talking about my dad. You're not supposed to wave hidden things – ancient things – around at parties, for fun. I had been feeling wigged and uneasy from the second I took the sword. I didn't know exactly what was going on, but I was desperate to get home and put the blade back where he belonged again before—

"Before someone finds him," I whispered.

"Are you talking to me?" Jack asked.

"No, I'm muttering to myself. All part of tonight's delightful package of crazy." I pulled open the French doors, letting in a whoosh of freezing air that smelled of damp earth and exhaust fumes. "Hell. Our coats are in the dining room."

"Hang on a second and I'll get them. I'll grab Natalie if I see her and tell her we're off too."

"Thanks, Jack. You're a bright shiny star."

"Damn straight."

The noise of the party made me wince as Jack slipped back into the living room. I thought it would be a while before I wanted to dance again. I'd be lucky if my freakout didn't end up being the number-one story when I got back to school in January, and by that time Chinese Whispers would have made it common knowledge that I'd done a topless lap dance for Kylar and projectile vomited on Natalie.

The chilly air felt good. I breathed in deeply, stepping past the threshold of the sunroom and looking out at the night. *Calm down. You'll be home soon. You can hide the sword soon.*

The room was built onto the side of Natalie's house, so next door's wall was straight ahead. The garden – just a little patch of grass with a few shrubs, like mine at home – was on the right side, and the gravel parking area in front of the house on the other. The streetlights twinkled too brightly through the bare branches of the trees, making my eyes water.

I blinked and squeezed my eyes shut, but when I opened them, coloured dots were still darting through my vision. They came together in the shape of a man.

He was turned sideways to me, so that I could only see his profile in shadow. He wore a robe – no, it was a kimono – that gleamed dully with gold embroidery. A costume, like mine? Except that it didn't really look like a fancy-dress outfit. And he didn't really look like he belonged at this party.

He was very tall, but sort of slender, like a kid, with arms and legs that seemed too long for his body. Something about the shape of him was subtly off, the proportions skewed. The more I stared, the more *off* he seemed. Abruptly I was convinced that he wasn't anyone Natalie had invited here. He was ... wrong.

The man turned his head towards me. The light reflected from his eyes – no, no, that wasn't the light. There were twin holes in his face, glowing eerie white. They had no iris, no pupil. Those weren't *eyes*.

For a second I was so frozen with fear that I felt like I'd turned into a piece of the wall behind me. This guy was real. *Real.* And he was so, so wrong. I couldn't even explain how terrifying he was. He could have pulled out an AK47 and aimed it at me and I wouldn't have been able to whimper, let alone run.

He could see it too. He smiled a triumphant, gloating smile.

And just like that, I was mad. More than mad. *Furious*. This guy was trying to scare me on purpose. I didn't know why, or how, but he was trying to drive me crazy, and he thought it was funny. My feet came loose from the ground and I flung myself down from the doorway, gravel crunching under my feet, my breath making wheezing noises in my ears. The noise of the party had faded away to silence behind me.

"Who are you?" I said. My voice came out shockingly loud; too many drinks.

He carried on smirking. "I am the Zenpyou. You would call me … a Harbinger. The bringer of fate. I come to remind you, child of the Yamato, of your sacred duty to protect that which you bear; a duty you seem to be taking far too lightly. Has your family already forgotten the consequences of failure?"

He stopped, like he was waiting for me to say something back. Waiting for me to get on my knees and grovel?

"Are you high or something?" I demanded. "What are you on about?"

His smile faded abruptly; his stare turned assessing. "You? No. It cannot be."

"What do you want?"

He made a sound of disgust. "I have told you." He turned away with a restless, contemptuous shrug.

"Remember what I have said, sword-bearer."

He began to walk towards the road. His back shimmered like a mirage as he moved into the light.

"Where do you think you're going? Get back here!" I charged after him, so angry that I didn't stop to think about what I was doing.

The shimmering light spread out behind him, a wake in the air, like the disturbance a ship makes in calm water. The straight, everyday lines of houses, trees, streetlights, the pavement under my feet, the sky above me, all rippled, streaming and blurring past my eyes. I forced myself to keep running. I couldn't tell the ground from the sky, but my feet were still hitting solid earth and I could still see the man's lanky shape ahead of me.

"Mio! Stop!"

It was Jack's voice, shrill and frightened.

The streaming ripples brightened until they blinded me. I threw up my hands to protect my eyes. There was a noise, coming closer, a rising wail, like a—

A car horn.

CHAPTER 4

BLOOD FROM
A STONE

Have you ever been hit in the face? Really hit? So your head snapped back and you landed on your rear end wondering what the hell happened? You don't actually feel it at first. The harder the blow is, the more numb you go. I mean, your face just seems to disappear, and for a minute you think your eyes are going to drop right out of their sockets because they're the only thing that still seems to be working.

I suppose that explains why I didn't feel the car hit me. There was no pain. Just a sort of … nudge. I flew up, and the world did a gentle roll around me, everything coming apart, lights and trees and cars scattering before my eyes like colourful pieces of broken glass.

Then I hit the ground. I landed on my front and skidded for a few feet before I came to a halt. I still couldn't feel anything, and it was *quiet*. I'd say "dead quiet", except that's too accurate to be funny. I never realized how loud my heartbeat was until it stopped.

And all I could think was, *Thank God I landed on my front. Thank God I didn't destroy the katana. Thank God.*

Then it started to hurt. Pain was closing in on me, cold and dark, like a vice, compressing me from all sides at once, crushing down until everything was reduced to a bright chink in the agony, a gap that let me hear Jack screaming and see her running feet. The gap kept closing down, getting tinier and tinier until it was nothing but a pinprick and it just seemed easier to close my eyes...

Heat pulsed on my back like the heartbeat of some massive creature. It broke through the agony for a second, and in that second, I heard another voice. *Mio*, it whispered. *Take my hand. Don't let go.*

I knew his voice. I had never heard it before in my life, but I knew it. Mentally I reached out through the darkness and the cold, and felt that same warmth close around me, embracing me, lifting me up, up, away from the pain—

And I was somewhere else.

The light was red. The sun was setting beyond the forest, streaking the sky with fire, shining through the autumn leaves that shivered down on to the battle.

A man and a ... a creature fought beneath the trees. The man weaved, leapt and spun, avoiding the nine slashing tails of the creature. He moved faster than any human should be able to move. He was a black hurricane, a whirlwind of flashing silver blades and flying dark hair. I could not see his face – but his big, tanned hands were clenched white on the handles of his swords.

His swords...

In one hand he held a short wakizashi blade. In the other he held a black and gold katana that glittered in the red light. My katana. Mine.

But here it was his. Everything about the way he moved, the confidence with which he wielded it, shouted that. And he fought furiously, as if the survival of everything he loved depended on winning.

The creature was a thing of terrible darkness, its body rippling and shifting in the air like oil on the surface of water. Long tentacles of that darkness lashed and whirled at the warrior, scraping white chunks out of tree trunks and gashing great holes in the earth. Its face was the most awful thing of all, a nightmare that melded human with feline – red lips and fine brows, an elongated jaw and bristling needle fangs. Yellow, inhuman eyes.

The man moved into a complex pass that turned the blades into a silver blur. Two of the creature's limbs went flying. Black liquid spattered over the red leaves. The warrior darted forward into the gap and struck deeply, cleaving a hole where the creature's heart should be.

The creature let out a high-pitched shriek that shook the

trees. The man leapt back, swords at the ready. More black liquid gushed out of the wound as the thing writhed, its limbs drawing in with a convulsive movement, like the legs of a dying spider. The drifting mantle contracted, folding in on itself.

The man's muscular back seemed to relax a little, but he took another, wary step back before he lowered the blades to his sides.

The creature shrieked again. One of its limbs shot out, streaking across the clearing like a black whip. A jagged claw hit the man squarely in the chest and then ripped away in a spray of blood.

The short sword dropped from the warrior's left hand with a clatter. He clapped his palm over his heart. Staggering slightly on his feet, he watched as the shadow creature convulsed. The beast twisted down into a knot of blackness, and … solidified. A second later it was no more than a rough stone figure, barely a foot tall, in the shape of a cat.

The man sighed, shoulders sagging as if a terrible weight had been lifted from him. Blood spilled through his fingers with the movement, cascading down his chest, soaking the material of his kimono. Almost gracefully, he crumpled, still clutching my – his – katana in his right hand.

He fell among the red and copper leaves and I saw his face for the first time.

He was young. Much younger than I'd thought when he was fighting. Not a man, after all. A boy, maybe only a couple of years older than I was.

His skin was golden, turning pale now as his blood drained away. Long hair lay in a shiny pool around the strong, angular planes of his face. His eyes were almond-shaped, long-lashed, endlessly dark. There was no fear in them. They were as calm as still water, reflecting the sky. This boy was beautiful, and unafraid. And he was dying.

His lips shaped a word I could not make out. I stared at his mouth, moving closer as I tried to understand what he was saying. Those peaceful eyes shifted, just a little, until they almost met mine.

He smiled painfully. Peacefully. "Mio."

I heard footsteps crunching stealthily through the fallen leaves. The boy's eyes flicked away from me as a shadow fell over him.

A green, leaf-shaped blade flashed down. Darkness fell over me like a thick, velvet cloth.

No!

I shot upright, my fingers clawing at the air. I had to go, I had to. I had to get to him, to help, to hold onto him…

Wait. My head throbbed and tears made my vision swim and blur. I blinked rapidly, putting both hands over my face. *Wait. I remember…? I remember.* A forest. A monster. A boy with – with my sword. The boy who said my name. He was dying, lying there *dying* – he was calling for me – and I didn't help him. I hadn't done *anything.* I let him go. I rocked backwards and forwards in agony as a terrible sense of loss pierced through me. *Why did I let him go...?*

"Mio, please stay still! Please! Can you hear me?"

The pleading voice finally got through. I forced myself to look up. Jack was kneeling next to me, and the light from the moon showed tears pouring down her face. I was sitting on tarmac. In the middle of the road. "Jack?"

"Thank God," she said, fumbling for her phone. "You're going to be all right, OK? I'm calling an ambulance."

"What?" I whispered. The suffocating feeling of grief was beginning to fade. I looked around, bewildered. "What – what happened?"

"Just stay still!" Jack reached out, then hesitated, her hands hovering in the air, as if she didn't dare touch me.

"Did I fall?" Then I gasped. "Oh no!"

I whipped my arms back – ignoring Jack's yelp of protest – to pull the katana out of the shinai carrier and inspect him. Not a scratch. I turned him over and over, double-checking, and let out a sigh of pure relief. He was pristine.

There was a weak pulse of warmth under my hand on the grip. For a second I held the sword to me, taking comfort in the familiar/unfamiliar weight and shape. I stroked my fingers along the saya once and felt the last of the Dream's grief dissipate. I sighed again, easing him back into the shinai case. Then I got quickly to my feet.

Jack sat on the ground for a second, gaping at me. As

she swore and scrambled upright, her phone popped out of her hand and hit the tarmac with a clatter. We both bent to pick it up; I got to it first. As I straightened, I looked around again. Why were we in the middle of the road outside Natalie's house?

I froze. "There was a car."

"The bastard didn't stop. You – you flew twenty feet. You flew! You shouldn't even be conscious. I thought you were dead."

Slowly I stretched out my arms and legs, staring at them in the strong moonlight. The sturdy fabric of my kendogi was ruined – shredded in some places – and covered in dust and dirt and bits of glass. But the skin showing through the holes didn't have a scratch on it. I touched my face. Rolled my head experimentally. Nothing. Even the headache was gone.

"I'm OK," I said, hearing the surprise in my own voice.

"How the effing hell can you be OK?" Jack demanded shakily.

"Good question," I muttered.

I dreamed again. I dreamed right here in the middle of the road. The same Dream as always, but this time – this time *I remembered* it. Who – who was that *boy*? That boy with eyes full of the sky...? Why did I feel like I was supposed to save him? Like it was up to me to hold onto him?

And why wasn't I dead?

"Mio…" Jack's voice broke.

I reached out and shoved her phone into her skirt pocket, then hugged her hard. The bare skin above her fairy wings was icy cold, and her whole body was trembling.

"I don't know, Jack. I just don't know. Hey, you think I should get a lottery ticket?" My own voice cracked.

Jack let out a strangled laugh and smacked me lightly in the shoulder with her free hand. "You idiot.. You ran right out into the road. What were you doing? I told you to wait for me. Why didn't you wait?"

"I don't really know that either. I saw something…" *The Harbinger.* I shuddered. "Look, I'll try to explain later. Can we just go home for now?"

"Are you crazy?" She pulled back to stare at me. "We have to go to the hospital!"

"Look at me, Jack. There's nothing wrong with me! I don't even have road rash. No one's going to believe I was hit by a car. If we go to A&E they're going to think we're wasting their time. They'll throw us out. Or worse – call Rachel." I was shaking myself now. Too much had happened tonight, and I couldn't process any of it. "Please, Jack."

Jack studied my face, then looked around help-lessly. A few houses down a young couple was coming out, swaddled against the cold, with a Labrador puppy on a lead. They were pointing up at the dark streetlight outside their house, shaking their heads. This year's top boy band was blaring out from Number Five. Everything looked completely normal.

Jack grabbed my hand. "Fine. Let's go before my head pops."

Square chunks of safety glass crunched underfoot as we stepped up onto the pavement. I squinted down at the mess, realizing belatedly that it was unusually dark because *all* the streetlights were out. The only reason I could see to walk was because of the nearly full moon. "What's all this glass? And what happened to the streetlights?"

"The glass is *from* the streetlights," Jack said wearily. "When you were lying in the road there was some sort of power surge. All the lights flared up – too bright to look at – and then … then they just exploded."

Bel Downing swore when the lights in her tiny office started to flicker. Her finger slammed down on the "Save" icon and she sighed with relief when the command executed without the computer crashing. Damn power surges.

She reached for her mug of tea, found it contained only cold dregs, checked the time and swore again. No wonder her back was killing her. She had to stop doing this. It wasn't like the British Museum was going to spring for overtime when she was writing her own dissertation.

When the lights had stopped blinking, she shut down her computer and had a long, spine-cracking stretch, trying to decide what takeaway to hit for dinner. She was weighing up noodles versus pizza when she heard an unmistakable sound echo down the empty corridor outside.

"What—?"

There it was again. For God's sake! How had a cat got into the museum?

Remembering the chaos wrought by a trapped pigeon a few months before, Bel got up hastily and pushed the door of her office fully open. She peered up and down the shadowy corridor, but there was no sign of any living creature there.

She internally debated fetching one of the night watchmen. What if the cat was on the move? In the five or ten minutes it would take to get help, the stupid animal could have got into anything. Another meow made her mind up. The sound was coming from the Japanese rooms. She headed in that direction, passing the shadowy statue of Kudara Kannon as she entered the first room. Her footsteps echoed softly. Did she dare put on the powerful overhead lights? She couldn't walk around in the pitch-dark, but she didn't want to scare the cat into hiding with a sudden flood of light. After a moment she switched on the display lights instead. The soft spots highlighted the exhibits and gave her enough light to move around without falling over anything.

Bel heard another pitiful meow and felt a momentary pang of pity for the lost cat. She wasn't much of a pet person, but all this noise must mean that the poor thing was frightened and wanted to be found.

"Here, puss," she said, making kissy noises as she moved deeper into the gallery. "Here, kitty. Where are you? Come out."

There was another meow, this time from right behind her. She turned quickly and sucked in a sharp breath, mouth falling open.

One of the exhibits – an ancient stone grave-offering, about a foot high and roughly carved in the shape of a cat – was broken. Shards of rock glittered in the display case amid a pool of dark liquid. The liquid flowed, thick as blood, down the sides of the broken exhibit's pedestal and had somehow squeezed out under the sealed glass of the case to drip onto the floor. Torn between disbelief and fascination, Bel hesitated, then took a step back.

Her shoe squelched. She looked down and saw that in the few seconds she had stood gaping, the black liquid had circled her feet.

The hairs all over Bel's body raked up as a low, wicked chuckle echoed through the gallery. One by one, the display lights began to wink off, plunging the room into deeper darkness.

This can't be happening. This isn't real.

Bel turned to run.

The fluid surged up in front of her, long rivulets gathering like an upside-down waterfall to form into a tall shape. A shape that was not human.

The mocking laughter warped and changed, taking on

the ululating quality of a cat's yowl. The last light flicked off. Bel saw eyes in the darkness. Yellow eyes. Cat's eyes.

She tried to scream, but it was already too late.

The familiar dull roar of city noises outside made the silence in the attic seem even deeper. I felt as if I was wading through it, knee-deep, as I searched for the old metal case, my emergency torch blazing in one hand and the katana clutched in the other.

I have to put him back. I have to.

The light flashed over the white-painted exterior, dazzling me. I snapped my eyes closed, taking a deep breath.

Do it. Just do it. You know you have to. You have to.

It was incredibly hard to get myself to kneel down in front of the box. My legs twitched and seized up, like my own muscles were fighting me. My fingers clenched spasmodically on the saya, the slightly raised imprints of the golden cherry blossoms biting into the skin of my palm. I landed ungracefully on my backside, and cringed as the thud sent something toppling over in the dark recesses of the attic room.

I propped the flashlight on the seat of a wonky chair near by. The vivid yellow beam gleamed off the dust-choked surfaces and made dense black shadows in every nook and cranny.

Lid up.

Stiff, ancient silks unfolded.

There was a gentle dip in the bottom of the box, perfect for the katana to rest in. Maybe designed for it.

I took the sword in both hands. Head bent, my forehead resting gently on the curve of the saya, I whispered, "I'm sorry. I should never have taken him out. I'm sorry, Ojiichan. I'm sorry, Hidden One."

So, so sorry...

I slowly eased the katana back into the box. After clumsily flipping the silks over the shining black and gold, I lunged for the lid and shoved it down. The hollow boom of the two halves of the case coming together rang in my ears like a church bell.

I rested like that for a little while, both hands on the lid, holding it down. Holding me up.

Finally I eased to my feet, grabbing the torch. My legs wobbled. Sickness surged in my stomach, and emptiness yawned in my chest. I wrapped my free arm around my midriff, trying to breathe around that awful, wrenching sense of wrongness. *Mine.* He was mine. And I was leaving him. I was leaving him trapped here alone, shut up in the dark...

"Just a sword," I panted between chattering teeth. "Just ... a ... sword."

It was nearly over. Now I just had to get out of the attic. I just had to get away.

My first step was slow, wobbly, as if I had forgotten

how to use my legs. The high, singing note inside me hadn't cut off with the closing of the box this time. It was like a cord tied inside my ribs, stretched taut as a violin string, screaming with tension; shrill, desperate.

The second step, even slower than the first, made my breath sob in my ears and cold sweat spring up all over my body. My heart reached back for the sword with everything it had. Or maybe it was the sword reaching for me.

Don't go. Don't go. Don't let go.

The third step broke me.

I couldn't move another step without ripping out my own heart.

My legs gave way. I fell down onto the dusty floorboards, gasping for breath.

Misery. Emptiness. Fear.

No light. No air. Icy cold and dark, nothing but darkness. Oh God, I can't leave him. I can't let him go, not like this, I can't let go. I can't. I can't…

He's mine.

I didn't make a decision to move. Before I knew what was happening, the box was before me again, the lid flying back. I ripped away the embroidered cloths.

The warm silk of the grip and cool lacquer of the saya leapt into my hands.

Relief swept over me – a gentle tide of sheer *rightness* like some beautiful piece of music reaching straight into my spirit. My stomach stopped churning. My head stopped throbbing. The high, screaming vibration that had shaken me and choked off my air turned golden and sweet, twining around me like an affectionate cat. The painful emotions dissolved into blessed calm. Joy. Warmth. Happiness.

I could feel the katana pulsing faintly in my grip, and a deep, thankful sigh shuddered out of me. I hugged it close.

You're all right. I've got you now. I've got you. I won't let go again.

I won't ever, ever let go.

CHAPTER 5

THE BOY WITH THE SKY IN HIS EYES

I t was nine-thirty in the morning. I stared up at my bedroom ceiling and contemplated my options.

One: I had got so drunk at Natalie's party that I'd tripped out and had a really elaborate and disturbing dream which I found impossible to distinguish from reality.

Two: I had experienced one of those psychotic breaks that people were always going on about, and from now on I was never going to be able to distinguish dreams from reality.

Three: Everything I had experienced last night was real. The antique sword I had pinched from my parents' attic was … something else. Something more. So much more that it had somehow fixed me when I ought to have been dead and had been starring in the recurring dreams I'd had since I was a kid.

Personally, I was thinking that Option One looked pretty fricking good. Especially since the minute I started seriously considering Number Three, I'd be a candidate for Two.

I groaned and rolled over, squashing my face into my pillow. My eyes felt like someone had poured sand into them. Last night the Dream had left me alone for the first time in weeks – but only because I couldn't sleep. How could anyone sleep after what I'd seen last night?

It couldn't be real. It couldn't be. None of it. Could it?

I didn't know what was going on. Maybe Jack was right and someone had spiked my drink. Or maybe... Maybe there really was something uncanny about Ojiichan's sword. Either way, I knew I should try again this morning to put the katana back. I knew I should. I couldn't get away with hiding an ancient deadly weapon under my bed for ever. What would happen when Mum went to hoover under there? If I put it away, all this would stop. Everything would go back to the way it was before.

Right?

The memory of the agony I'd experienced in the attic last night made me shiver. I curled up into a ball as icy sweat prickled up on the back of my neck.

The quiet knock on the door had me jolting upright, my hand shooting down over the side of the bed to where I'd stashed the katana.

"Mio? Are you awake?"

I sagged back against the pillows. "Yeah. Come in."

Rachel pushed the door open, a mug of tea in her hand. "Hi. How are you feeling?"

"All right," I said warily. "Why? What'd Jack tell you?"

Rachel put the mug down on the nightstand and immediately started nosing through the contents of my bookcase, taking the haphazardly piled paperbacks off the shelves, whacking the dust off against her jeans and then putting them back neatly, spine out. "Just that you came over a bit funny at the party and had to come home early. She said you might need a doctor's appointment."

"No!" I heard the echo of my own voice and swallowed as Rachel turned to me in surprise. "I mean, I don't need to see a doctor. Honest. It was just really hot and I'd been dancing and maybe Jack should have let me eat dinner—"

"Hey," Rachel said. "Are you sure you're all right? You look a bit feverish."

I glanced away from her, shamed by the concern on her face – and realized that the torn-up, dirty remains of my kendogi costume were lying half out from under the bed. In a burst of adrenaline, I leapt up and dropped my duvet over the telltale swatch of tattered black fabric.

"Look," I said, doing a little spin on the rug. "I'm totally fine. If I go to the doctor you'll need to tell Mum and Dad, and I really don't want to worry them on their holiday. They deserve some time off."

Rachel's face softened. I could read the words *She's such a considerate little thing* scrolling through her brain. There are times when looking puny and defenceless can work for you. The bunny rabbits on my pyjama bottoms probably helped, too.

"There's no need to do cartwheels – I'm convinced," she said. "But I think Jack feels guilty. Since it's an alien emotion for her, she doesn't know how to deal with it. The moping is getting on my nerves. Drink your tea and come cheer her up."

"Right-oh. Will do. Thanks," I said, herding her swiftly towards the door.

When it had shut behind her, I yanked the duvet up and stared at my kendo uniform. It was in tatters. That was proof *something* had happened. Some parts of what I remembered had to be real. *But which parts?*

I knelt down next to the bed and dragged the katana out into the light, holding the saya in both hands. As soon as I touched it, a familiar warm, tingling sensation started in my palms.

"Is this really all about you?" I whispered. The tingling turned into a sharp buzz under my fingers – almost like an electric shock. I flinched, dropping the sword onto the bed. He lay there on the white sheet, the glossy black lacquer and golden flowers gleaming in the morning light. He was beautiful, but he was just a sword. *It* was just a sword. A *thing*.

I picked him – it – up again.

The saya and hilt pulsed gently in my hands this time, like a heartbeat. *Mine. Mine. Mine.* I felt the sense of possession like a deep ache in my chest. Even the cherry blossoms that decorated him linked him to me. "Mio" meant cherry blossom. This katana was … special. More than just a sword. More than just an heirloom.

Mine.

I stroked the silk-wrapped hilt, stopping with a muttered swear word when I realized what I was doing. God, I was really losing it. I needed to talk to Jack.

Ten minutes later I was dressed in skinny jeans, boots and a long-sleeved T-shirt that read SPARKLIEPOO in pink glitter – and I had to decide what to do about the katana. I couldn't exactly slip it into my pocket and skip off with it. But I didn't have the strength to try leaving it behind again either, not yet.

Back when I was doing kendo practice three times a week I'd worn my wooden shinai in its carrier over the top of my school coat and never had any trouble from anyone. It felt a bit risky to try it with a real sword. In the light of day, with me dressed in normal clothes, no one was going to assume it was a fake, just part of a costume. And what would Jack and Rachel say if I arrived at their place fully armed?

76

In the end I put the sword in the shinai carrier and shrugged my duffle jacket on over the top, hoping that the diagonal bulge across my back wasn't too conspicuous. The sword was about the same length as my torso and the blade and saya had a slight curve that allowed them to fit naturally into the shape of my body. The biggest giveaway I could see in the mirror was a slight bulge where the top of the shinai carrier protruded a little over my left shoulder. It wasn't perfect, but it would have to do.

When I let myself into Jack's flat, she was sprawled on her stomach on the sofa with her feet sticking in the air, while Rachel was curled up in an armchair watching the news.

"It's believed the police were unable to find signs of forced entry at the museum, although they would not confirm that the destruction of the artefact and death of assistant curator Belinda Dowling were an inside job. It has been reported that the murdered woman died of blood loss. One floor of the British Museum will be closed until further notice, and a security guard has been taken in for questioning."

A picture of a woman with long, dark-red hair, blue eyes and a friendly smile appeared on the screen, with a caption underneath: MURDERED MUSEUM EMPLOYEE.

Jack sat up and raised her eyebrows at me. *You ready to talk?*

I shrugged a little. *If you are.*

"Hey, Rach, I forgot to get a Christmas card for Auntie Ruth," Jack said, not taking her eyes off me. "So I'd better nip out. Won't be long."

"Well, be careful," Rachel said absently. "God, look at this. Even museums aren't safe now! There's a lot of nutcases out there."

"No kidding," I muttered as Jack put on her purple biker jacket.

The air was icy and the sky between the buildings was that pale, metallic blue you only see in winter. Traffic roared past. Voices drifted out as we walked by the shops on the corner. The silence between us felt like a concrete slab attached to my chest.

Jack waited until we were moving through the warm, brown coffee miasma outside the local Starbucks before she spoke. "So – let me get this straight. You were … hallucinating. You ran out into the road after something I couldn't see. A car hit you. All the streetlights exploded. And somehow you're fine."

"Um. Yeah."

"This stuff is crazy. I was there, and I don't even believe it."

"I know."

"I literally have no clue what happened. But I can't pretend it *didn't* happen."

"Right."

"You ran out in front of a car. You should be dead, Mimi. Or in the hospital. I'm so glad you're not – don't get me wrong – but I need to understand why."

"Yes."

"Plus, I really hate it when you try to hide stuff from me. Which I can tell you are."

"Sorry."

"You should be."

There was another long pause. We'd passed the shops and cafes now and were walking along the back of the Royal Courts of Justice. The huge, Gothic building loomed over us, its grey stone blocks and narrow-arched windows seeming to suck up the light. On the other side of the street was one of those office buildings that look like a load of shoeboxes stacked one on top of another. There were a couple of vans and cars parked along the road, but we'd left the traffic behind and there were no people in sight. The office building's windows were mirrored, blank and empty.

"Are you going to say something?" Jack asked, stopping abruptly. "Or just let me go on until I stop asking because I feel stupid?"

"I'm not trying to make you feel stupid." I ran my fingers through my hair, then tucked it behind my ears. "I'm trying to figure out how to tell you what's going on without convincing you that I've done a Charlie Sheen."

"Mio, I'm your best friend. I know you're not mad.

You haven't even tried to shave your head or anything. Just spit it out."

I took a deep breath, my gaze wandering past Jack to fix on the tall, wrought-iron fence at the end of the road ahead of us. Most of the fence was hidden by pasteboards and tarpaulin covers with a construction company's logo on them. The fence made the road seem very closed-off and lonely. Jack leaned back on a lamppost, making herself comfy. "Still waiting."

"OK, OK." I took a deep breath. "I think it's to do with the sword." Jack started to speak, but I hurried on. "Remember how, as soon as I got him from the attic, the lights started playing up everywhere we went?"

"I suppose," Jack said doubtfully.

"And pretty soon after, I started seeing things. Really scary things, Jack. Something was already wrong, even before we got to Natalie's. I felt freaked out, and I wanted to hide him. Then I saw this guy, and I'm not sure if he was real or what, but he said some really strange crap to me – so I ran after him. I didn't realize I was in the road. Everything went sort of blurry. And then when the car hit me, I heard this voice…" I could see by Jack's face that she was not buying it. I shrugged helplessly. "I don't know."

"*You* don't know? How do you think I feel? What are you trying to tell me here?"

I rubbed the back of my neck. "The sword is old. I don't even know how old. My grandfather told me that the Yamato family have been hiding and protecting him for at least five hundred years. He said it's... It's our purpose. I think there's some kind of – of power in him and ... I shouldn't have messed with it."

Jack looked at me hard. Finally, she nodded. "I suppose I can live with that as an explanation. Spooky antique sword. Messed you up. Made you imagine stuff. So now that you've put the sword back, things'll go back to normal. Right?"

"Um..."

Jack's eyes narrowed and she came away from the lamppost. "Right?"

"Jack, I meant to put him back. I really did. I tried."

"What do you mean you *tried*?" she demanded. "How hard is it? Just put the effing thing down and walk away."

"I can't."

"Why not? What's stopping you? You're not making any sense here, Mimi."

"I know that! I'm not trying to pretend that it makes sense, OK? I'm just telling you what happened. I went up into the attic last night after we got home. I put him in his box, I closed the lid and – and *I couldn't walk away*. It hurt, Jack, really physically hurt. I was a mess. I couldn't do it. He – he was calling me back."

"*He* called you back," she repeated slowly.

"This isn't an ordinary sword," I said hopelessly. "It's

like he's trying to communicate with me, like we're connected. And I've been having these dreams. For a long time, I never remembered them, but now I do and the sword is in them. It's not... I can't explain any better than that because *I* don't understand. I can't leave him behind. I can't let go of him."

"Mio," she growled, her gaze suddenly riveted to my shoulder where the lump from the padded top of the shinai carrier showed. "Where is this sword ... right now? Please, please, please tell me that it is back in the house where it's legal."

My face must have given me away. She smacked herself in the forehead with her palm and did a quick circle on the pavement, exasperation leaking out of every pore. "Oh come on! This isn't funny. I don't care if that thing – and by the way, have I mentioned how monumentally creepy it is that you keep calling a hunk of metal 'he'? – I don't care if *it* sings 'I Will Always Love You' and tap dances around your bedroom. You cannot just go walking around London in the daytime with a two-foot-long samurai sword strapped to your back!"

"I didn't have a choice, Jack."

"Of course you—"

A scream rang out, cutting through Jack's rising anger. The noise died off with a wet gurgle that made goose pimples spring up over my entire body. Without a word, we both set off running towards the sound, Jack pulling out her phone as we went.

There was a narrow alley between the tarpaulin-covered railings and the ones of the red-brick building next door. I took one look down it and stopped dead. Jack, a step behind, nearly fell over me.

"Near the Justice building, on the corner of Carey Street and Grange Court," she was saying into her phone. "I think someone's been attack—"

Her voice cut off with a gasp as she looked over my shoulder. Faintly I could hear the 999 operator demanding more details. We both ignored her.

"Holy crap," Jack whispered. "Holy crap!"

I recognized the person in the alley – the pretty face and the long red hair. I had seen her on the news in Jack's flat before we headed out. It was the woman who'd been murdered at the museum. A dead woman. And she was ripping someone's throat out.

She looked up from the man she was holding, her teeth bared in a snarl. Blood was smeared across those teeth – teeth that were way too long and sharp to belong in any human's mouth. Her gaze fixed on me, and the bright blue of her eyes flashed yellow, like a cat's caught in the beam of a headlight.

Her victim groaned weakly, and she flung him down at her feet like trash. Ragged clothes and a straggly beard marked him as homeless. There was a lot of blood on those threadbare clothes. My first impulse was to go to him and try to help, but another part of me – a part that had been humming with tension since we heard the scream – held back.

"Child of the Yamatos," the woman said, and ice shot down my spine. Her voice was like a special effect from a film, a sort of cat warble with human tones underneath – but worse than that was the fact that *she knew who I was*.

Her bloody lips stretched into a smile that spread wider, wider, impossibly wider, revealing rows of needle-like fangs all the way back to her ears. "My Mistress was right. She said you were near, sword-bearer. Oh yes, the scent of power is all over you."

"Run, Jack," I whispered. I wanted to shout it, but my throat wouldn't work properly. "Run."

The woman's body was spreading, losing its human shape as it drifted out into a mantle of darkness with nine long, trailing tails. An overpowering smell of animal, dung and wet fur, and something sickly and rotting, rolled over me. I gagged on the stench as memories unfolded in my head. This was the creature I saw fighting the boy in my Dream last night.

Every night.

Desperately, I scanned the windows of the red building, but they were all veiled by thick grey blinds. The tarpaulins on the fence concealed us from the Courts of Justice. The street was deserted. There was a monster, a nightmare monster, right here, alive and walking around in daylight on the streets of London, and no one had noticed.

"Give me the sword." The creature was suddenly right before me. I hadn't even seen it move. "I know you have it. You awakened me when you awakened it. It is Hers. Give it to me." Black, jellylike tentacles reached out for my face.

Something shoved me hard. I fell, and the tentacles closed on air.

Jack hadn't gone anywhere. She was stood directly in the monster's path in a fighting stance, fists raised.

"No!" This time my scream worked. But it was too late.

The creature lashed out at Jack. Its tentacles thudded solidly into her midriff and swept her right off her feet. She went flying over my head and crashed into the rank of motorbikes parked behind me. They toppled like dominoes. Jack disappeared in the tangle of wheels and exhaust pipes.

"Jack!" Terror for my best friend shredded my insides. I surged to my feet.

A pair of tentacles shot in front of me, blocking my path. There was nowhere to go. The monster chuckled richly.

"Help!" I yelled, stretching my hand out towards the street as if I could touch freedom. "Somebody *help*!"

Sudden, almost painful heat pulsed against my spine.

I heard fabric – my coat – tear. A shining black shape flashed over my head towards my open palm. I cringed and then gasped as a familiar silk-wrapped grip slapped into my hand. My fingers closed around it as naturally as if it were part of my own body. My katana.

"Yes..." the monster hissed.

Mine!

I ripped the blade free of the saya and lunged at the creature in a wild, one-handed thrust. But I knew before the movement was half completed that it had no chance of connecting; Ojiichan would have despaired at the clumsiness of the strike. The creature billowed back unhurriedly, its body seeming to hollow out as it avoided the blade. I slashed desperately at its tentacles as they came near. It flicked them out of my reach. The extra limbs danced lazily in the air around me.

"Dear, dear, dear," it said, a deep chuckle grating through its teeth. "You're one hundred years too early for that, little girl."

Like a monster in an anime, I thought in dazed disbelief. *Is this really happening?*

With no warning, two of the black tails whipped forward and wrapped around my wrists. The cold, creeping sensation of the creature's flesh on mine made my stomach roll, and I thrashed and struggled furiously, almost choking with panic. *Get it off, get it off, get it off!*

It was no good. I couldn't budge the tails an inch.

The creature's face, which was growing more pointed and catlike as I watched – black-and-white fur sprouting around its eyes and mouth – drifted closer. The tentacles forced my arms up above my head so that the thing could peer at the katana.

"Veiled. Hidden all away. No wonder my Mistress's other servants have sought in vain. Oh, this will hurt," the thing whispered to itself. "It will burn. But She will reward me."

Slowly, as if reluctant, another of the tails crept towards the katana. The tip of the black tail made contact with the metal and the cat-creature flinched. Then, in a swift movement, it wrapped the entire tentacle around the blade.

A high, whistling noise, like pressurized steam escaping, filled the air. The tail touching the sword seemed to solidify, turning from jellyish black to dull brown marred with dozens of tiny cracks. The katana's blade glowed red, then white-hot. My fingers, wrapped around the grip, felt nothing more than the sword's normal pleasant warmth, but the monster was in agony. Its shadowy body writhed, head whipping from side to side. The tentacles that held me prisoner jerked and trembled.

The whistling noise grew louder as the glow of the blade brightened. It was like a terrible, agonized version of the singing that I knew; a cry of pain. I could almost hear a voice in it, almost hear words in it. It was as if the sword was screaming my name. The sound rent through me and I struggled harder, but it made no difference. The monster's limbs held me like steel cuffs.

The tentacle wrapped around the sword was beginning to crumble away like dried-out clay. The creature's head was tilted back, its eyes shut, deep growls rumbling out of its gaping maw.

Mio! It was a cry of agony from the sword. *Mio!*

In a burst of desperation-induced strength I arched my back. The muscles in my stomach tore as I swung my legs up and kicked out with everything I had.

Both feet hit the cat-monster square in the chest. I bounced off backwards, wrenching the katana with me. The tail holding the sword disintegrated in a cloud of brownish ash. The monster howled as it lost its grip on the blade.

There was a boom of thunder, so close that it seemed to go *through* my body. My bones rang together like bells. White energy exploded from the blade, ricocheting off the walls like the sparks of a Catherine wheel, blinding me. The sword's grip was ripped from my hands. At the same time the monster let go of my wrists. I fell to one knee, shielding my face from the light with my arms.

The beast screamed again. I forced my watering eyes open and stared in disbelief. A tentacle lay on the ground, sliced cleanly through. Dark liquid bubbled up from a wound in the monster's side.

Standing between me and the monster, my katana in his hands, was a man.

He wore a black kimono. Glossy dark hair streamed down his back almost to his waist. As I stared up at his profile, an electric thrill of recognition travelled though me.

It was the warrior from my dream.

I grabbed one of the railings and hauled myself up. "Who – who are you?"

He stared back at me for a wordless, timeless instant. I didn't think it was possible, but he might have looked as shocked as I felt. He sucked in a deep, ragged breath, as if to speak – but instead whipped his head round to stare at the monster again. Powerful muscles bunched in his back as he lifted the katana. Thick, black liquid dripped down the shining blade.

Then he spoke. He spoke with the sword's voice.

"My name is Shinobu."

CHAPTER 6

IMAGINARY FRIENDS

"**Y**ou?" The cat monster hissed at the boy fiercely, gobbets of spit spraying out between its fangs. "I ripped out your heart five hundred years ago in the red forest! You should be dead, dead, dead!"

"Five hundred years?" the boy repeated. He sounded shaken. The point of the blade trembled in the air. "It can't be…"

The monster's eyes gleamed. Its remaining limbs shot forward, sharpening into deadly black claws as they curved around the boy.

He snapped to attention. I saw a flash of a pale, set face, as the sword scythed out in a shining, silver arc. Two more of the creature's tentacles fell to the ground.

"Back!" the boy shouted.

The creature let out a high-pitched scream that made my eardrums vibrate, and scuttled away, trailing through its own black blood. "You shall not imprison me in stone again!"

"Well, it seems I failed the first time," the boy said grimly. "I must try harder."

"Vile humans!" the creature said, lips peeling back over its fangs. "You have no right to the sword! It is not for you. It belongs to my Mistress. Give it to me!"

Mine.

"No!" I cried out.

The boy's sky eyes flickered to me and the memory of his death speared me like a knife; the blood spilling through his fingers, his pained wheeze as he fell. *I can't watch him die again.* I shook with relief as I heard sirens echoing in the distance.

"The police! The police are coming!" I babbled. "They have guns! You'd better run now, or they'll shoot holes through you, you stupid cat. Can't you hear them?"

The monster's face showed confusion for a second. "Guns…" it whispered, grimacing, as if the word tasted bad. It stared at the boy, its tentacles lashing indecisively. Then a look of cunning crossed its face and it drew back, its shadowy form billowing upwards into an arch, like a frightened cat. The severed limbs on the pavement and the splotches of blood bubbled, running back towards the monster's body in black rivulets.

"I will return," it hissed. "And you will surrender the sword then – or die!"

The creature's front limbs sprang up towards the top of the house next to the red-brick building, its body stretching out into an impossibly thin, black bridge. Then, like a rubber band snapping, the back limbs left the ground and the rest of it shot up, disappearing over the edge of the building.

Roof tiles cascaded down into the alley. The boy spun, scooping me up with one arm and pushing me back against the wall. All around us tiles shattered on the pavement with a noise like gunfire, but he was between me and them, sheltering me with his body. A chunk of broken ceramic bounced off his shoulder. He grunted with pain and I heard the katana rattle on the concrete as he dropped it.

"Are you all right?" I gasped out.

He shook his head wordlessly. Silky strands of his hair brushed my check. They smelled of pine trees and smoke. My nose nudged his chin. I wanted to look up into his face, but my own tangled hair was in my eyes. I tried to blow it out of the way. He made a tiny sound that could have been a laugh – choked and rusty – and suddenly gentle hands were combing back the unruly strands, deftly tucking them behind my ear. The movement was so natural, as if he'd done it a thousand times before. His fingers lingered there, just brushing the skin beneath my ear, making it tingle.

Now I could see him. The darkness of his

almond-shaped eyes was filled with blue-grey curls, shapes like rising smoke, or the reflection of storm clouds moving over water. Didn't I know those shapes? The singing was rising up inside me, a true, golden note – telling me that I knew those eyes. I was conscious of a crazy urge to grab his face and hold it still so that I could keep staring at him until I figured it out. Only I didn't need to, because he was already holding still, staring back at me, searching my face for something – maybe for the same something I was looking for in him. Something … something…

There was a hoarse groan behind me. The boy jerked back, his hand falling away from my face as if he'd only just noticed we were touching. Shock and uncertainty flared in his eyes, cutting off whatever fragile thing had been starting to grow between us. For a split second I actually thought I was going to burst into tears.

And then I realized: that was Jack groaning.

I cursed and pushed away from the wall, snatching up the katana and its saya from the ground and flying across the street to where Jack lay half-hidden under a pile of motorcycles. I shoved the sheathed blade through the belt loop on my jeans, then grabbed hold of one of the toppled bikes by the wheel, trying to figure out how to heave it off her.

"Wait!" the boy said, appearing next to me. "Let me help you."

By some miracle of luck, several of the motorbikes

had got tangled up with one another as they fell, forming a cage around Jack rather than landing on her and crushing her. I couldn't see any blood, but years of watching *Casualty* and *CSI* told me that didn't necessarily mean she was fine. As the boy pulled the last bike off I dropped to my knees beside her, not daring to move her or even touch her, in case she had hurt her back.

"Jack. Jack, can you hear me?"

Her eyes stayed closed. Now I knew exactly how she had felt after seeing that car hit me the night before, and why she had been so angry that I hadn't put the damn katana away. *This is my fault. This is all my fault. Oh God, Jack. What if she's really hurt?*

The boy knelt next to me, took Jack's wrist in a careful grasp and laid the fingers of his other hand over the top. "Do not fear. She is alive," he said gently. "Her heart is beating strongly."

Jack groaned again and suddenly tried to roll over onto her side. I put my hand on her shoulder, holding her still. "Don't move, Jack. Please just stay where you are."

"Jesus, I feel like I got hit by a bus," she whimpered. "What happened?"

"It was a motorbike," I said. "Several of them. Help's coming, OK? Stay calm. You're going to be fine."

"Whoa," Jack said, blinking at me blearily. "Deja vu much?"

"I know," I said, swiping tears off my cheeks. "But

I don't think you're getting off as lightly as me."

"Your friend's pupils are the same size, and they are reacting evenly to the light," the boy said. "She recognizes you and understands you. I think she will be all right."

Fresh tears welled up and I scrubbed at them impatiently. "Thank you. I can't even ... for everything. Thank you."

"Ah, who's this?" Jack asked. "I don't remember... Oh my God, what about that *thing*?"

"It's gone," I said, not feeling any need to mention that it had promised to come back, Terminator-style. "And this is... This is..." I blinked a few times. "I'm sorry but who *are* you? I mean, one minute I was all alone and the next you were just – there."

"My name is Yamato Shinobu," he said, sitting back a little and letting go of Jack's wrist. "But where I came from, I cannot say, for ... I do not know."

The sirens wailed much closer now. I could hear tyres screeching as they circled, looking for signs of a disturbance. Shinobu's head tilted as if he were trying to make sense of the sound – then his eyes lifted to the buildings surrounding us for the first time. He looked around, his expression part confusion, part awe. "This is a strange place," he said softly. "I had not realized before how truly strange."

I shook my head. Lots of people were called Yamato,

but… "You don't know? You don't *know* where you came from? Or – where you are?"

"I…" The boy glanced over his shoulder and got swiftly to his feet. "I think I must look at this old man. There is a lot of blood. Do not concern yourself, Mio-dono – stay with Jack-san."

Before I could form a question that would encompass even half of what I wanted to know, he had slipped away to where the homeless man still lay in the alley.

"What did he just call me?" Jack whispered.

"He called you Jack-san," I said absent-mindedly, watching him from the corner of my eye. "Which is like … Japanese for 'Miss Jack'."

"Right. Cute. What did he call you?"

I gulped. "I don't know."

"Liar." Despite her position on the ground, Jack managed to look menacing. "Spill."

"Er – well, if I remember my anime subtitles right – he called me … 'Lady Mio'."

Jack blinked a few more times. "Hold up. Am *I* hallucinating now?"

"Maybe it's contagious," I muttered. "Because I never told him our names."

Rachel doodled on the edge of her Jung essay in red pen. Her attempt at a rose had become a pool of blood, so she added a bloody hand print and then a curved, red-dripping dagger. Finally she swore, threw her pen down and tried her sister's mobile for the seventh time.

For the seventh time she got a recorded message saying that the phone she was trying to reach was unavailable. She muttered under her breath and switched to Mio's number.

"This is not funny," she enunciated clearly once she had got through to the answering service. "I expect this kind of behaviour from Jacqueline, but not from you. You've been gone for hours. Ring me back and tell me where you are and what you're doing *right now* or I'm calling my mother. That's right, you heard me. And don't think I won't call your parents too, Mio!"

She hung up, dropped her phone onto the table in the Yamatos' kitchen – where she'd brought her essay after the girls had left, hoping that the light and space would help focus her brain – and prowled backwards and forwards under the glass roof of the extension, staring up at the bruised grey clouds. It had been sleeting steadily for the past two hours. Where were they? If they'd gone indoors somewhere and decided to stay for lunch they ought to have let her know, dammit. If they got into trouble it'd be her ass in the fire.

She snatched a banana from the fruit bowl and ate it moodily, wondering if she really did dare call her mother, and if so, whether watching Jack quail under their parent's wrath would be worth getting a scolding of her own for not looking after Jack better. Like she was supposed to put an ankle bracelet on the kid or something. Jack never listened to her anyway.

She tried both phone numbers again while she finished off the banana. Still no answer. She left another snappy message, then went to toss the banana skin into the rubbish bin and swore when she found that it was stuffed full. The lid wouldn't even go down properly. Disgusting. Grumbling and muttering the whole time, she changed the bag and tied the full one up, then pushed open the glass door that led out to the Yamatos' tiny back garden, where they kept their wheelie bins under the overhang of the garage roof.

She squinted up at the sky, then made a run for it across the scrubby grass. The sleet bored straight through the thin fabric of her jumper in icy needles, and by the time she reached the bins she was shivering, damp, and more annoyed than ever. Taking out the rubbish was Mio's job. It was amazing how Mio, with her angelic face and perfect manners, managed to slither out of almost anything she didn't want to do. And got away with it too, far more often than Jack, who always had to make a big deal out of everything. Rachel shoved the bag of kitchen waste into a wheelie bin, slammed the lid and braced herself to run back from the shelter of the garage overhang.

Then she heard something.

It was a pitiful mewing noise, weak and squeaky, like a tiny kitten. Rachel's heart melted instantly. She made soft clicking noises with her tongue, creeping slowly round the edge of the garage, towards the thick yew hedge that separated the Yamato garden from the narrow alley at the back.

"Here, puss, here, cutie," she whispered. "Come out, darling."

Another pathetic little meow drew her forward, even though she could barely see where she was going. It was so dark back here that it was like night had come on without her realizing it, and the cold was intense. She needed to get the poor stray inside before the weather got any worse.

"Come on out, precious. I'll look after you."

There was another mew, close enough that Rachel was sure the cat must be nearly at her feet. She crouched down, extending her hand ahead of her, expecting to feel a tiny, shivering body and wet fur at any second. "There you are, puss. Are you hungry, hmmm? Are you hungry?"

The cat meowed again, right in her ear. Rachel jumped, and her hand made contact with something. Something clammy and gelatinous, like a giant slug.

It wriggled under her fingers.

She jerked back with a cry of disgust, but a weight hit her shoulders, crushing her to the ground. The wind left her lungs in a pained wheeze. She could feel something crawling across her back, and she struggled to suck in enough breath to scream, but another damp, rubbery thing slapped across her mouth, choking the cry back down her throat.

"Oh, yes…" whispered a low, gloating voice. "Yes, little girl. I am very hungry indeed."

I had a moment's panic as the emergency services finally arrived; the sword was still tucked at my waist and highly conspicuous. I didn't have time to get my coat off and put it in the shinai carrier. I cursed myself. *You'll get arrested!*

The boy – Shinobu – leaned towards me. "What is the matter?"

"I can't let them see…" I gestured to the katana, turning my back on the ambulance personnel swarming around the homeless old guy and Jack.

Shinobu frowned, then nodded. "Stay still."

"What?" Before I could say anything else, the sword had disappeared from my belt loop. I gasped. I'd barely seen Shinobu's hands move.

There was a tug at the neck of my coat. In the next instant the solid, reassuring weight of the sword was in its place in the shinai carrier on my back and the flap of torn coat was flipped back over the top. Shinobu stepped away, his head turning as he checked if anyone had noticed. "It is hidden."

"How did you…?" My voice trailed off. I already knew the answer. He was incredibly fast. *Inhumanly fast.* I shrugged a little and felt the sword's contented purr of energy as it settled into place. "Um. Thanks. Again."

He bowed solemnly. "You are welcome."

As the medics bustled around, stopping the homeless man's bleeding and checking Jack's skull was intact, the two police officers started peppering us with questions. I met Jack's eyes once, and she nodded slightly. That was all it took. Our answers were identical.

"Did you see your attacker?"

Yes. It was a woman.

"Can you describe her?"

She had long, red hair. She was youngish, probably in her thirties. And wicked strong – she threw us both around like we weighed nothing. Maybe she was on drugs or something?

"Did you know her?"

No, she was a stranger.

"Had you ever seen her around before?"

Nope, sorry.

"Would you recognize her if you saw her again?"

Maybe, but it was all so fast and scary, you know? We never really got that good a look at her.

I kept waiting for one of them to single out Shinobu for a question. He loomed behind us, a giant, kimono-wearing shadow, apparently torn between watching the EMTs work, and staring at the buildings, the road, the police cars and ambulance. Even the streetlights. It was like he'd never seen them before. I wanted to reach out and reassure him somehow, but I didn't want to draw attention to him. He already couldn't have looked more out of place if he'd tried. He seemed … lost.

We got lucky. Maybe they assumed he didn't speak

English or something, because the police ignored him the whole time. So did the medics, which was strange considering they insisted on giving me a check-up, even though I told them I was fine.

Finally the paramedics loaded the homeless guy into the ambulance – he'd lost a lot of blood, but he was going to be all right – and asked the police to bring me and Jack to the hospital so that Jack could have x-rays. Jack argued about that, but half-heartedly enough that I knew she must be feeling pretty bad. I helped her to her feet, and put my arm around her.

One officer – a woman – walked ahead to open the door of the police car for us. Jack took two steps and staggered as her boot caught on an uneven bit of paving. She weighed a lot more than I did and my knees were still shaky anyway; for a second I thought we were both going to do a face plant. In a flash Shinobu was on Jack's other side, propping her up effortlessly.

"Thanks," she mumbled.

We got to the car. I loaded Jack in and went to follow her, then noticed that Shinobu was standing back, obviously confused about what he was supposed to do next. A motorcycle whizzed past us and he flinched and reached for the red sash at his waist as if he expected to find a sword there. I took hold of a fistful of his kimono sleeve. "Come on," I said firmly, trying to tug him after me. "You're going with us."

At first it was like tugging on a steel banister attached to a concrete wall. He stood motionless, staring at the car, and at the vehicles passing on the road. His fathomless eyes were confused and wary. Despite the towering size of him – he must have been over six-feet tall – there was something strangely vulnerable about him right then.

I stopped pulling at his sleeve and closed my hand around his arm, squeezing gently. A little electric thrill sizzled across my palm. "Shinobu?"

He looked at me. Some kind of weird understanding flashed between us: *It's all right. I'm here. You're not alone in this.*

He nodded wordlessly. He let me pull him into the car after us.

I took the middle seat. It was a good thing I was small. With two large and extremely muscular people book-ending me, there wasn't much room left in the back. Being squashed against Jack wasn't really a novelty, since she and I usually got the same Tube or bus home from school. Having my shoulder and thigh pressed into the boy's was something else altogether. My skin tingled everywhere that was in contact with him, like he was giving out some form of radiation that only I could feel. It made me too aware of him.

The male police officer climbed into the passenger seat and looked at us in the rear-view mirror. "Are you two all right back there?"

"Two?" Jack repeated slowly. "But—"

A couple of small puzzle pieces clicked together in my head. *No wonder no one asked him any questions!*

I grabbed Jack's hand and squeezed it hard. She snapped her mouth shut. We both turned our heads to stare at the boy. He looked back at us gravely, eyes shadowy in the dim interior of the car.

"We're fine," Jack said. "Thanks."

The female officer got into the driver's side and the car pulled away from the kerb, following the ambulance into traffic, where it immediately got stuck. Under the sound of the engine idling, Jack whispered, "Can they not … see you?"

"I don't believe so," he admitted. His voice was low, but definitely not a whisper. I looked at the back of the officers' heads. Neither of them so much as flinched.

"I noticed earlier that they were looking through me. You were too occupied to realize," he said, in answer to our shocked faces. "I don't know how. Or why it is that you can see and hear me, when they cannot."

Jack put her hand over her eyes with a groan. "Maybe I hit my head harder than I thought."

"Are you going to be sick?" asked the female police officer urgently. "I'll unlock the back door so you can lean out."

"No – she's just got a headache," I said. "Don't worry."

"Who is this guy?" Jack muttered. "Where did he

104

come from? What really happened back there? I think my skull is going to pop if someone doesn't tell me what the eff is going on."

"Look, you have to know something about all this," I said quietly, looking at the boy out of the corner of my eye. "You knew who we were, our names even. How did you know that?"

Shinobu's expression was bleak. The chill of it made my tingling skin go numb. "You will think I am insane."

That was eerily similar to what I'd been saying to Jack right before everything went to hell. I bumped his knee gently with mine. "After all the stuff I've seen in the past couple of days? I'm pretty sure *I'm* insane. So just spill it. Whatever it is."

He swallowed audibly. "I have seen this city and all these strange and wondrous things before. I have seen the both of you before. In my dreams."

CHAPTER 7

REMEMBRANCE

"Once upon a time, when all the lands that floated on the sea were new," Ojiichan had said, "two powerful beings came into existence as suddenly as sparks of lightning blazing to life among the stars. The first being was to be a king, and he was handsome and commanding. The second was to be his queen, and she was beautiful and gentle. And these two fell in love, of course."

"Of course," I muttered, my feet jiggling restlessly under the covers. Normally there was nothing better than one of my grandfather's stories at bedtime, but that night I wasn't interested in fairy tales. "Ojiichan, you said you'd tell me about…" I hesitated, then pointed at the ceiling. "You know."

One who remembers. One who endures. One who is hidden. Mine.

Ojiichan raised his eyebrows. "And so I will. Are you

going to listen? Or would you rather we read about Peter Rabbit?"

I snorted with laughter at the threat, flopping back onto the pillow. "No, thank you."

He smiled. "Then no more interruptions. Now, for a time, the two were happy with only each other for company, but at last they decided that they wanted to have children; children that would be as perfect and beautiful as they were themselves.

"It was here that for the first time something did not go as planned for the king and queen. Perhaps it was the queen's desperation or the king's arrogance, but their first children were not perfect, not beautiful. Their son was born without bones, and him they called Leech Child. Their daughter was horribly deformed, and her they called Faint Island. The queen wept over her poor children and their suffering, but the king… Oh, the king raged and stormed and cursed, and, at last, disgusted and unable to stand the sight of these imperfect children any more, he made to cast them into the sea."

"He's horrible," I whispered.

"Oh yes, he is. His wife intervened, weeping and begging him not to murder their offspring. Instead of flinging the children into the water to drown, she made her husband put them into a reed boat, in the hope that they would float to a new land where someone would find and care for them. But that was all she could do for the unwanted babies, for she knew that if she tried to keep them, her husband would never be satisfied until he had killed them and wiped their ugliness and his failure away.

"The king and queen tried again for children, and this time their efforts were rewarded, and the queen had many good, strong babies that were lovely enough to satisfy her husband.

"But just as their happiness seemed perfect, something went wrong again. The queen gave birth to a child that was too strong, too powerful, whose power was as great as the fire of the sun. And in giving life to the child, the queen died. Again the king raged and stormed, his fury fuelled by the agony of his grief for his beloved mate, and this time there was no compassionate wife to beg for mercy for the child. The king killed him, and in the same insanity of sorrow, he broke open the great gates of Yomi, the Underworld, where all immortal spirits dwell in eternal darkness, and began to call out for his dead queen, his lost wife, to come back to him.

"For days the king wandered through the pitch-blackness of the Underworld, searching for the queen. Finally he found her, knowing her by the soft touch of her hand and the musical beauty of her voice, and his joy was great. But the queen was horrified that he had come, and told him that he must go back, must leave without her, for she had eaten the food of Yomi and could never now return to the lands of the living.

"The king was not swayed by these words. He told her that his love for her was as wide as the ends of the earth, as deep as the bottom of the sea, and higher than the highest peak of the sky, and that he would never leave Yomi unless she came with him at his side. The queen was convinced of his devotion and agreed to travel back with him into the light again. In his happiness and his eagerness to leave that chill and shadowy place, the king forgot himself, and forgot that Yomi is dark for a reason. And so he lit a torch in order to guide them quickly from that realm of shadows. The moment the light flared the queen cried out. The king quickly turned to her, and then cried out himself, for he saw—"

A loud bang at the bedroom door nearly made me jump right out of the bed. But it wasn't a creature from the Underworld; it was my dad, angry with my grandfather for telling me "ghoulish" stories that he was convinced would give me nightmares. Banging on the door was Dad's way of telling my grandfather to stop. If Ojiichan didn't emerge from the room in a minute or less, then he'd come in and shout at us.

After Ojiichan had kissed me on the forehead and wished me good night, he promised in a whisper that he would tell me the rest the next day. But the next day when I got up, I found Ojiichan lying in a boneless heap at the bottom of the stairs. He'd had a massive stroke.

He was dead a day later.

I know that no one likes hospitals. But ever since Ojiichan died, the way I feel goes beyond that. I hate them.

The moment the police walked us into the A&E, it was pretty much all I could do to stop myself from running right back out again. I balked at the second lot of electronic doors as a gust of that sickening hospital smell smacked me right in the nose. Shinobu stopped just behind me, and I could feel the warmth of his hand hovering at my back, not quite touching me.

"Are you all right?" he murmured.

The sight of Jack's anxious face turning back to look for me forced me to nod and take that step inside.

They separated us almost at once. While Jack went to have x-rays as a matter of urgency – the female officer right behind her – I was left in the bustling emergency waiting area. There didn't seem to be much else to do but sit down. As soon as I did, the male police officer sat in the seat next to me. Shinobu had stopped at the entrance, putting his back to one pale blue wall as he stared around at the hospital with wide eyes.

I caught his gaze and tried to indicate to him with a jerk of my head that he ought to take the seat on my other side. The policeman gave me a funny look. But Shinobu hesitantly came forward and dropped down onto the uncomfortable plastic seat so it seemed worth it.

We sat like that for about half an hour. The police

officer asked me a few more questions – mostly the same questions, actually, but phrased slightly differently – noted down my answers in his little book, then finally decided to go and look for his partner.

He didn't come back.

Sticking to my role as a mild-mannered, innocent, bewildered teen hadn't taken much effort. It was pretty close to the truth anyway. But at least it had been something to concentrate on. The second the officer was gone, my brain started to go haywire.

I'd come within an inch of dying an hour ago. Not dying in a car crash or some normal accident that could happen to anyone – *murdered*. Killed by a monster so awful that it shouldn't even exist in people's nightmares. Only it did exist in mine.

Then I was remembering Ojiichan, lying in the bed in the High Dependency ward, and the dry rasping noises of his last breaths, the sight of the skin around his mouth crinkling up like tissue paper, that dull milky sheen on his eyes.

Stop it, I told myself fiercely. *That's not helping. Just think about something else!*

Like what? Like the sight of Jack lying under that pile of metal debris? Like how it felt not to know, for a minute, if she was even alive or dead?

"Oh God," I whispered, putting my hands over my face. They blocked out the too-bright lights reflecting off the cold blue walls, but not the constant background noises of suppressed panic and pain that grated over my senses or that hospital smell that was choking my lungs. Why didn't they spray some freaking air freshener? It smelled nearly as bad as that thing – that awful thing – and it's cold, creeping tentacles. God, what *was* it? Could it possibly be real?

Why did it come after me? Why did it want my sword?

"Mio-dono?"

It was freezing in here, icy blasts of air coming in through the door every time a new casualty arrived. I could feel myself shivering, but sweat was standing out on my face, sticky and uncomfortable.

What is happening to me?

"Mio!"

I jumped, pulling my hands away from my face. The boy was crouched on the floor in front of me, staring up into my face.

"Look at me," he said, his voice low, a little rough. He leaned forward protectively. "I'm here. Don't be afraid."

Reluctantly I met his eyes. There was real concern there, as if he knew me. As if he cared about me. Without understanding why, I felt myself start to relax a little.

"Who are you?" I whispered shakily. "I don't mean … I remember what you said, but who *are* you? Why—" I almost chickened out, then forced myself to say it. "Why have we been dreaming about each other?"

Suddenly he had that wary, vulnerable look again. "You have seen me in your dreams?"

"Yes. For a long time. Years." I tried to figure out his expression. "I saw you fighting that monster. I saw you turn it into stone, and then I saw... I saw you ..." *Die.* "... fall."

His lips pressed together. "The connection runs both ways then. Did you see anything else? Did you see what happened after that?"

A green blade flashing down in the red light... I frowned as the memory jolted through me. "Not really. What did happen?"

"Mio-dono, the last thing I remember that is real to me is the battle you saw in your dream. I was struck down, and I thought I would die and go to meet my ancestors. Instead ... when at last I awakened, I was trapped. I know not where. There was no light. No nothing. Only confinement and blackness and cold. Endless cold. There was no time for me in that place. I might have been trapped for minutes or days or months or ... longer. I faded in and out of awareness, and I wondered, when I could make space within my suffering to wonder, if I was in Yomi, punished, or exiled, or forgotten by the gods."

"That's – that's horrible."

"But then something changed," he said, leaning further into me. "I began to see things in the dark. See and hear and feel. I saw an impossible place, with buildings

113

like mountains, where people spoke a strange, garbled tongue. I saw monstrous machines, and great wonders. And I saw…"

"Me and Jack?" I finished, remembering what he had said before.

"When you were together, yes. Mainly, I saw *you*. Felt you…" His eyes dropped to my lips. "I saw everything that you did. Heard what you did. I felt what you felt, and knew when you were sad, hungry, angry, afraid… It is from you that I learned to speak this language – English?"

I nodded dumbly.

"I have seen this world before, through your eyes. Though it is very different being here in my own body. Being able to see and hear for myself, being able to touch…" His tanned fingers flexed on his knee, millimetres from mine. His hand was long and bony, and flecked with tiny white scars.

"Then when you said you didn't know how you'd got here or where you came from, you *literally* meant that. The last thing that happened to you was—"

Death.

He nodded, his face grave and set.

"And then" – I snapped my fingers – "you're free, and you appear here, just in time to save me from a horrible death?"

His eyes flashed up to mine. A beautiful, slightly crooked smile spread over his face, lighting it up like a sudden blinding flash of the sun through thick clouds on a cold day. And just as suddenly, it was gone, leaving him thoughtful again.

"Yes," he breathed. "Just in time. Mio-dono, I was with you yesterday when you entered the dark room upstairs in your parents' house and took out the sword – my sword. But I saw something you did not see. When you laid hands on it you … you burst into light, into white flames that swirled around you and through you. Almost at once you began to feel things and see things. Shades, shadows, things that weren't there. Those flames did something to you. The sword did something to you."

"Wait. What about that guy? That guy who called himself the Harbinger. Was he real? Did I hallucinate him too?"

"No," Shinobu said emphatically. "He was real. Even in the cold and dark I could feel his power. I do not know what he is, but he is … inimical to humans."

"Then I got hit by that car," I said slowly, following events back in my mind. "I thought I was going to die, but I heard a voice, telling me it would be all right. It was your voice."

He lifted his head again. His eyes almost nailed me to the seat with their intensity. "You were dying. I could feel it. I reached out and tried to pull you back. I tried with everything I had. I strained and fought the blackness as I had never had the strength to fight before. Something …

cracked. Within me or within my prison. Energy spilled out – more white flames – and for a moment you and I and the flames were … *one*."

"Miss Yamato?"

I leapt up as if my seat had burned me. A new police officer – not one of the ones who had brought us here – stood near by. *Oh my God*. He couldn't see Shinobu, so it must have looked as though I was having an intense conversation with thin air.

I forced myself to answer. "Yes, that's me."

"Your friend has had her x-rays. She's asking for you, and I have some questions for you both. Then we can get you home. Come this way."

Despite the reassuring words, the man's voice was strangely flat and metallic, like he was really furious about something and trying to hide it. I tried to check his expression, but he had already turned away from me and was heading past the rows of seats towards a door on the other side of the waiting room.

"I think I'm in trouble," I muttered to Shinobu as I followed the policeman, concealing the movement of my lips with a fake cough.

"You have done nothing wrong," Shinobu said. "They cannot punish you."

"Shows how much you know about the British legal system," I said weakly.

The policeman pushed the door open. He gestured

curtly for me to step into the room ahead of him. Shinobu slipped in silently, and the door clicked shut behind us.

It was an ordinary examination room, with a desk crowded with messy papers and an ancient computer, a curtain on a rail surrounding a high bed, and metal blinds over the windows. Jack was perched on the edge of the bed, looking bored. Her face lit up when she saw me. She opened her mouth, but before she could say anything, Shinobu shouted.

I spun round.

He was frozen in the middle of the room, hands outstretched as if he had been trying to reach for me. His eyes were completely blank. Like a shop dummy. I looked at Jack to see if this really was my imagination, or something real again. She was caught mid-movement too, one foot on the floor, eyes glazed over.

It was as if someone had hit the pause button on both of them.

Someone?

For the first time I tried to look straight into the policeman's face. I couldn't.

Even in the bright fluorescent lights, even standing right in front of him, I still could not see him. My eyes just wouldn't focus. It was like looking into a black hole.

"What are you?" I whispered.

He dissolved into darkness.

The room filled with a wild, screaming wind that

lifted me from my feet and threw me backwards into the wall. My head bounced off the plaster, and I cried out. I felt the katana rip through the material of my coat again, shredding what was left of the shoulder to pieces.

I hung helplessly, feet dangling above the ground. Papers flew around me, shredding in the air. The blinds rattled like bones. My back and ribs screamed with strain. The wind was trying to push me right through the plasterboard.

The seething mass of darkness was directly in front of me, warping and stretching, changing. It became a human torso in a long, black kimono, the fabric covered with strange patterns of gold. Something pale slid up into view, the shadows trickling away from it like water down a window. A face.

Its proportions were strange, subtly skewed, too long and delicate to be right. Its eyes were closed, and its expression was blank. It was the man from Natalie's party.

The Harbinger.

Nothing was holding me to the wall. He wasn't even touching me. But I couldn't get free. My breath gulped and sobbed as his power drummed at me, pummelling my skin, my bones, my hair, my teeth: *Worship me, worship me, worship me...*

When his eyelids lifted his eyes were gone. There were only shining, white globes, rooted in his skull, burning into me.

He held the unsheathed katana in one hand. The saya lay carelessly discarded on the ground at his feet. Tiny sparks of pale energy danced up and down the blade, bounced off his hand. I could feel the singing vibration of the sword reaching out to me, trying to find me, but something blocked it. He blocked it. He had taken my sword from me.

"What a small, ugly thing you are," he said, contempt and a vast weariness edging his voice. "But you are the last of your line, so I shall preserve your life. Since your family seem to have neglected your education, I now do you the honour of enlightening your appalling ignorance. Listen to me closely, for I am the one whom it is your purpose to serve. Never forget that. You belong to me. This sword belongs to me. *Everything* belongs to me." He lifted the sword and allowed the tip to hover at the vulnerable curve of my throat. The proximity burned, as if he was aiming a laser at my skin. The katana was crying out for me, but I couldn't move, and it *hurt*.

"You are Yamato. You exist to protect the katana, as generations of your ancestors have done before you, stretching back to the day I first chose them. You will not fail me. If the sword is lost, you will die, hell shall open, and shadows and blood will devour this world. Do you understand?" The words reeled out of his mouth almost by rote, as if he had said them a thousand times before.

I nodded, the tiny, pained movement the only one

I was capable of. My fingers clenched and my toes curled as the constriction on my chest increased. I could barely breathe.

The Harbinger sneered and turned away, removing the blade from my neck. He lifted the sword, pointing... Pointing to Shinobu.

Shinobu jerked back to life. He took one look at the situation – me hanging from the wall, the man standing in front of me, the katana in his hand – and blanched. Fury filled his face. He leapt forward.

The sword shrieked, the sound of its pain vibrating through me.

Lightning sparked at the tip of the blade.

Stakes of crackling white energy shot through Shinobu's body. He let out a hoarse cry, doubling up in agony. *No, no, no!*

"Don't." It took every bit of strength I had to force the word out. My voice was slurred and stumbling, as if I was drunk.

More bars of light sliced through Shinobu, impaling him to the floor. His voice cut off as if he had no more breath, but I could still see him moving, struggling, his hands clutching at the lino floor. His head flung back and I could see the shape of his mouth stretched into a silent scream.

"Stop it!" My back arched and was slammed against the wall. "Why?"

The Harbinger made a tiny tut of disgust. "So very stupid. I am repairing the damage – the damage that you have carelessly allowed, girl. Be grateful you are the last Yamato or I would have punished you for that carelessness."

The bars of light sparked. Shinobu convulsed as if he was being shocked, his eyes rolling back in their sockets.

Then he began to fade. Literally fade away. The colours seeped out of him, like a watercolour if someone spills liquid on it. I could see the pattern of the lino through his back. He was disappearing right in front of my eyes. White fire flared up on the katana's blade, rippling along the shining black-and-white curve. The steel almost glowed with relentless solidity as Shinobu disappeared.

He's dying…

I screamed.

"Be silent," the Harbinger snapped.

I can't watch him die again. I can't! My heels drummed at the wall as I fought the unbearable, suffocating weight of the Harbinger's power. *I can't let him go. I have to hold on!*

I screamed again. Screamed Shinobu's name.

The sleek shape of the katana flashed. One moment it was firmly grasped in the Harbinger's fist. The next it was gone. The Harbinger's head snapped round, shock and sudden fear contorting his face.

The hilt of the katana hit my palm and my fingers snapped closed around it. Strength surged through my body, freeing me from the force that had held me to the wall, freeing me from the Harbinger's death-grip on my mind. My feet hit the floor and my arm whipped the blade out like an extension of my own bone and muscle.

The Harbinger dodged so quickly that he blurred. But not quite fast enough.

My katana scored a long, shallow line diagonally across his torso from shoulder to hip, ripping the fabric of his kimono open. White fire burst out along the torn edges of the black fabric.

The Harbinger yelled: *"Mio?"*

The room shook. The windows shattered. Glass shards blasted through the air.

Everything went black.

CHAPTER 8

OF
DARKNESS

Icy cold droplets pattered down onto my face and hands. Rain. It was blowing in through the broken windows. A fire alarm screeched close by. I blinked and realized that I was on the floor, slumped against the wall. My legs had given out beneath me.

The room was wrecked. Furniture had been overturned and flung away into the corners, the lino floor was marked with a starburst of long, black scorch marks. Overhead, ceiling tiles had melted, exposing pipes and electrical wires. The metal strips from the blinds had torn loose from the windows and were embedded in crazy patterns all over the walls. I was covered in broken glass.

I couldn't stop staring at the devastation. It was like a scene out of a nightmare.

"Yo, Mimi! Snap out of it!"

The familiar voice made me blink. I tried to focus, but it was as if something had shaken loose in my brain. I lifted my hands to rub them over my face and realized I was still clutching the sword. My fingers had locked around the hilt and I couldn't let go.

A large, warm hand settled over my bloodless fingers and carefully prised them away from the grip, then chafed the skin, massaging until the blood began to flow back. My hand burned fiercely where the silk and the golden menuki had bitten into my palm.

"Mio-dono, please." The deep voice was urgent. "Are you hurt? Does anything hurt?"

I squeezed my eyes shut for a minute, feeling the fractured pieces of my consciousness start to slide back into their normal places. I knew these voices. I knew the hand holding mine.

When I opened my eyes, I saw Jack and Shinobu crouched in front of me. Jack's face was streaked with soot and Shinobu's was drawn and grey.

"Did you hit your head?" Jack waved her hand in front of my face. "What the hell happened in here?"

I felt the tears well up in my eyes and spill down my cheeks. "The policeman was a monster," I managed to say, sobs shuddering out of my chest. "The Harbinger. He froze you. Oh God. I attacked him. I tried – I tried to k–kill him!"

I lifted one heavy arm and grabbed the front of

Shinobu's kimono. The fabric was whole, unmarked. It showed no signs of the white energy that had torn through it – through him. I pushed the material aside and ran my fingers over the bare, golden skin of his chest, searching for scars. "You – you were – you were scream-ing. The light went through you like knives."

Shinobu gently caught my wrist, stilling the frantic movements of my hand. His face, pale a moment before, suddenly looked flushed. He cleared his throat. "I am uninjured."

"Jack? Are you—?"

"I'm fine," Jack said. "The x-rays were clear, and I feel all right. But I don't remember anything after you walked in with Shinobu and that policeman. It was like I blinked and woke up on the floor."

"He wasn't a policeman," I whispered, shaking my head. "I can't – he wasn't *human*. Oh God."

"I think she's in shock," Jack said.

"Why is this happening?" I asked, leaning forward to grab the front of Shinobu's robe again. "What am I sup-posed to do?"

"Listen, I want answers too, but we can't stay here while we get them," Jack interrupted firmly. "It looks like we tried to blow the place sky-high. Let's make a run for it and with any luck no one'll realize we were in this room. We just have to cross our fingers there aren't CCTV cameras pointing this way."

Shinobu nodded sharply, even though half of what she'd just said had to be gobbledegook to him. He picked up the katana, sheathed it and, after a moment of hesitation, offered it to me.

Mine. My hands moved before my brain could decide whether it was a good idea or not. I took the sword from him, reached over my shoulder and, in a single movement, shoved it through the gaping hole in my coat, back into the shinai carrier. It buzzed softly against my shoulder blade, and I patted the top of the hilt absentmindedly, then stared down at my shaking fingers in shock.

"Wait. What … what about the real police?" I asked, struggling to get my head together. "Aren't they waiting for us? What are they going to think if we just leave?"

"I don't know where they are. I've been sitting around waiting on my own for forty minutes," Jack said. "Maybe that fake guy got rid of them. Anyway, we don't owe them anything. If they want statements, they're just going to have to come round to the house. Come on."

I braced myself on the wall and struggled up, with Shinobu and Jack helping me. Glass chunks showered off all of us. It was a miracle that we weren't cut to pieces.

Shinobu steadied me on my feet and released me. "Mio-dono—"

"I'm not a lady," I said woozily. "You do know that, right?"

Shinobu ignored my words completely. "May I borrow your coat?"

I blinked. "I–I suppose." Clumsily I shrugged out of it, grabbing Jack's shoulder to keep me upright. "Are you cold?"

Shinobu wrapped the thick duffle material around his arm. "I do not want to risk you or Jack-san cutting yourselves as you climb out. Stand back, please." Using the wad of fabric, he began to clear the window of the remaining jagged shards still clinging to the frame.

"You can tell he's not from around here," Jack said, impressed. "That's what they call a real gentleman."

Shinobu was already coming back, shaking the glass off the fabric. He moved behind me, holding the coat out so that I could put it back on easily over the shinai carrier. Fingers whispered gently across the exposed nape of my neck. I shivered. Then my arms were in the sleeves and he moved around me, examining my face with a frown.

"I think we should go," he said. "Now."

"You don't have to tell me twice!" Jack caught the edge of the window frame – which was waist height for her – and climbed over it without any difficulty, although her movements were a bit stiffer than normal. She was more bruised up than she wanted me to know.

Shinobu knelt down and cupped his hands, giving me an expectant look.

"Wh–what are you doing?" I asked him.

"You will need a leg up," he said, as if it was obvious. "You are not as tall as Jack-san."

Normally I would have grumbled and muttered – I hated having my shortness pointed out – but the sight of him patiently waiting there on his knees made me feel … odd. Like Jack said, I wasn't used to this kind of behaviour from boys.

I made sure there was no glass on my boots, then very carefully placed one heel in Shinobu's cupped hands. He supported me as if I weighed nothing. I got my other foot up onto the frame and dropped down on the other side. A second later Shinobu landed soundlessly beside me.

As he straightened he suddenly staggered. For a moment I thought he would actually keel over, but one hand shot out and he managed to catch himself on the wall. The golden skin of his face had gone even paler and the hand he had pressed against the bricks was shaking visibly.

Just like that, fears about my own actions, about the sword, about what was coming next, even the dizziness, all compressed into a shadow in the back of my brain so that I could concentrate on worrying about Shinobu.

"You *are* hurt, aren't you?" Instinctively I shoved my shoulder under his arm and put my arm around his waist to support him. Rock-hard muscles trembled under my hand. "Why didn't you say something?"

Jack hurried to help, propping him up on the other

side. "Dude, you look awful."

"Not hurt," he said faintly. "Whatever the Harbinger did – there was – pain. I think … it has been a long time since I felt pain. Since I felt anything. "

Jack and I exchanged a worried look. "Let's get moving," I said.

Supporting the much taller Shinobu as well as we could, we moved through the silent ranks of cars. As soon as we turned the corner, I saw that the hospital was in chaos. Staff and patients from A&E, driven out by the explosion and the fire alarm, were milling around everywhere or huddling under the roof overhangs outside the entrance, trying to avoid the icy rain. No one was going to notice us slipping away.

Walking to the Tube station, swiping our passes through the barriers and then boarding the train had a strange, dreamlike quality with Shinobu in tow. Every time someone's gaze skated over him I expected them to react, but it was clear that no one saw anything more than a pair of dishevelled teenagers who needed to apply serious quantities of soap and water. It made me doubt myself again. My eyes kept flicking to his face, not just to see if he was OK, but to make sure he hadn't disappeared.

Thankfully, as soon as he sat down his colour started to come back. When the Tube moved he stirred himself to turn and stare out of the window at the darkness and to reach up and tap at one of the fluorescent lights. By the time we stumbled off at our normal stop, a few minutes' walk from home, he was able to stand on his own again, and the pinched look of strain had left his face. By unspoken agreement – neither of us wanted to have to deal with Rachel right now – Jack and I guided Shinobu in the opposite direction to home, heading for a favourite hang-out spot. It was a big, old, second-hand bookstore, and part of the ground floor had been converted into a coffee shop. The prices were good and the coffee was better than Starbucks. More importantly, it felt safe. It was an open public place where nothing would be able to get at us.

When we went through the old-fashioned glass door, the place was deserted apart from the sleepy-looking barista behind the counter. It must have been later than I'd thought.

We headed for a leather-lined booth in the back corner. As soon as we sat down, I pulled out my phone. What with one thing and another, I'd forgotten to turn it on this morning. I winced when I did. It was not only a lot later than I'd realized, but I had about twenty missed calls and a dozen messages. A few were from Rachel's number, probably wanting to know where we'd disappeared to. I deleted them. I would have to listen to her rant once I got home anyway; no need to make time for bonus yelling. I felt strangely uncomfortable when I saw that I had two texts from Kylar Grant, wanting to know if I was OK after last night. I deleted those quickly too, refusing to look at Shinobu. The rest I ignored.

Jack patted her jacket down and swore. "Damn. I've just realized – I lost my phone. It must have gone flying when that cat-thing hit me."

"Nekomata," Shinobu corrected. "It is called a Nekomata."

"A what-in-the-who now?" Jack shook her head, running her fingers through her hair. "Never mind. I can't believe this. Mum's going to kill me for losing my phone and I can't even tell her why."

"I'll think of something to tell her. Don't worry about it now," I said, shoving my own phone away, along with the questions for Shinobu that were burning on my lips.

I was queasy, my head was pounding, and even though the real shaking had stopped, my hands were weak and trembly. Jack looked worse than I felt. It was harder to tell with Shinobu; he looked all right now, but then … I didn't really know him well enough to be sure. One of us was going to pass out – again – at this rate. I was pretty sure that people in shock were supposed to need hot, sweet drinks.

I scrounged some cash from Jack and went to the counter to get a large, double-shot latte each for me and Jack and, after a minute's thought, a large mug of tea for Shinobu. As I stood waiting at the end of the counter, I found my eyes constantly straying to the big, plate-glass window and glass door, nervously searching the street outside for anything that looked out of the ordinary. I nearly jumped out of my skin when the espresso machine let out a loud hiss.

Finally I carried the drinks back to the booth, distributed them and then sat down next to Jack. Shinobu was opposite us. He sniffed tentatively at his cup, pulled a face, and put it down without tasting it.

Jack knocked back half her coffee like it was vodka. "Mimi, I want to know what happened while I was out. At the hospital. *Did* a bomb go off?"

I took a fortifying mouthful of my own coffee, cupping my cold hands tightly around the mug for warmth. "No, I told you," I said, staring down at the foam, "it was me."

"More words than that, please."

Sighing, I gave them a bare bones account of what I had seen while they were both frozen and admitted to Jack that I had met the man – or whatever he was – who attacked us before. Last night at the party.

"Whoa. I'm almost glad I don't remember anything," Jack said, with a shudder of her own. "I can't believe you were brave enough to go for that guy like that. I'm really glad you did, but... Hey, remember how Kobayashi Sensei used to say you weren't aggressive enough – that you could've been the national champion if you'd just had a killer instinct? Shows what he knew."

My fingers tightened around the warm coffee mug as I stared at it again, not wanting to meet Jack or Shinobu's eyes. "I didn't actually want to hurt anyone in kendo," I mumbled.

Liar, liar, pants on fire! The truth was I'd always had a killer instinct. Right from when Ojiichan first started training me in our back garden, I'd loved slashing at the air, slicing up imaginary foes, getting out all my unhappy emotions. Attacking a practice dummy and killing it had made me feel better every time. But things changed as I got older and the sensei started pairing me up with other kendo trainees at the dojo. Sparring wasn't like cutting up the air. Suddenly you were taking out all your anger – your jealousy, fear, unhappiness – on *another person.*

I'd plugged away faithfully at kendo until I was fourteen, for my grandfather's sake, even though his death had taken all the joy out of it. But when Kobayashi Sensei started pressuring me to enter the bigger tournaments, started telling me that I needed to be more aggressive, I freaked out and quit. And I hadn't picked up any kind of a sword – wooden or otherwise – since then.

Until last night.

"It was well done," Shinobu said, breaking into my grim thoughts. "You saved us all."

Pricklingly aware of Shinobu's knee touching mine under the table, I flushed and ducked my head. I was grateful when the barista appeared, perky ponytail swinging, a tray propped on her hip.

"Hi guys," she said. "Is everything OK for the three of you?"

Shinobu went very still. Jack choked on a sip of her coffee and I reached out and pounded her between the shoulder blades, turning a politely baffled look on the girl.

"Three of us?"

She blinked a couple of times. I literally saw her pupils dilate as she stared at the mug of tea sitting abandoned in the middle of the table and then at the place where Shinobu was sitting. She laughed uncertainly. "Oh, wow – sorry, I thought I saw a bloke sitting back here with you. Weird. Must've been an optical illusion or something."

"Yeah. Weird. We're fine, thank you," I said, willing her away.

She walked back to the counter, still giving us uncertain looks over her shoulder.

Shinobu looked after her, then down at his long fingers, turning his hands over as if he'd never seen them before. The glossy mass of his hair slid forward over his shoulder, the overhead light gleaming blue on the dark strands. "I *am* here. I can touch things, feel pain – so I must be a part of this world. Why cannot all inhabitants of this place see me as you can? Why did that girl seem to perceive me at first and then not?"

"Dude, this is too weird. Are you seriously *invisible* to everyone else?" Jack wiped her mouth with the back of her hand. Her shock made me realize that I hadn't filled her in on any of the things Shinobu had told me while we were stuck in the hospital waiting room. But it didn't seem right for me to just blurt out what he'd said; irrationally, I felt as if Shinobu had been confiding in me, that his honesty about his suffering was for my ears only.

"Shinobu," I began hesitantly, "is it all right for Jack to know about what you told me? You know, about … where you've been? What you remember?"

He considered both of us. "I have not told you everything yet. Perhaps I should begin at the beginning and relate to you everything that I can remember. It will be easier to tell it all at once and be done with it."

Jack nodded eagerly. I was a little less eager, not sure everything he was going to tell us would be particularly pleasant to hear, but I nodded too.

"I was born in the country that your language names Japan," he began, "and if the Nekomata spoke the truth, then my birth was over five hundred years ago. I was orphaned as a young child, but friends of my parents – the Yamatos – took me in and raised me as their own. They were good people. My adopted father was a swordsman who had retired with much honour from the service of his master to live in the small village of his birth. He taught me kenjutsu, the way of the sword. He taught

135

me … everything a boy needed to know." He paused, his eyes suddenly blank. I realized with a chill of horror that the family he talked about were long dead. Shinobu was never going to see his father again.

Then he shook his head, and just like that, the moment passed. "The rest is confused. I must tell you everything, because I do not know which parts are truly important and which seem important only to me.

"Just after I turned seventeen, a newcomer settled in the village. He was wealthy and well-mannered, although he was considered a little strange with his solitary habits. But within a few weeks of his arrival, people began to go missing from the village. They simply vanished – from their fields, their beds, their baths. None of us had any idea of where they had gone, and they were none of them the kind of people who would run away and leave their families.

"One night one of the missing, a young girl, came back. At first she seemed exactly as normal, and her family were so happy to see her that they welcomed her into their arms with few questions, and did not doubt her when she said that she could not remember anything from the time she had been gone. For two days the village rejoiced. On the third day, her family were found slaughtered in their beds. Each of them, from her baby brother to her ancient grandmother, had been sucked dry of blood. There was no sign of the girl. But bloody tracks led from the house of death to the house of the newcomer."

Jack gulped audibly. I sat frozen against the booth, the coffee glugging uneasily in my stomach.

"Many people wanted to drag the newcomer out and kill him, believing him to be a demon. Hearing the commotion outside his house, the newcomer threw open his doors and told us that he knew what monster haunted our village and how to destroy it. He claimed the beast, sensing he knew this, had stalked his house in the night, but had been unable to enter it because of the protections he had put in place. And when we looked, we saw bloody hand prints and claw marks, signs that something had tried to get in but failed.

"The newcomer brought out ancient scrolls and papers and showed us pictures and descriptions of just such events as had overtaken us. The nature of the beast was that of a nine-tailed cat which supped on human blood. Having fed from a man or woman, it could take their form and all their memories so that it might slip unnoticed into their life and prey on their loved ones. It was a Nekomata. It could be killed, but only by one with great strength, speed, and skill. One who was willing to risk his life for his village."

"You," I whispered. "Your village picked you."

His shoulders tensed, and he let out a long, slow sigh. "I volunteered."

"God," Jack breathed. "I can't even... That was so brave."

Shinobu shook his head again. His eyes were shut now, and his back hunched. "It was not bravery. It was fear. It was very clear by then that no one was safe, and I had already lost my family once. I could not endure the thought of losing anyone else. I could not bear to watch and wait for it to happen. I needed to do *something,* to fight, even if that was selfish. She – they begged me not to go." His hands clenched on the table top. "Begged me. I ignored their pleas. For myself, for my own sanity, I volunteered. I thought – I thought the worst that could happen to me was death."

The worst *that could happen?*

I wanted to climb over the table to him. To put my arms around him. To tell him that it was all right now, it would all be all right. Anything to make him sit up out of that defensive ball of agony and open his eyes again. But it wouldn't be all right. It would never be all right.

He had lost everything, and he didn't even know why.

Nothing I can possibly say or do will make it better.

"I saw the fight in my dream," I prompted softly, trying to drag him back from the memories.

"Huh? Hang on, are these the dreams you were babbling about before?" Jack asked.

"Yes. I didn't remember them until last night when I... Well, you know after the accident, when I was out cold.

I've been dreaming about him for years. I saw him…"

I saw him die. And he had seemed to see me, *recognize me*, as he lay dying. It made no sense. It had happened hundreds of years before I was born. "He beat the Nekomata, but it got him before it turned to stone."

"I was careless," Shinobu admitted, opening his eyes at last. "Over-confident. I thought the monster was done-for after I wounded it."

I hadn't thought he looked all that confident. I thought he'd looked as if he'd gone into that fight prepared for, even expecting, death. I wondered if the ones he cared for so much had ever really appreciated the depths of his love for them, a love so great that it had been easier for him to embrace the probability of dying than live with the risk that they might be hurt.

What would it feel like, to be loved like that?

"So what happened then?" Jack asked. "I mean … did you die? How did you get to be here, alive, in London, five hundred years later?"

Shinobu spread his hands. "I do not know. That is the truth." He explained to Jack – more plainly and bluntly than he had to me – how he had found himself trapped in a timeless, inescapable prison. "If it was death, then I could never escape it. There seemed no hope. Until…" He looked at me, and the tense, unhappy expression on his face lightened a little. "Until I began to see Mio-dono, in the darkness. She was a child that first time, tiny and delicate, her hair long and her feet bare. She held my sword – this sword – in her hands, though she could barely lift the weight. I saw her, and I had life again. A half-life, surely, but better than what had come before. From that moment, I have been connected to her. Like a shadow, I have trailed in the wake of her brightness."

"That's … sweet? And also kind of creepy…" Jack said uncertainly.

I sat bolt upright in the booth, both hands flying up to my face. "You saw that? You saw me with the sword, when I was a kid? With my ojiichan? You were with me all these years?"

Shinobu nodded warily.

"Oh my God. I know where you were. I know where you were trapped. You were in the sword."

CHAPTER 9

CAT FIGHT

was…?" He stared down at the weapon.

"You were dying," I said slowly, working it out. "You had the sword in your hand. And somehow – I don't know how – something happened, and you ended up inside it. Like a genie in a bottle. It makes sense. That's why you remember me from when Ojiichan first showed me the katana. I *felt* that connection. I felt something respond to me. That was you. That's why I have been dreaming about you all these years. Shinobu, the blade was your prison."

"The blade?" Jack repeated doubtfully. "He was in a sword? Is that possible?"

"Is a giant nine-tailed demon-cat possible?" I asked, rather sarcastically.

She blinked. "Fair point."

After glancing at the barista to make sure her attention

was elsewhere, I drew the katana out through the hole in my coat and laid it on the edge of the table. Shinobu stared down at it. His hand stretched towards me, as if to touch the sword, and then drew back. "I think..." he said. "I think you are right."

"Ojiichan said the katana has been in our family for generations. Your Yamatos must be my ancestors. After you … disappeared, the Yamatos kept your sword." I frowned. "The Harbinger said something about that. He said *he* had chosen us to protect the sword. But the sword already belonged to you, to us."

"The sword has changed since it was mine," Shinobu said softly. "It feels different; it pulses with a strange energy now. My sword was just a sword, a fine sword that I was proud to carry, but no more. The Nekomata showed no interest in it. It sought only my death. Now..."

"Now it's obsessed with it. And it said it was coming back for it."

There was a little pause.

"Wow, Mimi," Jack breathed. "What are we going to do?"

"I don't know. I don't know how to fix this. I tried to put the sword back last night, I did. I couldn't do it. Why did I ever take it out in the first place? Why?" I drew in a shuddering breath.

"This isn't your fault," Jack said.

"That's not what you said earlier," I reminded her.

"You *told* me to put him back in the box."

"You could not have known the danger," Shinobu said to me. "To punish yourself now for that innocent mistake would be wrong. You would not judge another so harshly. Would you?"

Tentatively he reached across the table again. His fingers stopped a whisper away from mine, which were curled around the katana's sheath, as if he couldn't quite bring himself to bridge the tiny distance.

He had rubbed my bruised fingers in the hospital room, and I had dragged him onto the Tube, but those touches were different. As I stared at our hands so close together on the wooden table top, I could almost feel that breath of air between our skin spark with electricity.

My gaze connected with Shinobu's. There was a physical jolt, like two magnets jumping together. Like two perfect musical notes meeting and singing as one.

"Guys?" Jack's concern had transmuted to curiosity. Her gaze was like a heat-lamp burning the side of my face.

But I couldn't look away. I didn't think Shinobu could either. It was beyond either of our control. Because I knew those eyes... I *knew* those eyes. Didn't I? The pattern of blue-grey flecks that moved in them and the lightning-quick thoughts and feelings that flickered behind them? His smell, the rhythm of his breath ... so familiar... I knew how his silky hair would feel in my hands. I *knew*.

The door of the coffee shop opened with a cheery tinkle of the bell.

"You can't bring them in here," the barista called anxiously. "Only assistance animals are allowed."

Have to hold on. Don't let go.

The green blade sliced down—

"Shit!" Jack spat out the word.

I jumped, blinking, and shook my head dazedly, conscious of Shinobu suddenly sitting back on the other side of the table. *What just happened?*

"They're not mine," said a woman, sounding annoyed. "There's loads of them hanging around outside. You ought to call the RSPCA."

Jack's hand clamped down on my shoulder. "Sorry to interrupt your moment, but I don't think that's a good sign. Look!"

I turned and saw the barista with a tray in each hand, desperately trying to shoo a pair of cats outside. One of them was obviously a stray, with mangy-looking tabby fur and ragged ears. The other was a sleek and well-fed grey, wearing a collar. Both of them were spitting at the poor barista. As soon as she opened the door to try and nudge them out, ten more swarmed inside. The woman who had just entered the coffee shop shrieked. The barista slammed the door hastily as the animals ran between her legs.

The cats formed a bristling wall, inching towards us

in our booth in the corner. Outside, I could see more cats, dozens of them, pressing up against the windows and the door. Their eyes almost glowed. I could hear the low, mesmeric notes of their cat-yodelling through the glass.

The white-faced barista fled to the shelter of the counter, where she fumbled for the phone. She picked it up – then stopped and stared down at it like she couldn't understand why it was in her hand. The woman by the door looked around in sudden confusion, her eyes sliding away from the wall of hissing, spitting felines like melting butter sliding off a knife. "Weren't there...? Huh."

The barista shook her head, put the phone back on the hook and smiled at the woman. "How can I help you today?"

The customer stepped over to the counter, already rummaging in her handbag. "Sorry, I zoned out there for a second. Can I have a large, double-shot cappuccino to go?"

Within seconds both women were back in their routine, acting like nothing had happened. That, even more than the eerie noises of the animals as they edged towards us, made fear quiver through my body.

"Is there another way out of this place?" Shinobu asked, easing to his feet.

"Must be," Jack said. "Fire regulations and all that." She shoved me out of the booth in front of her, giving me one second to shove the katana back into its carrier on my back before she grabbed my hand. "Come on."

Shinobu took my other hand in a hard grip. The pair of them hauled me out of the cafe area into the narrow aisles between towering, haphazardly stacked bookshelves, Shinobu in front, Jack half a step behind. The overhead lights weren't enough to fully illuminate the shadows back here, and the smell of dust and damp paper made me sneeze.

"I've never seen that many cats before," I said breathlessly. "Where did they come from?"

"The Nekomata," Shinobu answered, voice grim.

A moment later I heard a glassy crash behind us. The bell above the door jangled discordantly.

From the corners of my eyes, I saw dozens of small, sleek shapes flashing into the stacks around us. My ears filled with dry, papery, rustling sounds. I whipped my head around and caught sight of yellow and green eyes glowing everywhere in the shadows between shelves.

Overhead, piles of books began to shift. Scraps of browning paper fell down like dirty snow. A tattered Mills & Boon paperback fluttered past me, almost grazing my nose. An Agatha Christie mystery bounced off Shinobu's arm. Jack dodged a massive, leather-bound Reader's Digest of Myths and Legends.

"Look out!" Shinobu shouted. He hauled me forward, and I yanked Jack after me, just managing to avoid a landslide of back-issue magazines that filled the aisle.

A large, black cat dropped into the space ahead of us, its back arched, hackles raking up as it growled. More felines landed behind it, adding their voices to its threatening song.

Shinobu whipped a massive encyclopaedia off a shelf with his free hand and winged it at the cats. The black one went flying and the others scattered.

"Ouch!" Jack kicked out without breaking stride and two more cats went sailing away. "I'm not into animal cruelty but if any more of these little buggers try to claw me I'll turn them into earmuffs."

I ducked to avoid a falling Stephen King and saw a green glow ahead, to the left. "There's the fire door!"

Another pile of books toppled over into the aisle ahead of us. Shinobu turned and caught me around the waist, lifting me effortlessly over the obstruction. I had to let go of Jack or have my arm wrenched out. Jack scrambled over the books with a muffled "Oof!", landed next to me and zoomed in front. She grabbed the metal bar on the emergency door, forcing it down. An ear-splitting wail sounded.

"Getting really sick of sirens!" Jack shouted as Shinobu and I shot through the exit. She slammed the door shut behind us. There were several heavy thudding sounds and a couple of yowls.

We stood in the narrow alley that ran behind the shop, catching our breath. Windowless, graffiti-covered walls closed in on either side. Most of the space was taken up with a huge industrial skip that overwhelmed the fresh, bready smells drifting from the bakery next door. The concrete made sticky noises underfoot.

"Actually, that was kind of fun," Jack said.

I gave her a blank stare. "I don't like you any more."

She stuck out her tongue.

"How far is it from here to the house?" Shinobu asked, sounding tense.

"Ten minutes' walk," I said. "Why?"

Shinobu pointed. On top of the overflowing skip, a trio of cats was creeping into view.

This time it was me who swore. The first of the cats pounced. Shinobu spun away. It hit the wall where he had been an instant before.

We scrambled out of the alley on to the familiar road. Overhead, heavy, brownish-grey clouds pressed down, turning the afternoon as dim as twilight. People hurried by with their heads bowed and their eyes firmly fixed on their feet.

"Hostiles at twelve o'clock," Jack snapped out.

"What does that mean?" Shinobu and I asked in unison.

"Cats straight ahead! You idiots both need to watch *Top Gun*."

"Run for it!" I yelled.

As we pelted down the road, cats of every colour,

size and condition leapt down from walls and rooftops, flying at us with savage hisses and sharp claws. Shinobu ploughed straight ahead, forcing them to scatter or be crushed. I put both arms over my head, grateful for the thick fabric of my coat, and jumped and swerved wildly, trying to avoid them. Next to me, Jack was kicking like Jackie Chan on ten cans of Red Bull, knocking out would-be attackers by the dozen.

Every time I looked up I expected to see bystand-ers staring at us in shock or filming our antics on their phones. But even when I charged into a couple and acci-dentally knocked the woman's briefcase out of her hand, no one else seemed to see what was going on. Their eyes just flicked over us and then away, as if we weren't there. It was terrifying. We could be eaten by feral cats right in the middle of the street and *no one would notice*.

We swerved round the corner, and I felt a dizzying flood of relief as I caught sight of my own front door. I shoved my hand into my pocket, wrenched out the key and flew up the stairs, passing Shinobu. As I fum-bled with the lock, Shinobu yelled behind me. A huge marmalade tom – a cat which belonged to one of our neighbours, and which I had known all my life as a lazy, friendly pet – flew out of the bush next to the steps with a tearing growl and went for his throat.

Jack seized the cat's tail in midair and whipped it away into the street.

"You are very fast," Shinobu commented, sounding impressed.

"Ten years of karate," Jack gasped. "I wish I could say the same for Mimi, though. What are you doing? Picking the effing thing?"

The lock clicked and we all piled inside. The moment we were in, I threw the door shut, snapped the deadbolt and locked it again. Jack sat down on the bottom step of the stairs with a thump and Shinobu leaned against the door. There was silence except for the harsh sound of our panting.

"You know what?" I said. "I am never asking my parents for a kitten again."

CHAPTER 10

RACHEL'S FATE

A door slammed at the back of the house. Feet stomped heavily towards us, sending *Tyrannosaurus Rex* vibrations through the floor.

"What time do you call this?" Rachel erupted into the hallway. "Where have you been? Why didn't you call and let me know where you were and – and what the hell happened to you?"

She rushed forward, anger melting into shock and concern as she saw the ragged, dirty state of us. She knelt on the bottom step and cupped Jack's face carefully between her hands. "You've got a black eye."

"Get off, Rach!" Jack tried to brush her sister away and was firmly ignored.

"Start talking. Was there an accident? Did you get mugged?"

"Um…" Jack rolled her eyes desperately, and I noticed

for the first time that there really was a dark, purplish shadow forming around her left eye socket. It must have happened when she hit the motorbikes. I supposed I'd been too busy to take stock before.

"Yes," I said, quickly. "Or, rather, not really. There was, like, a street fight, and we walked into the middle of it. We got a bit beaten up. The police—"

"The *police*?" Rachel shrieked. The sound echoed off the high coving and made us all wince, including Shinobu, who was standing motionless at the door.

Rachel paused, cleared her throat and began again. "Let me dial that down a notch. OK. What about the police?"

"Jack called them, and they came and broke things up and then took us to the hospital to get checked out. We're both fine. But Jack lost her phone – and it totally wasn't her fault," I added. Jack gave me a grateful look. I went on, "By the time I remembered to check mine we were practically home anyway so it didn't make sense to call and freak you out. Sorry."

"Oh God," Rachel moaned.

"Don't stress," Jack said, her voice a bit muffled by Rachel's grip on her cheeks. "I had x-rays and I'm in perfect condition, honest."

"You don't understand. I'm going to have to tell Mum, and Mr and Mrs Yamato."

I began hastily: "I don't think that's a great—"

"Why couldn't you both have glued yourselves to the couch and watched TV until you turned into drooling, emotionless drones, like the rest of your generation?" Rachel said, reproachfully.

"You don't have to phone anyone," Jack said quickly. "You heard Mimi. This wasn't a big deal."

Rachel finally let go of Jack and sat back with a sigh. "Nice try, kiddo, but getting mixed up with the police and being taken to the hospital *is* a big deal. Don't worry – it's my skin that's going to get roasted, not yours. You'll probably have to save up for a new phone yourself, though."

"Curses," Jack said, though I could tell she was secretly relieved that Rachel seemed to be on her side.

"Ach, I need caffeine before I start phoning people. Come on. I'll make you both a cup of tea."

She stood up and headed back towards the kitchen. Jack flicked a look at Shinobu, then raised her eyebrows at me. *What do you think?*

I shrugged. *She wasn't that distracted. I definitely don't think she can see him.*

Shinobu cleared his throat. "Excuse me, Rachel-san?"

Rachel kept walking without any sign that she had heard him. I sighed, not sure if I was relieved or disappointed. It was definitely easier not to have to explain why there was an armed warrior-boy trailing around after me, but at the same time, we had to do *something* with Shinobu, and it was going to be hard to work that out, long-term, if no one else could see him.

"Oi," Rachel called. "Get in here! I want to keep my eyes on you two delinquents."

"Coming!" Jack called, jumping up and hurrying forward. I followed more slowly.

"Let us smooth Rachel down a bit," I whispered to Shinobu. "Then we'll head upstairs where we can be private and talk."

Shinobu nodded and slipped into the kitchen behind me, positioning himself against the wall by the door in his bodyguard pose. I perched nervously on one of the breakfast stools at the central island next to Jack, who was already back to her normal self.

"That's like punishing me for being attacked," she was arguing. "You can't punish the victim, sis."

"Tell Mum, not me," Rachel was saying patiently, as she set cups out on the island in front of us. "I'm not the one who'll have to shell out to replace it."

The kettle was boiling in front of me with a homey, rumbling noise. I looked around – at the pale-green walls that I had helped Mum paint and the little pots of herbs on the windowsill that Dad was so proud of growing – with a sense of being in a dream. Even the faint smell of coffee and hand cream, so much a part of home that I normally barely noticed it, seemed unreal. The world was suddenly askew. I was out of place in my own house. My own skin.

We almost never saw this place again. We almost never got home today.

I sucked in a deep breath, distantly aware that Shinobu was standing alert by the kitchen door, looking around. Probably waiting for me to signal to him what to do next.

I don't know, Shinobu. I just … don't. Rubbing my hand over my face, I took another couple of deep breaths, trying to wriggle my skin back into its proper place.

Jack was still going on about her mobile phone. "If anything, I ought to get rewarded for being a good citizen and calling the police. Right, Mimi?" She appealed to me as Rachel moved behind us to open the fridge. "If Mum makes me pay for a new phone out of my own money, I'll turn into a troublemaker for sure."

"Like you aren't already," Rachel said, rummaging around for the milk.

I seized the distraction and reached into my pocket for my own phone. "Maybe it's not lost for ever. If someone picked it up, you might be able to get it back."

I forced myself to focus on the phone display, selected Jack's number from my contacts and pressed "Dial", then I lifted the phone to my ear.

"Yeah, right. You must be crazy if you think that – er – anyone who was around there would hand it in."

"You never know. It's ringing."

The tinny sound of Jack's ringtone – "Take My Breath

Away", from that cheesy *Top Gun* film – rang out. It took me a minute to realize that the noise was in the room. In the kitchen. With us.

Me and Jack stared at each other.

"What is the matter?" Shinobu asked, sensing my sudden fear. I couldn't answer.

I swivelled round on the stool, following the sound to its source.

Rachel slowly straightened and eased the fridge door closed. She turned to face us, her right hand creeping into the pocket of her cardigan. She pulled out Jack's phone. The plastic case was battered and grazed, as if something had tried to chew on it. "Oops."

"Rachel?" Jack whispered.

"Sorry, Jacqueline. I needed it for the scent trail, you see. And the cats had to know who to chase and where to chase them to."

"What are you talking about?" Jack's voice had gone shrill. "How did you get that?"

"No time for questions now, kiddo. Big sister has some business to take care of."

Rachel looked at me. Her grin stretched wider, wider, splitting her face in half. Rows of razor sharp teeth gleamed behind her lips. "Told you I'd be back," she said. She dropped the phone, and her hand shot towards me, fingers elongating as black, obsidian claws burst out of the skin.

I spun on the stool, my outstretched arm scattering the mugs on the island as I seized the kettle. I threw it instinctively, with no time to aim. The pot hit Rachel squarely in the face. Boiling water and hot steam sprayed over her. She let out a high-pitched screech, falling back against the fridge. The ringtone cut off.

"What are you *doing*?" Jack yelled. "That's my sister!"

"It's the Nekomata," Shinobu said, suddenly right behind me. He grabbed my hand and the back of Jack's jacket, hauling us both off the stools and towards the door. "It fed from your sister and took her form to trap us. Come on!"

"No!" Jack tore free of Shinobu's grip. Her eyes were fixed on Rachel, who was slumped on the floor, curled into a ball, arms over her face.

Shinobu shoved me forcefully behind him and ran back for her. I reeled sideways, hitting the wall next to the door. Shinobu caught Jack's arm just as she reached the fridge. She fought him, her free hand stretching out towards her sister.

"Rachel! Look at me!"

Rachel's human skin burst. Flesh-coloured shreds flew out in long streamers, turning black, thickening into tentacles. She surged up from the floor, her pretty face sprouting black-and-white fur, eyes flashing yellow.

One tentacle flicked and knocked Jack's legs from under her, sending her crashing to the floor. Two others cracked out like whips and wrapped around Shinobu's arms. He pivoted on one heel, kicking high. His foot smashed into the Nekomata's face. It flinched and hissed viciously. "I've had enough of you."

One of its free limbs flew up, sharpening into a wicked point.

I sucked in a deep breath that felt like it lasted for ever. Then I darted forward, breath roaring out of my throat. "Shinobu!"

The katana appeared in my hand. I wrenched the blade from the saya and spun it in a one-handed strike, slicing cleanly through one of the tentacles that was holding Shinobu. Thick, black blood spurted. He ripped free of the second tentacle as I whirled past.

"Get Jack!" I shrieked to him over the sound of the Nekomata's catlike scream.

"I will eat you!" The monster's voice no longer sounded anything like Rachel's. "I will suck the marrow from your bones!"

Shinobu hoisted a stunned Jack up into his arms. He carried her to the kitchen door, but instead of running, he dumped her outside and turned back. His eyes scanned the kitchen, looking for a weapon. I backed warily away from the Nekomata into the sunroom, really, really hoping that he would find one.

It's in my house. Oh God, this thing is In. My. House.

The monster shot four tentacles at me, the ends

sharpening as they flew, like arrows. To my astonishment, I managed to dodge two of them and slice a long line into the side of the fourth before the injured tail whipped furiously and caught me a ringing blow to the side of my face.

Pain exploded across my cheekbone. I staggered but managed to keep on my feet, turning the movement into a dive that took me behind the dining table.

"You have got stronger already," the Nekomata said, sounding surprised. "But not strong enough. Give me the katana! Give it to me!"

A forest of talons thudded into the table and chairs. The hardened oak exploded. I flung myself away, screaming as needle-sharp shards of wood sliced through the arm and shoulder of my coat. I hit the kitchen tiles hard, knocking over one of the island stools. Blood trickled down my wrist and pattered onto the wreckage of smashed cups and wood chunks as I scrambled up.

The Nekomata laughed, a wicked, gleeful gurgle. "Foolish little girl. You do not have the power to hurt me."

"But I do," said Shinobu.

As the Nekomata whirled to face him, Shinobu lifted the nozzle of our kitchen fire extinguisher and depressed the grip. White foam surged out of the mouth and hit the Nekomata full in the face.

The monster shrieked and scuttled back towards me, tails clawing at the bubbling foam. I could hear its skin sizzling.

"Aim for the heart!" Shinobu shouted at me.

I sucked in a deep breath and lifted the katana. Droplets of my own blood dripped onto my face as I stared at the thrashing knot of darkness on my kitchen floor. *The heart? Aim for the heart? Where the heck is that? I don't know how to do this!*

"Jack," Rachel's voice cried from under the bubbling foam. "Jack, please don't let them hurt me."

"Mimi." Jack was standing in the kitchen doorway, clutching the frame. Her eyes were huge, pleading. "That's still Rachel. We have to save her."

"That is not your sister, Jack-san," Shinobu shouted. He looked like he was about to try and jump over the Nekomata and wrench the katana off me. "Mio – strike now!"

Tentacles uncoiled from the knot around the creature's face and flew out, wrapping around my wrists and dragging me forward. I stumbled one step and dug my heels into the floor, resisting with everything I had. "Help!"

The Nekomata's eyes were swollen almost shut, its face scalded by the foam, but the terrible mouth gaped impossibly wide, filled with snapping, bristling fangs. The monster's hot breath blasted my nose with the stench of rotting flesh. My hands, and the sword, were within an inch of its mouth.

I heard a crash – the door into the garden flying open

– then Shinobu's voice, raised desperately, shouting in Japanese. I only understood one word: *Kitsune.*

The Nekomata's crushing grip on my arms loosened for an instant. I twisted sideways and managed to rip one hand free, but the hand holding the katana was still firmly caught. I looked around frantically for another weapon – a knife, a chunk of wood, anything. Then I realized that the Nekomata was making no attempt to pull me closer any more. It had frozen, its puffy yellow eyes riveted on something behind me.

I peered over my shoulder to see Shinobu just outside the back door, in the scrubby little garden. His black figure was limned with fire, outlined against the red glow of the setting sun.

But it was hours until sunset and the sky was black with clouds.

The light was coming from the big, unruly myrtle bush next to the garage wall. Fiery rays shone through the leaves, turning them scarlet and bronze and gold, as if the centre of the bush was on fire. The foliage rustled with a soft, sibilant sound like a roomful of people whispering secrets.

A small fox, slightly mangy and greyish, like all city foxes seemed to be, emerged from under the bush and sat calmly, bathed in the glowing light. It stared at me though the glass wall of the extension with what I could have sworn was humour. One of its ears twitched.

The red glow intensified, and as I watched, the fox's mangy, grey fur melted away to reveal a vivid, copper coat with a lustre like polished metal and a shining blaze of white on its chest. The fox stood up on its back legs, body lengthening, transforming, as it grew. A final burst of light made me blink.

When I looked again, the light was gone and in the fox's place there stood a slender young man. Glorious, copper hair fell well past his waist, and he wore a formal white kimono. His face was heart-shaped, with a pointed chin and a smiling mouth. A glossy, white-tipped tail poked out of the bottom of the kimono.

"Shinobu of the old country," the young man said. His light, tenor voice was formal, but there was a lilting note to it that made me feel he was on the verge of laughter. "You have called upon the Kitsune of this city for assistance, and, in accordance with the promise made to you by our king centuries ago, we will lend it. What is it that you wish of us?"

Shinobu let out a sigh, slumping with clear relief. "Thank you. I beg of you, Lord Fox, banish the Nekomata from the house, and make this place safe from the invasion of harmful supernatural creatures."

The fox spirit tilted his head, a narrow, white grin spreading across his face. "Your request shall be granted. And just between us? Awesome wish, man."

The tip of his tail began to crackle, fur turning

incandescent like a long, white flame. The Nekomata's tentacles released me, flinging my arm away so hard that I spun round and stumbled over the fallen kitchen stool.

"No," it yowled. "This is not the business of the Kitsune."

"Sorry, cat-breath. You made it our business when you messed with Tall, Dark and Handsome here." The fox winked at Shinobu. Shinobu cleared his throat.

"I will take vengeance. My Mistress will take vengeance!" the Nekomata cried.

The fox laughed. "Yeah, good luck with that. If I were you, though, I'd stop whining and start running."

The fox lashed his bushy tail once, twice, then whipped it forward. A bolt of sizzling blue-white lightning shot from the white tip and hit the glass wall.

The electricity bubbled and spread on impact like glowing gel, multiplying, crackling along the joins of the windows, springing up on the skirting boards of the kitchen, surrounding the doorway, roaring out of the cupboards. It even dripped out of the taps.

I looked down to see it burning under my feet, licking along the tile grout. The blue-white flames didn't consume anything. They didn't even feel warm. But the Nekomata let out a squeal of utter terror and scuttled back towards the kitchen doorway, where Jack was still standing.

Jack's eyes widened. She scooted through the entrance, missing the Nekomata's tentacles by inches.

The Nekomata didn't even notice. Its rolling eyes were fixed on the fox fire that was engulfing the kitchen and swarming towards it. The drops of its blood on the kitchen tiles fizzled and disappeared with tiny puffs of black smoke under the flickering light.

"This is not the end," the Nekomata snarled at me. "I still have your friend's sister. If you do not surrender the sword by sunrise, I will devour her. Surrender by sunrise, or Rachel Luci dies!"

With a parting yowl, the Nekomata turned tail and ran.

CHAPTER 11

FAVOURS
AND PROMISES

I heard the front door fly open, despite the fact that I'd locked it. I scrambled to my feet and peered down the hall in time to see the Nekomata's tails disappearing out of the open doorway just ahead of a wall of blue-white flames. The flames shot up around the frame and lintel, then the door slammed shut with a thud and the dead-bolt engaged again. The fox fire roared up for a second, then snuffed out completely, leaving no sign that it had ever been there.

The Kitsune sighed. "Shame. One more second and it would have been Stonesville for Kitty. Well, this was fun, guys. See you around."

"Wait!" Jack ran past me and leapt out of the back door to confront the Kitsune. "Don't go!"

Crap. I couldn't remember most of the stories that Ojiichan had told me when I was a kid, but something that had stuck in my head, possibly due to subsequent years of anime-watching, was that while fox spirits could be friendly to humans, they could also be temperamental and tricksy. If Jack wasn't careful she would end up getting turned into a rice ball.

"Jack—" I began, hurrying out into the garden after her.

She ignored me. "You kicked that monster's ass, man. You have to help us get my sister back."

I edged forward, preparing to grab Jack, but Shinobu met my eyes and shook his head slightly. When I looked at the Kitsune's face, I saw why. He was gazing at Jack's spiky white, pink and purple hair, purple jacket, black fingernails, skin-tight black pants and knee-high biker boots with the dazed, admiring look that men usually reserved for someone who looked like Jessica Alba. In a bikini.

He bowed reverently. "I'm Hikaru. What's your name?"

"I'm Jack. Jack Luci," Jack said. She bowed back, a movement I recognized from martial arts. "And my sister—"

"Is Rachel. I heard," Hikaru said. He looked torn for a second, then sighed. "I wish I could help. Honestly. But you saw that thing. It had nine tails." He waved his own tail apologetically.

Jack gave him a bewildered look. "It was terrified of you."

"Not *me*. I was here representing the London Kitsune.

That's why I got the awesome entrance, with the light and everything. I happened to be closest when your friend here called in his favour, so I was imbued with the authority of my king. And the king can call on every Kitsune in the city. I'd never be a match for a nine-tails otherwise." Seeing that Jack still looked confused, he explained: "Animal spirits like us grow a new tail every hundred years, right? That thing's been alive at least a thousand years. I'm not even a hundred yet. So it's ten times more powerful than me. It'd eat me for a light snack. And I mean, literally."

"There's a Kitsune king?" I said slowly. "There's a Kitsune king in London?"

"Yeah. Anywhere there are foxes, there are Kitsune," Hikaru replied absently. He was still staring at Jack.

"And he owed you a favour?" I asked Shinobu, since Hikaru obviously wasn't going to give me the time of day.

Shinobu nodded. "When I was a little boy, before the Yamato family adopted me, I came across a fox caught in a snare in the woods. I felt sorry for it, so I set it free. He turned out to be a Kitsune. He spoke to me, told me that he was a prince, and that he was in my debt. He promised to repay me if ever I called on him, no matter where or how.

"That prince is the King of the London Kitsune now," Hikaru said. "Lucky coincidence. But Kitsune never forget their debts, and all the kings come from the same family. Even if you'd been in the Antarctic, the nearest foxes would have tried to help."

"Then won't he help again?" Jack asked. "If he's Shinobu's friend—"

"It's not like that, Jack-san. The Kitsune are honourable, and they always keep their promises, but the debt is now paid. They no longer owe me anything."

"We don't get involved in human business these days," Hikaru said, matter-of-factly. He averted his eyes from Jack with what looked like a painful effort. "I mean, it's not like you guys are all that friendly to foxes, you know? Rat poison, traps, guns. And that's just in the city. So, I really should be going now..."

Jack ran her fingers through her hair and tugged at it. The white tufts sticking up through her fingers made her look like Goth Tinkerbell. "We're not like that. Rachel loves animals. She's always putting food out for strays and hedgehogs and birds. She'd help you, if it was the other way round. You can't just leave her to get eaten. Won't you do *anything*?"

Hikaru, who was halfway back to the bush, stopped. "Me? What am I supposed to do?"

"I don't know! I don't understand why any of this is happening, but this is my sister. She didn't do anything wrong. Please help us!" Jack moved towards him and caught the trailing edge of one of his sleeves. She tugged on it, an uncharacteristic, helpless gesture.

The fox spirit gazed into Jack's face, clearly torn. "Look, I don't want that thing running around my city any more than you do. But there's not much I can do about it, really. I just don't have the juice." He sounded genuinely upset. I suppose he wasn't to know that he was the wrong sex to ever have a chance with Jack anyway.

"I'm small fry," he went on. "If you were going to have any chance of standing up to Nightmare Kitty, what you'd need to do is get the king on your side. Which, er, would be tough. Although … it's not exactly normal human business when a nine-tailed vampire-cat-demon is involved…" He shook himself. "Hey, how did you kids get mixed up with a Nekomata anyway? That's old magic. Are you a sorcerer or something?" He gave Shinobu a narrow-eyed look, as if he suspected him of somehow dragging me and Jack into a bad, nine-tailed vampire-cat-demon-hobnobbing crowd.

Shinobu raised an eyebrow at me. A little reluctantly I brought out the katana, which I had been hiding behind my back. My injured arm twinged sharply with the movement. "The Nekomata wants this."

Hikaru's mouth dropped open. He took a step towards us, as if unable to resist. His eyes flicked from me to the sword and back again. "That's where the power aura is coming from? I thought it was this immortal dude." He jerked his head at Shinobu.

Shinobu began: "I am not immortal—"

Hikaru flicked his hair over his shoulder impatiently. "Whatever, man. You're, like, five hundred years old. Just own it."

"I am not immortal," Shinobu repeated patiently. "But until very recently, we believe that I was imprisoned within the sword. We don't know precisely where its powers came from, only that the Yamato family have been its guardians for centuries."

"Your family?" Hikaru asked me, slightly reluctantly.

I nodded.

"But that's a meitou."

Jack and I exchanged a blank look. "It's a what?" I asked.

"A legendary sword! A spirit sword! I don't know how you're even holding it – it should be burning your hand off. How would a human family get hold of something like that? How would you possibly protect it?" He hesitated, then blew out a deep breath. "All right. This changes things."

"In a good way or a bad way?" Jack asked anxiously.

"Well, on the one hand, a Nekomata plus a meitou equals not ordinary human business. So I guess that's good for you. But, on the other, this is obviously a lot bigger than a random Nekomata visiting London. That sword … it's an object of power. You sure you can't take care of Nightmare Kitty yourself?"

"If I could, I would," I said fervently. "The Nekomata

nearly killed us twice. Whatever power the sword has, it's not mine to use."

"You sure about that? Looks to me like it's working on you already."

I stared at him blankly. "What?"

He squinted at me, his gaze unexpectedly shrewd. Then he looked at Jack again. Finally he nodded sharply. "Screw tradition. I'm going to beg for an audience with the king. Maybe he can make sense of this mess. I'll come back an hour after sundown and give you the skinny. In the meantime, stay in the house. Nothing can get in while our protections are on it. You'll be safe."

"You will come back?" Jack asked. "Promise?"

Hikaru's face took on a stern, noble look. "My word is truth. I shall return."

"Thank you," Jack said tremulously.

The fox spirit's face softened. His hand lifted as if to touch Jack, hesitated in the air, then fell. Finally he stepped back and bowed again. "See you after sunset."

As he turned away his shape whirled into a tornado of copper and white that compressed his human form down to a much smaller one. A second later a beautiful young dog fox trotted towards the myrtle bush and disappeared into the leaves.

I bundled Jack upstairs to her own flat before she broke down. I knew it was coming and I knew she wouldn't want to do it in front of Shinobu, or even me. Ever since her dad had walked out, Jack hated anyone to see her like that. She let me open her front door for her, then pushed me firmly out into the hallway, staring at the wall behind me rather than meeting my eyes. "Going to get cleaned up. Might be a while. I'll come down when I'm finished." Her voice broke on the last word and she slammed the door in my face.

Inside the flat, there were a series of bangs and thuds, and a smashing sound. Finally the low humming noise of the shower came on. Maybe Jack would feel better when she'd washed off the dirt.

Right. Monsters are flying at you like confetti and your sister is being held prisoner by something out of a horror film. A hot shower will make everything dandy.

Awareness whispered across the back of my neck, and I turned to see Shinobu standing guard on the stairs behind me.

"You didn't need to follow us up here," I said in surprise. "You heard Hikaru – the house is safe."

"You are still safer if I am near, Mio-dono."

I sighed wearily. "You have to have worked out by now that I'm not a lady." *Not much of anything, really...*

"You are *my* lady," he said quietly, looking away.

Something unbearably sweet moved inside me, forcing a short, shaky sound – half-laugh, half-sob – out of my lips. I tried to straighten away from the wall, and wavered on jellylike legs. Shinobu came forward quickly, reaching out to steady me. His hand closed around my bad shoulder and I hissed with pain. He snatched his hand back, staring at the blood streaking his palm. "You are hurt!"

"Oh, yeah. Some splinters got me. I thought you'd noticed."

"If I had noticed, I would have attended to it before," he said, almost angrily. "Where are your medicinal supplies?"

"Um … like a first-aid kit? My dad has them all over the place. There'll be one in the big bathroom, I suppose."

"Take me there at once," he commanded. He gently wrapped his arm around my waist, pulling me against him to support my weight.

"I can walk," I protested half-heartedly as he guided me towards the stairs. He ignored me.

Within a few moments I was perched on the edge of the tub. Shinobu, who had already opened the first-aid kit, was swiftly laying its contents out on the bath mat. He'd had to ask me what most of the things were, since the packaging was unfamiliar to him, but he seemed to know what he was doing. As he worked he muttered something under his breath in Japanese.

"What was that?" I asked suspiciously.

"Nothing. But if you are ever hurt again and you fail to tell me…" He let his voice trail off threateningly.

"What?"

He stared at me, hard, before saying, "I shall be cross."

I pressed my lips together, trying to hide my smile.

"You may think it funny," he said seriously. "But your suffering also hurts me."

"*What?* Like, physically?"

"No." His gaze faltered, and he turned away. "Inside."

I stared at his straight, broad back as he tied up the long sleeves of his kimono and began scrubbing his hands. Did he realize that he'd said the one thing that would force me to listen to him? I couldn't bear to think of my actions causing anyone pain like that. Especially not him. He'd had five hundred years of suffering already.

When his hands were clean, Shinobu carefully started peeling off my battered coat. It was … harder than it sounded. The lining of the left arm was glued to me with dried blood. I had to grind my teeth together to avoid whimpering as Shinobu tugged at it.

He muttered under his breath in Japanese again. This time I didn't ask.

After a minute he took a face cloth, wet it with warm water and began sponging the fabric. It stung like – well, just about like you'd expect. The adrenaline had definitely worn off and my whole arm was throbbing, sending spikes of pain up my neck and down to my hand. Eventually the blood cement came unstuck, and Shinobu managed to ease the left sleeve off. He tossed the coat into the bath.

We both looked down at my arm and stared in appalled silence.

The shoulder of my long-sleeved T-shirt was soaked with blood. Several needle-like splinters, an inch or so long, poked grotesquely through the fabric. Shinobu turned away abruptly and started washing his hands again.

I bit my lip. This was a weird situation. People sometimes say, *This is going to hurt me more than it hurts you*, but you always think it's bull. I got the feeling that as much pain as I was in right now, Shinobu really was feeling it just as badly, if not more. I had a bizarre urge to apologize.

Hands clean for the second time, Shinobu knelt on the floor beside me. He was so much taller than me that this made our faces level. He leaned over to peer at the injured place on my upper arm, picked up a pair of tweezers, and then cupped the inside of my arm with his other hand, holding the wounded area steady. His knuckles brushed the side of my breast.

I shuddered convulsively, then felt my face flood with heat as Shinobu went still.

When he spoke, his voice was hoarse. "Tell me if anything is too painful to bear."

I fixed my eyes determinedly on the mirror over the

sink. The face staring back at me had a feverish look, with spots of colour high up on its cheeks and eyes that glittered strangely. I looked like some other version of myself, a Mio I had never met before.

He began to pull out the splinters embedded in my arm. The first couple came free with nothing more than an uncomfortable itching sensation. The third made me twitch; my hands balled into fists.

Shinobu stroked my inner arm through my T-shirt, murmuring in Japanese. The gentle treatment should have made me feel like a little kid. It didn't. Even the sight of my own face was too much now. I clamped my eyes shut.

"Can I go on?"

I nodded.

"That's the last one I can see," he said, after what felt like an hour. He dropped the tweezers back on the towel, and his hand slipped away from my arm. "Are you a skilled seamstress?"

I opened my eyes, baffled. "No."

"Then this garment is beyond repair," he said, and ripped the arm of the T-shirt off.

"Whoa!" I nearly fell backwards into the bath. He grabbed me just in time, his large hands easily encircling my ribcage.

"A little warning next time," I said feebly.

"Hopefully there will be no next time," he said.

"I have done a shameful job of protecting you so far."

I chewed on that as he quickly cleaned the wounds in my arm – most of them were nothing more than small puncture-wounds or grazes – picked out a few more tiny splinters and then applied antiseptic and plasters to the worst of the cuts. He nodded, satisfied, and got to his feet to clean up the mess.

"Shinobu," I said as I eased off the edge of the bath to help him. "You realize … you know that if it weren't for you I would be dead, right? You saved me three times. No – four. " I stopped and shook my head. "The point is that without you today I'd have been toast. I owe you my life. A few splinters are nothing compared to what could have happened. You can't feel guilty about this."

He had his back to me again, but I could see his shoulders tensing up. "You don't understand."

"Don't understand what?"

There was a short silence before he spoke again, a new, stubborn note in his voice. "I have to protect you."

"Why? I mean – I am incredibly grateful, don't get me wrong. But you don't … *owe* me anything."

He didn't answer and kept his face turned away from me. I went on. "I'm not your responsibility. I'm not some duty you have to fulfil. You're not a slave. You have your own body again, and – and choices, and a life. You have to believe that."

His gaze snapped to mine. The depths of emotion there turned my tongue to rubber.

"You have no idea—" His voice choked off, then he began again, low and hoarse. "For an eternity, I was trapped in shadows. Barely alive. Aware only of frozen cold and confinement. If I had been sane enough, I would have begged for death. I had no hope, no warmth, nothing. Nothing but that endless dark." He swallowed hard. "Then I heard a voice. It reached me there in that prison and it drew me up, out of the blackness and cold. I felt a heartbeat that thrummed like a bird's, quick and excited. I saw a pair of eyes – so beautiful, the colour of polished rosewood – smiling. Warmth. I will never forget the embracing glory of that warmth. The warmth of your eyes."

The silence sang between us.

"You're talking about when I was a kid, aren't you?" I whispered. "I … I only touched the sword for, like, five minutes."

"You gave me a part of yourself, and that was everything I had."

One of Shinobu's hands lifted slowly, almost reluctantly. A single fingertip traced the line of my hair, not quite grazing the skin. He moved towards me until his breath was on my lips. "You woke me. You saved me. And from that moment I was yours. All I want – all I have ever wanted – is to protect and serve you. Please, my lady. Tell me that I may."

I nodded wordlessly as I stared up at him, fighting to think straight. He was going to kiss me. I could see it in the way his eyes flicked to my lips, how he tensed to move forward, to bridge that tiny distance between us. His hand would curl round my throat. Our mouths would meet. And when they did…

Then what?

The realization flashed through my brain like lightning: I didn't know him. Not really. Suddenly the intensity of his gaze was scary. The strength of what I felt was terrifying. I'd never been like this before. It was too much. Blindly I put both hands up and pushed at his chest, trying to get a little space between us. It was like pushing at a wall.

"I don't – I can't – I'm…"

Shinobu blinked, his hand falling away from my face. He looked dazed, a little shocked, and then abruptly horrified. He straightened up fully and backed away from me until he was pressed against the shower. "I apologize, Mio-dono. I am sorry."

"No, don't – you don't have to. I–I just need some room to—" Oh God, I was making it worse. *I have to get out of here.*

A lunge for the exit, a scrabble at the handle, and I was out in the hall with the door firmly closed behind me, taking slow deep breaths and trying to understand what had just happened. It took a few minutes for the buzzing in my brain – and my body – to calm down. Had he…? And then I…? Oh *no*. I grabbed my head with both hands and groaned as I realized I'd literally abandoned him in there without even saying thank-you. Or sorry.

I could not be a bigger freak if I'd trained up and taken an exam in it.

I swallowed hard, turned round, and barged the door open, marching back into the bathroom.

"Shino – oh!"

Shinobu had unwrapped the sash that held his kimono closed at the waist, and the garment was half off, held up only by the sleeves hooked over his wrists. My gaze wandered helplessly over the vast expanse of taut, golden skin and the round, bulging muscles standing out on his arms and chest. He had almost no body hair, except for a thin, fine line that trailed down over the smooth flatness of his lower belly…

"Is something wrong?" Shinobu hurriedly shrugged the kimono back over his shoulders and pulled it closed.

I snapped my eyes away from him and fixed them on the showerhead. "No, everything's fine. So … I just wanted to say, you know – use the shower. Although apparently you were, um, way ahead of me there." I cleared my throat. "Towels are under the sink. I think some of my dad's clothes will probably fit you. I'll leave them for you outside the door, OK? Take your time."

"Thank you," he choked out. A darting glance at

him showed me that every bit of visible skin was going a deep crimson shade. *Oh, good – at least I'm not alone in my mortification.*

Luckily my legs waited until I had closed the door behind me again to give out.

CHAPTER 12

LOYALTY AND LIES

Andy Greaves checked his watch, sighed, and heaved himself out of the comfortably sagging chair in his Portakabin. It was time for the forty-five-minute perimeter patrol. He took the high-visibility security coat off the back of the chair and put it on, tugging his walkie-talkie off the front of his belt as he stepped out into the grey afternoon and slammed the door behind him. The sleet had stopped at least, but his breath was still clouding in front of his face, and he could feel his old joints stiffening up.

"I hate winter," he muttered as he depressed the button on the walkie-talkie to contact the two other security guards in the second Portakabin on the opposite side of the building. "Hey Phil, it's Andy. Send Islam out and I'll meet him on the east corner."

The walkie-talkie let out a high-pitched squeal. Andy's ears rang. He cursed, nearly dropping the walkie-talkie.

Interference – feedback on the channel, maybe?

He tried again, shouting this time. "Phil! You there, mate?"

There was a weird, almost-human groaning sound, then another shriek. Andy held the transmitter away from his ear. "Come in?"

Nothing but white noise. Andy sighed and hiked his trousers up with one hand. Standing about in this cold made his bad knee worse, and Islam was probably already out patrolling anyway. He might as well just start walking.

He hooked the walkie-talkie back onto his belt, shoved his hands into his pockets, and started his routine walk around the outside of the building. The concrete scuffed noisily under his feet and he amused himself by trying to whistle the tune of *Star Trek* in time to the sound. He ran his eyes over the chain-link barriers around the outer walls, but he wasn't really expecting to see anything. Officially the old station was a high-value target, but in reality the only people who ever tried to get through security were students on a dare or photographers. They were usually shocked to find that they weren't just allowed to come in and wander around and beat a hasty retreat when they saw the security banners. Andy blamed *Dr Who*. They shouldn't have set an episode here. It was asking for trouble.

He was so used to his route that his eyes wandered over the dark stain without registering it the first time. When he did realize what he'd seen, he ground to a halt.

A large spill of thick, black liquid was pooled on the

concrete by one of the sealed-up entrances. Oil? Andy nudged it with the toe of his shoe. The pool … rippled. Like jelly. Weird. A leak from somewhere?

Andy looked up at the brown-brick wall and saw long streaks of the same liquid there, glistening in the dim light. It was like someone had climbed up the wall holding a bucket of black paint and dripping it as they went. Only this stuff wasn't paint. And it definitely hadn't been there on the last patrol.

Andy ripped his walkie-talkie off his belt again. "Phil! Islam! Come in. I think a vandal's got through the barriers."

The radio frequency hummed with white noise.

"Come in! Where are you?"

Still nothing.

Andy swore under his breath and turned back, jogging round the side of the building towards his Portakabin. It was against company policy to carry a mobile with you – his was back on his desk inside, along with a landline phone. He was calling the bloody police…

The walkie-talkie in his hand suddenly crackled to life. "Andy…"

"Islam? Is that you, mate?" Andy ground to a halt again. His fingers clenched around the walkie-talkie as he willed the other security guard to respond.

"Help…"

"Are you all right?" Andy's heart was stuttering irregularly in his chest now. He'd left the army over twenty years ago, but the old instincts were still there and the prickle on the back of his neck reminded him of fighting out in the Falklands, of that wary feeling right before something went belly-up.

"Get ... out. Get—"

Islam's voice cut off with a choking noise. Andy was about to press the button to speak again when another noise sounded. A low, nasty laugh that went down Andy's back like an icy cold razor blade.

The channel went dead.

Andy stared at the walkie-talkie for a split second. Then he threw it down and ran for the Portakabin. He wrenched the door open, seized the mobile he had left lying on the pile of papers and jumped back out again. He had to help the other lads. He had to know what was going on.

His bad knee crunched painfully as he sprinted along the outside of the building towards the second Portakabin where Islam and Phil were stationed. His fingers fumbled over the buttons of the phone, trying to unlock it.

"Hold on, mate," he muttered to himself. "I'm coming."

He saw more of the black liquid spattered and pooled across the concrete under his feet as he turned the corner. The river spread out before him, gunmetal grey, deserted and lonely, icy wind whistling over the surface. The door of the second Portakabin was hanging open. One of the tiny windows had been smashed, and black liquid dripped down the outer wall. Fine red droplets misted the door and the broken glass.

Andy froze, suddenly more frightened than he'd ever been in his life. He turned in a slow circle. There was no one in sight. Apart from the wind and the distant noises of the city, there was nothing to hear.

His fingers finally pressed the right combination of buttons to unlock his mobile. He got as far as dialling the first nine before there was movement in the shadows of the cabin.

"Andy?" someone said. "Is that you out there?"

"Phil?" Andy asked, flooded with relief. He moved forward, his fingers stilling on the mobile as he squinted, trying to see through the broken glass. "Are you hurt? Where's Islam?"

"Well, to tell you the truth, mate," Phil's voice said, "I'm a bit beaten up. I need your help."

Andy stepped cautiously through the doorway of the Portakabin. "What do you need—"

Phil was in the cabin, all right. His body lay sprawled across the smashed desk and the mess of fallen papers. His eyes stared blankly at the ceiling, blood trickling slowly from his neck.

"What I need," Phil's voice said from the shadows, "is your blood."

Andy opened his mouth to shout. Something black uncoiled from the back of the cabin and shot towards him. He jerked away instinctively. One foot slipped in a puddle of the dark liquid. Andy fell with a crash, the back of his skull hitting the splintered edge of the desk.

For an instant, the pain was overwhelming. It blocked out fear, shock, anger. He saw something black and white moving over him, but his vision was fragmenting, blurring, going grey at the edges. The sudden pain was already fading. He closed his eyes with relief.

He was gone before the Nekomata's teeth sank into his neck.

Jack was waiting for me downstairs in the living room when I finished my shower. She was leaning against the back of the big, leather sofa in front of the TV, arms folded. Her wet hair was slicked back, all her make-up had been scrubbed off, and her eyes were red and puffy. Like me, instead of throwing on some comfy PJs, she'd dressed to go out again, in jeans, boots and hoodie. The black eye she'd got this morning seemed to have darkened a few more shades.

"We need to talk," she said flatly.

I tumbled into speech. "I know, Jack, and I'm so—"

Jack held up her hand. "Shut up a minute and let me get this out." She took a deep breath and rolled her shoulders, like she was warming up for a fight, then started: "Mimi, you're my best friend. Whatever you're into, I'm down with it. But Rachel isn't a part of this. She's not a fighter. She doesn't know what's going on. She just got dragged into it, and what that thing might have done to her…" Jack paused, shook her head fiercely, and fixed her eyes on mine. The look made my stomach lurch.

"I need you to promise me something," Jack continued. "I know the sword has been in your family for a million years, and it's precious and dangerous and you're, like, supposed to protect it and all that stuff, but if you have to make a choice ... if it comes down to Rachel or the sword ... you have to swear to me, *swear*, that you will do the right thing."

The right thing?

A million thoughts swirled through my head. I wanted to remind Jack that we had no guarantee the Nekomata would give Rachel back to us even if I did surrender the sword. The sword was so powerful, even Hikaru, an immortal, had seemed frightened of it. But I didn't. I forced myself to put the katana down on the back of the sofa. Then I went towards her and threw my arms around her – ignoring the hot, warning throb from my injured arm – and squeezed her until she made a wheezing noise.

"I swear," I whispered. "We're going to get Rachel back. It doesn't matter how. We will get her back."

Jack let out a shuddering sigh that was almost a sob, and we clung to each other for a minute.

"OK, that's enough of that," she said finally, her voice trembling, as she pushed me away. "Don't be such a girl."

"Sorry, but I am a girl. I have all the right girl parts and everything."

"Euw!" Jack said, snorting unsteadily. "Don't talk

about your girl parts! I'll need mental bleach."

"You love it," I said, making a kissy face. Jack lightly smacked the back of my head.

Just like that, things were all right between us.

And those conflicted thoughts that were still clamouring at the back of my head? That alarmingly loud internal voice that was crying out in protest? I slammed the door on them, hard. They belonged to some other person. Some other Mio that I didn't know. And didn't want to.

"Did you, like, grow or something?" Jack asked, frowning.

"Since when?" I rolled my eyes at her. "This morning?"

"I don't know, but—" She put her hand on the top of my head and then brought it forward in a straight line. It hit the bridge of her nose. "You can nearly look me in the eye, and you're not even wearing high heels."

I blinked, took a step back, and realized she was right. "Huh. I thought this T-shirt had just shrunk in the wash." My bra had been a bit uncomfortable too. I'd ended up putting a stretchy Lycra tank top on instead.

"Long-overdue growth spurt?"

"Maybe. It wouldn't be the weirdest thing that's happened recently," I said, sliding past her, snatching the katana up again, and collapsing on the sofa. "Argh, I'm exhausted." *And frightened and freaked out and worried…* My hands opened and closed around the saya and hilt of the sword, never quite letting go.

"I ordered pizza," Jack said, sitting next to me. "We – we need to keep our strength up, you know? Rachel would be telling us we needed to eat..." Her voice broke a little at the end.

I nodded, swallowing hard. It felt heartless to even mention food, but that was probably why Jack had done the ordering instead of leaving it to me, like normal. Neither of us had eaten anything today. We couldn't afford to pass out. And I wasn't going back in the kitchen right now. I noticed that Jack had closed the sliding doors that separated the living room from the kitchen. I was grateful. The room was wrecked. How was I going to explain that to Mum and Dad?

Mum and Dad.

Hell. I dived for the cordless house phone standing on top of a stack of books on the coffee table, snatched it up, and then collapsed back on the sofa, clutching my bad arm. "Eff, that hurts."

"What are you doing?" Jack asked.

I checked the phone and saw a little symbol of a tape with "x3" flashing next to it on the display. "Oh, *hell.* Of course they phoned up to check on us. Mum will be worried and Dad will be furious. What am I going to say to him?"

"Why are you panicking?" Jack asked. "You're good at this stuff, Mimi. Phone your mum's mobile and just tell her that we didn't hear the phone."

"How am I supposed to explain the fact that no one answered the phone *all day*? I bet they tried my mobile too, and yours," I pulled my phone out of my pocket, and sure enough, Mum had started phoning right about the time we'd been fleeing from the cats in the coffee shop. "She probably called Rachel as well! No answer from any of us? We'll be lucky if they're not already on the way home! What if they called your mum?"

Even Jack looked daunted by that.

"What's wrong?" Shinobu's voice made me and Jack jump violently. I looked over the back of the sofa to see him leaning against the doorframe. I momentarily lost the power of speech.

He was dressed in the soft, worn jeans that I had dug out of the bottom of my dad's chest of drawers and a plain black T-shirt that my dad used to exercise in. On my dad they were loose, boring, ordinary clothes. On Shinobu's larger frame they clung faithfully to every muscle. I could clearly see the outline of his pectorals and abdominals shifting as he breathed.

I had a sudden, nearly uncontrollable urge to lay my head on that chest, to feel it gently rising and falling with the movement of his lungs, to hear the slow, steady rhythm of his heartbeat. The feeling was so intense that it was as if it had already happened, as if I had done it a hundred times before and it was my absolute right to do it again whenever I wanted. It felt less like wanting and more like … more like … remembering…

A leaf-shaped blade flashed in the red light as it sliced down—

"Mimi!"

I jumped again as Jack shrieked in my ear. "Whoa! What?"

Jack shook her head at me. "You're embarrassing yourself."

"Shut up," I muttered, flicking a humiliated look at Shinobu. "I was thinking."

"What were you thinking about?" Shinobu asked, coming forward. He looked suddenly intent and a little wary. Like my answer mattered to him. A lot.

"Yeah, right, you were 'thinking'," Jack said, making quotation marks in the air with her fingers. "Can we please get back to working out how to handle your parents, before they call my mum and they all come back to London and get eaten by demons? Cos I, for one, am not ready to be orphaned."

I didn't bother pointing out that Jack's dad was still alive. Since he'd gone off to California with his new girl-friend he might as well be dead to Jack.

"OK, OK, let me think." I put the phone down on my lap and ran the hand not resting on the katana through my damp hair, carefully keeping my eyes on the phone and away from Shinobu. I didn't want to zone out again. *Zone out* … aha!

"I've got it." I found Mum's mobile number on speed dial and pressed the button, ignoring Jack and Shinobu's baffled expressions.

The phone only rang once before Mum answered. "Mio? Is that you?"

Her voice was the perfect mixture of parental fury and parental concern. This was going to have to be *really* good.

I let my voice take on a shrill, anxious note. "Oh, thank God! Mum!"

Mum instinctively responded to the anxiety in my voice. "Mio, are you all right? What's happening over there?"

"I've been trying to reach you for *hours*!" I babbled. "We all have. We just kept getting a 'Service not available' message. I tried calling from Rachel and Jack's phones. Nothing worked. I was so worried. Did you get there OK? What about Dad?"

"We're fine, sweetie," she said soothingly, automatically flipping into Mum Reassurance mode. Thank God my dad hadn't answered. "You didn't need to worry about us."

"But I didn't know what was going on," I said, putting a bit of a tremble into the words. "I kept thinking about train crashes and stuff, but there was nothing on the news…"

"Now, don't be silly. There's no need to be a drama

queen! We're absolutely fine. There must have been some sort of disruption on the line when we moved into the new service area, that's all."

I sniffed, playing it up a little bit. "You're in the hotel?"

"Yes, we are, and it's lovely! You can just see the Eiffel Tower from our balcony. It's so beautiful, Mio. You would love it – although it's a good job you didn't come, really. Everywhere is booked solid. We'd never have got you an extra room at short notice."

"So you're having a good time?"

"Wonderful. It's even sunny here! And I've already seen this amazing coat that you're going to love…"

We chatted for another few minutes. I could tell that Mum was going all out to coax me out of my fake panic attack. It made me feel queasy.

"Now, listen," Mum said, as we got to the end of the call. "There's broadband in the lobby here, and I'm going to go and sign up for it. If there are any more problems with the phones and you start getting worried, just send me an email, OK?"

"Thanks, Mum," I said. "Um. Give Dad a kiss for me?"

"He's right here, Mio. Why don't you talk to him for a minute?"

Crap! "No, that's fine—"

"Mio?" My father's deep voice growled down the line. "You gave us quite a scare, you know. Your mother was about to start packing to come back."

194

"Yeah, it's been pretty scary over here too," I admitted.

"You're all fine? No problems?"

You have no idea, Dad. "Nothing I can't handle."

There was a pause. "Why does that sentence fill me with dread?"

"I don't know. Maybe because you're paranoid and incapable of trusting me?"

"When you prove yourself worthy of trust, then I'll stop being paranoid. What are you up to? You haven't wrecked the house already?"

My eyes shot guiltily to the closed kitchen doors. "Dad!" I snapped. "Why do you always have to start with me? You know what – just put Mum back on the phone."

"Mio—"

"Put Mum back on the phone or I'm hanging up."

Now he was the one sighing. "Fine. Take care. Don't blow anything up. See you in a few days."

Mum was laughing when she came back on the line. "Seriously, you two! That was – what? Thirty seconds before you started fighting?"

"I didn't start it," I said. "He was... Oh, it doesn't matter. I've got homework and stuff to do, and I bet this call is costing loads, so I should probably go."

"Hang on a second, love. Is Rachel about? I want to have a word with her."

Argh!

"She's in the kitchen making us curry. You know how

she always wants to feed me when I get stressed out? It smells amazing, but there are about six pots on the go. I'm slightly scared to go in there."

Mum laughed again. "Well, never mind then. I'll talk to her next time. You give both her and Jack a hug from me. Night, honey. Sleep tight, and don't let the bedbugs bite."

"Night, Mum," I whispered. This time the tremble in my voice wasn't faked. I hung up and buried my face in a cushion.

CHAPTER 13

FAIRY TALES

"**M**io—" Jack began. The front doorbell rang, cutting her off. She leapt up. "Pizza!"

"Don't go outside!" Shinobu and I burst out simultaneously.

"Make sure you keep your feet on this side of the threshold," Shinobu said.

"And don't … invite him to step inside or anything," I added nervously. "Just in case."

"Fine, fine," Jack said, pulling money out of her jeans pocket as she went out into the hall.

Shinobu waited until Jack was gone before he came to rest his free hand on the back of the sofa next to – but not quite touching – my shoulder.

"You should be proud of yourself," he said quietly.

"What for? Lying my ass off to someone who trusts me?"

"I know it was not an easy thing you just did. To take the whole burden of this thing, and the truth of it, upon yourself. But if your parents returned they would only become hostages to be used against you. You have saved them from that."

The tension leaked out of me in a long sigh. It was true. My parents were the last people in the world who could deal with monsters. They were dentists, for crying out loud. I ran my fingers around the complex piercing on the katana's guard, looking at Shinobu from the corner of my eye. "How do you always know just the right thing to say?"

"Do I?" He looked surprised. Then he smiled his crooked, shy smile.

I blinked a few times. I was a twenty-first-century woman, and I was not going to be conquered by any random facial expression. No matter how adorable it was.

"It might be strange for you to think of it this way," he said. "But I do know you quite well. I spent … a long time thinking about what I would say to you, if only you could hear me."

I nibbled on my lip. "Will you tell me something?"

He nodded, the smile fading into a grave expression. "Of course."

"You were there when my ojiichan promised me the sword, showed it to me for the first time. Do you remember what he said to me?"

"I think so."

"I'm trying to fit it with what the Harbinger said. He – or it, or whatever he is – said that he'd chosen our family to guard the sword. Didn't Ojiichan say something about bad people looking for it?"

"Your grandfather spoke in vague terms, suitable for a child, but … yes. Yes, he did say that. He promised that he would explain and tell you the stories of the sword later—" Shinobu broke off.

"Only he died," I said, a pang of old grief going through me. "He expected to be around to guide me and explain what he knew, and he wasn't. If the Harbinger did do something to the sword, and then turned it over to us to hide for whatever reason, he had to have told the Yamato family something, otherwise Ojiichan wouldn't have known to say that bad things could happen if the sword wasn't hidden. He knew 'bad people' might be looking for it. He knew – he had to have known – that it had some kind of power. So why – *why* – would he give it to me? Allow me to connect to it that way? I was, like, ten. I didn't even understand what I was feeling, what this weird connection was. It wasn't—" I cut myself off.

It wasn't right. That was what I wanted to say. But I couldn't. Because this was Ojiichan I was talking about. My grandfather, who'd loved me more than anything. My grandfather, whom I'd worshipped, and still worshipped. He wouldn't ever have put me in danger. He wouldn't.

Would he?

Shinobu hesitated. "It does seem strange. You were a small child, incapable of protecting the sword, or even yourself. At the same time, your father was an adult, yet, as far as we know, he is not even aware that the katana exists. If your grandfather needed to pass on the sword, why not to him?"

"Cos her dad would have laughed in his face," Jack said. She was leaning against the doorframe with two pizza boxes, a six-pack of Diet Coke and a pile of paper napkins in her hands. She came into the room, dumped the food on the coffee table and then opened one of the boxes to reveal that she'd opted for her favourite combo of pineapple and pepperoni on a deep-pan base. Ick.

I reached out to check the other box and was relieved to see that she had taken pity on me and got an Italian-crust Margarita.

"This is food?" Shinobu asked doubtfully, coming round the side of the sofa. He sat down gracefully on the floor beside the coffee table, folding his legs beneath him.

"It is." I handed him a large slice of the plain pizza, with a napkin to shield his fingers from the hot, stringy mozzarella. "And it's good. What did you say, Jack?"

"You've told me about your dad and your granddad. They could never, ever get on, right? A bit like you and your dad now. It seems like your dad was pretty determined to leave everything from Japan behind and just be British. Be modern. Never look back. Your granddad had this sword, but he must have realized fairly early on that it would be no good trying to convince your dad to hide it and guard it with his life." Jack swallowed a mouthful of pizza. "Your dad would probably have wanted to sell it and do roof repairs or something."

"You're right," I said, staring blankly at my pizza. "Dad is like that. I've always wondered if it was because he lost his mum so early. He was five when she died. It must have been pretty awful for him. He and Ojiichan came to England soon after that. Maybe it was part of Dad getting over it – just leaving all the memories of Japan behind. He always seemed like he wanted to leave Ojiichan behind too."

"I have known people like that," Shinobu put in. "People who dealt with sorrow by shutting it out."

I nodded, feeling more puzzle pieces click into place. "So instead of passing the sword on when Dad was sixteen, Ojiichan had to wait. And wait. But he didn't wait until I was sixteen. He showed it to me as soon as I was big enough to pick it up..." *As soon as Dad threatened Ojiichan with taking me away.*

Dammit, Dad. Why did you have to be such a pig to him? You left him no choice.

"It was a dangerous strategy," said Shinobu, putting his piece of pizza back in the box, untouched.

"We don't know if her granddad knew about the monsters, though," Jack said. "What actual sane person would imagine all this was going to kick off?"

"It wouldn't have, if I hadn't taken the sword out," I said guiltily. *It must always, always be hidden.* Why had I waited until it was too late to remember that?

"It is also what broke me free of my prison," Shinobu pointed out. "Would you wish me back there again?"

I sighed. "Fine. I can't go back, I get it. I just wish that Ojiichan had the chance to tell me what he knew. Tell me the rules, or something. Anything!"

Shinobu frowned thoughtfully. "Your grandfather tried to prepare you physically by training you in sword work. He must have tried to prepare you in other ways. He must have told you something. Perhaps something which did not seem important at the time?"

I threw my nibbled crust down. "I don't think so. I'm sure I'd remember. I mean, he never spoke to me about the sword before he showed it to me that day, not ever. Mostly he just told me stories, you know? He'd tuck me into bed and tell me fairy tales about Japan. I loved them, but Dad didn't like me hearing about that stuff, so we kept it a secret. Gods. Monsters. Demons and heroes. Princesses who were born in bamboo trees and flew off to live in the moon. A hero who turned his girlfriend into a hair comb to protect her and then cut the head off a dragon."

"Those are both common fairy tales," Shinobu said.

"My mother told them to me as a child too."

"Is that it?" Jack asked, disappointed.

"Pretty much. I remember the day he showed me the katana – I mean, that night – he told me a new story. I'd never heard it before and it was kind of … dark. It was about this king and queen who couldn't have children."

"Like in *Snow White*?"

"Er, no. It went something like the king and queen were the most beautiful people in the world, and they loved each other very much, but they had children that were – not right. Deformed. And the king only loved beautiful things, so he threw the babies into the sea."

"Whoa. What a dick."

"Yeah. And then the queen died. Her husband refused to accept that she was gone, so he followed her into the land of the dead, but when he found her she refused to leave with him because, you know, she was dead and it wasn't right. But the king said—"

"He would love her to the ends of the earth, and to the darkest depths of the sea, and to the highest heights of the sky," Shinobu broke in softly. "The world itself was not as great as his love for her, and he would never leave without her. And so she, weeping with joy, agreed to go with him, back out into the light."

There was a short, charged silence. I propped the katana against my knee and defiantly rubbed the goose pimples off my arms. "Is that a common fairy tale too?"

"It is the story of Izanagi and Izanami, the father and mother of all the Japanese gods."

"Gods?" I repeated.

"Correct."

Jack shrugged impatiently. "Well, that's a sweet, romantic story and all, but I can't see what it has to do with us or the sword."

"That is not the end of the tale," Shinobu said. "Can you remember the rest, Mio-dono?"

"No, because my dad came along. And the next day…" I took a deep breath.

"Oh, hell," Jack said. "That was when—?"

I nodded wordlessly. Jack shifted down the sofa and put her arm around my shoulder. Finally I managed to ask, "So what did happen next in the story?"

Shinobu took a deep breath. "The god Izanagi took his wife's hand and began to lead her out of Yomi—"

"Where?" Jack interrupted.

"Yomi. The Underworld. A place of endless darkness and endless night, populated with all the creatures of men's nightmares."

"Not a top holiday destination then," Jack said.

Shinobu cracked a tiny smile. "I would not want to visit it. Izanagi did not like it either. He had succeeded in his quest and was sick of darkness. So he took the comb from his hair and made it into a torch to light their way. His wife, Izanami, cried out, and when he turned to look at her ... he saw that she was rotting. Her flesh had decomposed, and her skin was covered in maggots and parasites. She had eaten the food of Yomi and was truly dead."

"Yuck," said Jack.

"Izanagi was terrified and disgusted. He could not stand anything that was flawed or imperfect and despite all his promises, his love for his wife was destroyed. He flung her away from him and ran. Izanami followed him, sobbing, broken-hearted and begging him not to abandon her after he had given her hope. But he ignored her. And she became filled with rage and hate and sent all the nightmarish monsters of Yomi after her husband to kill him, so that he would be forced to stay with her in the Underworld for ever. However, Izanagi's fear had given him swift feet. He reached the entrance of the Underworld ahead of his pursuers, and blocked it with a giant stone, so that Izanami could never escape."

"I stand by my original opinion. This guy is a dick," Jack said.

"Pretty much," I agreed quietly. "Is that the end?"

"Not quite. Izanagi performed the rites of divorce there, outside the entrance to Yomi. Izanami screamed at her husband through the stone that she would kill one thousand humans for every day that she was trapped in the darkness without him. And Izanagi, uncaring, replied that he would ensure one thousand *five hundred* were born each day to replace them."

"Lovely. Thanks a lot, Izanagi and Izanami," Jack said. "But I still don't get why Mio's granddad would make a point of telling her that story right after showing her the sword. There isn't even a sword in it."

"Again, it is a tale that all Japanese children know. It may mean nothing," Shinobu said. Despite the reassuring words, his face was troubled.

"You might as well say it," I told him.

He sighed, then reluctantly went on. "After her husband abandoned her, Izanami became the Goddess of Death. Mistress of Yomi and its denizens, the creatures of darkness."

It took me a beat to join the dots. Then the goose pimples I'd just got rid of prickled up over my skin again. "Let me guess. That's what the Nekomata is, isn't it? A creature of darkness. So when it kept going on about its 'Mistress'—"

Shinobu shook his head. "The monster could have been speaking of any supernatural creature more powerful than itself. The stories say that Yomi is teaming with malevolent spirits. We must not leap to conclusions."

I picked up the katana in both hands. It sat across my palms, glinting in the light. "Do we have anything else to go on?"

"The Goddess of Death," Jack repeated flatly. "Are you kidding me?"

All at once it seemed ludicrous. I groaned. "I don't

know. She's apparently been killing people off since the beginning of time without any help. Why would she need some big, macho sword to make her happy?"

"Bang goes that theory," Jack said, relieved. "What about this Harbinger guy? Where does he fit into things?"

"I have no idea. He said that if I didn't protect the sword – *boom!* – end of the world. That was when he skewered Shinobu to the floor." I shuddered.

Shinobu shifted to kneel beside the sofa. I felt a tentative touch on my leg, above my boot, and fixed my eyes on the pattern on the katana's saya, holding my breath. Long, warm fingers gently circled the delicate bones of my ankle. Little electric sparks of excitement bounced up and down my leg.

"There is no need to be upset," Shinobu said. "Although it was painful, I was not injured."

"It *was* injuring you," I said, risking a look straight into his eyes. "He said that he was repairing 'damage' to the sword. But I could see you dying. You were fading away into nothing."

"'Fading away,'" Shinobu repeated. His palm slid down to rest on my foot. I shivered and Jack rubbed my shoulder again, thinking I was still upset.

"So, wait," Jack said. "The Harbinger didn't want to take the sword for himself. He wanted to repair it? He was telling to you to protect it? Is it possible that he's one of the good guys?"

"No." I shivered again, and this time it was nothing to do with Shinobu. My grip on the katana tightened, fingers clenching until they felt numb. "The Nekomata has nine tentacles and fangs like knives, and it's still not as scary as him. Whatever the Harbinger is, he's definitely not one of the good guys."

CHAPTER 14

THROUGH THE LOOKING GLASS

Half an hour later, the pizza and Coke were all finished and Jack had just slumped into an exhausted sleep on the other side of the sofa.

I slid down to the floor to make a pile of the boxes and cans on the coffee table, tucking the katana in next to my right leg so that I could feel it close.

My left knee bumped into Shinobu's thigh.

His long legs were lying, slightly bent, under the coffee table, and his elbows were propped on the edge of the table top. I glanced up at him. His eyes dropped hurriedly from my face. I waited for him to look at me again, but when he did, I found my gaze slipping away from his.

"So, earlier," I began, slightly rushed, as I arranged empty Coke cans in a line. "You know, when I was fighting the Nekomata and you were all 'strike the heart'? Exactly where is the heart on that thing anyway? I mean, the middle of it moved around. A lot."

"When I fought it, I located the heart by observing the placement of the creature's head relative to the limbs in its mantle."

"Oh. Right." I tried to imagine "observing" anything in the middle of the screaming terror of facing that thing, let alone acting on it, and failed.

"Not something that you were taught in your kendo lessons," he said after a moment. His voice was gentle.

"Nope." I abandoned the mess on the coffee table and picked the katana up instead. Then I tried to make my voice sound light and careless. "They pretty much expected your opponents to have just the four limbs. And you don't aim for the heart anyway – that's not a point-scoring thrust."

He nodded. "It is a shame they did not teach you better."

My hackles went up. "I was one of the best in my class, actually."

"I know. Your form was always excellent, and you were fast and graceful. But your kendo is a sport. It teaches you how to score points. Not how to kill."

"I … I'm not sure anyone can teach me that. I'm not sure I've got it in me."

Is that really true? Or do I just wish that it was?

"Everyone has it in them. You must only be frightened enough, desperate enough, angry enough. The trigger is different for each person, but it is there, nonetheless. It is the dark side of our humanity, I think."

In my mind, I saw Shinobu attacking the Nekomata. The lightning-fast, ruthless movements, the way his body turned into a blur when he struck. How the Nekomata had cringed from him when he held the katana. *It* had feared *him*.

Shinobu was the one who had taken the monster down today. In the kitchen he'd practically laid it out for me, and I'd still managed to muff it up. Looking back, it seemed impossible that I hadn't lost the sword and my life. If it hadn't been for him, I would have.

There was a part of me worried that if I got that good, I'd end up hurting people. It had felt safer to get really good at blocking my killer instinct, my natural aggression. But the instinct was still there. It was what had saved Shinobu, and probably me and Jack, from the Harbinger in the hospital today.

Didn't that show something? If I kept holding myself back, was it possible I could get myself – or worse, someone else – killed?

Jack and Rachel needed me. And I needed help.

I gulped. "Shinobu, do you think you could teach me to fight like that? Because right now I feel ... completely unprepared. Actually, completely unprepared is an understatement."

"It would be my honour." To my surprise, he stood

up, pushed the coffee table into the gap between the two sofas and then stepped away, gesturing for me to rise.

"Right now? I don't want to wake Jack."

"Then be quiet," he said simply, his voice a low murmur.

He had me take up the beginning kendo stance and grip the hilt of the sheathed blade. My injured arm ached a little, but I pushed the pain down as Shinobu walked round me, examining me with focused, intense eyes. With a few words, he improved my grip, altered the placement of my legs and corrected my posture.

"Your teachers cared about making your form pretty. I care about you not dying. In a real fight the only thing that matters is drawing blood without gifting any to your opponent in return. The only point you wish to earn is to hurt or damage him enough that he will draw back and give you room to strike again, until he either retreats for good or falls down dead at your feet. That is your focus. Your own survival. Nothing else matters."

I nodded slowly. "OK."

"Try to relax your muscles," he said, standing behind me. Both hands hovered in the air above my shoulders. The warm, calloused skin of his thumbs brushed the back of my neck as he shifted. I nearly bit my tongue.

"The instinct to tense is natural," he went on. "But it works against you, telegraphing your strikes to an experienced opponent. In armour this risk is not so great, but fighting as you are now, it is a deadly weakness. Stay relaxed. Stay loose and flexible. Allow yourself to dodge and move quickly, to change course if you must, without giving your enemy the advantage of tracking your movements."

I nodded again, taking deep, calming breaths and hoping that he couldn't hear my heart hammering away against my sternum.

Shinobu instructed me to go through one of the basic kata, a set of minutely choreographed movements that drilled the elements of sword work into muscle memory. At first I tried to move quickly, carelessly, because I'd completed the kata so many times before, because my bad arm was itching and it made me impatient. He stopped me and made me begin again, slowly, so that he could correct me as I moved.

His body flowed through the space of the living room alongside mine. Unconsciously, I fell into rhythm with him, my limbs echoing the economic, unhurried grace of his.

"The sword is a part of you," he murmured. "Remember that. It is part of your own body, the razor-edged extension of your own flesh and bone. It is the shining point of your will moving through the world, making your intentions reality. A true warrior reveals his own soul with every flash of his sword. Remember?"

I kind of thought I did. This didn't feel like anything

anyone, even my grandfather, had ever taught me but – it felt right. *Natural*. Like some part of me did remember. Like I was reconnecting with something that I had always instinctively known, deep inside.

The pain in my arm faded. The awareness of Jack sleeping on the sofa faded. Everything faded except the sword and Shinobu. We flowed smoothly from one kata to the next, unspeaking. It was like a dance. A dance that we knew as well as breathing. One we had been born to dance. Together.

Finally, as if we had agreed it beforehand, we both came to a halt. I found myself standing in the shelter of Shinobu's larger body, the shape of him pressed lightly into my back, his hands lying over mine on the hilt as gently as a silk scarf wrapped around my skin.

I turned my face towards him, my head coming to rest on his chest. I could feel his heart pounding under the skin there. His eyes were already waiting for mine. The grey clouds in the darkness glowed with something like exultation. His gaze slowly drifted down to my lips.

He's going to try to kiss me again.

And this time I'm not going to stop him.

I felt my face flush, my heart rate flipping out of control. I drew in a shaken breath. "You're very good at this. Have you taught someone before?"

His face broke into a sudden, heart-breaking grin. It

was the most beautiful thing I'd ever seen. "Of course I—"

The words choked off. I felt a pained shudder travel through his body. He pulled away from me at once and half turned, rubbing his face with one hand, hiding his eyes.

Have you taught someone before?

My stomach churned as I realized what I had said. How could I – even I – have been stupid enough to ask that? His whole life had been *before*. Family, friends. People he loved and who loved him. A place in the world that was his. All gone. How could I have forgotten that? How could I have thrown it in his face?

"I'm so sorry. I – I didn't mean—"

"No." He didn't move, didn't look at me. His face was still hidden. It was like staring at a man-shaped rock. "I know. You should rest, like Jack."

With an awkward jerk he walked away and ended up on the other side of the room, in front of one of the living-room windows. His face was a pale blur, reflected in one glass pane, as he stared out at the gathering darkness.

I crept to the sofa and curled up next to Jack, fingers wrapped around the katana as tightly as metal vices, trying to take comfort from the low buzz of its energy. There was nothing I could do. Nothing could make up for all that he'd lost. No one could do anything for Shinobu. No one could give him his world back.

215

"Oh…" Someone sighed.

A voice.

A voice?

New sounds crowded in. I could hear. Hear sounds I had almost forgotten. I had not heard them – heard anything – for so long. I knew those sounds.

Breathing.

Heartbeats.

Life…

Light broke through the darkness, blinding, agonizing, amazing. Sunlight. It shone down patchily through dirty glass, turning long columns of dust into spiralling galaxies that were golden against the sleek, dark head bent over … the sword.

My sword?

Small hands clasped the hilt gently, and the tiny fingers were warm. Somehow I could feel that warmth. It pulsed through me, drawing me back from the endless dark and cold.

"It's so… It's … beautiful."

Oh yes, yes it was. The light. The warmth. Thank you. Thank you.

"He is yours, Mio," a deep, aged voice said.

Mio?

The dreamlike blur of black and gold sharpened painfully and I saw a pair of slanting chestnut-brown eyes, filled with surprise and joy, staring down. The little girl's fingers tightened around the sword. Something shifted inside me.

Mio…

The golden shafts of light brightened. I heard the echo of laughter, smelled the heady scent of ripening grass warmed by the sun. A breeze whispered sweetly through the tall fronds.

"Shin-chan! Shin-chan!"

A small figure, a blur of black and red and white, ran through the long grass. The wind tossed unruly, dark hair around a pair of laughing eyes. I reached out…

Pain ripped through my chest. I was lying on my back, looking up at clouds of red-and-copper leaves blurring as they danced, blurring as the world began to go dark.

I heard footsteps approaching. Someone leaned over me. I saw a long, pale face. A face that I knew. A twinge of surprise cut through the pain, through the slowly deepening darkness. Then I saw the sword. The red light glowed on its smooth, mottled brown and green blade. The man lifted it above me.

Why? Why, when I am already dying…

These are not your memories, Yamato Mio.

The voice echoed as if it came from a hundred miles away. The bright leaves, the glowing blade, the pain – all rushed away like water being sucked into a drain. I opened my eyes.

My own face confronted me. Involuntarily one of my hands lifted, and I touched a smooth, icy cold surface. A mirror. The face in the mirror blinked slowly.

I stared at my own eyelids for a second before I realized that my eyes were still open.

I started back. There was nowhere to go. The mirror curved around me, above me and below my feet. All I could see was my own face. My own reflection.

Except it wasn't me.

It wasn't me.

My reflection's eyes began to change. The inky blackness of the pupils dilated, spiralling out to engulf the irises and the whites. Her hands lifted, palms up, reaching towards me. They hit the other side of the glass and pressed against it, straining, turning red and yellow as they pushed.

You should not play in other people's memories, Yamato Mio.

Pitiless, black orbs stared at me, glistening and blank like a shark's eyes.

"Who are you?" I whispered.

You are afraid of me. So afraid… Once I was like you. Don't you see? Just like you. I was not always like this, *the voice said.*

It held a childish note of pleading that made me shiver – because the voice did not belong to a child. It was a grown woman's. She sounded like one of those people you come across sometimes in the city, sitting alone in a doorway or hiding in an alley, muttering to themselves in the shadows. People with shaking hands and ravaged faces that you flinch from because you sense instinctively that they aren't right somehow. They are broken.

And dangerous.

I shied away again, but the reflection was waiting behind me too, still pushing desperately against the glass. Her teeth were bared, her nails scraping at the mirror as she tried to get through to me.

Once I walked under the sky. Once I knew how to laugh, and sing, and run, and cry. Once I knew sunlight, and water, and breath...

The voice filled my head, echoing, pleading.

"I don't know what you want!" I screamed. *My voice was small and dead-sounding, as if the mirrors had sucked it up. The face behind the mirrors didn't change.*

I only want one thing. Only one. And I have killed so many people for it. Good and bad. Young. Old. Beautiful and ugly. I just keep killing over and over and over and...

I don't know how to stop.

Death is all I have.

I felt moisture trickling slowly down my cheeks. It was too warm, too thick. I raised my hand at the same time as the twisted reflection lifted one of her palms from the glass. We touched our faces at the same moment.

Oily, black liquid smeared my fingers and dripped onto my hands.

I was crying my reflection's tears.

Death is all I can give you.

"Mio-dono. Wake up."

I opened my eyes again. Shinobu knelt on the floor

next to the sofa, one hand outstretched as if to touch my shoulder. I was curled up into a ball, clutching the sheathed katana to me so tightly that my fingers had gone numb. I'd rolled onto my bad arm, and it was aching fiercely enough to make my eyes water.

I'd been having freaky dreams for most of my life – dreams which made me feel sad and frightened and awful – but nothing like that. That ... that hadn't felt like a nightmare or a memory. It felt...

It felt real.

"It is an hour past sundown," Shinobu said, his hand dropping away without touching me. "Hikaru-san should be here soon."

I sat up, still unable to speak, unclenching my fingers from around the saya with difficulty.

"Is something wrong?"

I couldn't answer. *Who was that woman? Who was that woman, and why did she have my face?*

"Mio-dono?" Shinobu sounded concerned. "Are you well?"

I couldn't talk to him about it. No way. That would make it seem more real than it already did. In fact, I didn't even want to think about it.

"Where's Jack?" I mumbled.

"She is ready to leave. I let you sleep for as long as possible, but you must get up now."

I nodded and rubbed my tingling fingers clumsily

over my face, struggling to get my brain working again. Just a dream. Just a stupid dream, that was all.

I looked up at him again, taking in his changed appearance. He must have gone searching in the cupboard under the stairs, because he was wearing my dad's long, black coat which I hadn't seen for years, not since the leather had started to dry out and crack under the arms. Obviously Dad had never got around to throwing it away. Shinobu had braided his hair tightly back from his face and in the severe, dark coat, he looked like a samurai again: too noble and beautiful to be real. He had my school coat folded over one arm. His face was calm, almost expressionless. Whatever devastating emotions had almost broken him before, he'd wrestled them down and locked them away. *And himself too.*

I cleared my throat and reached for my coat with my good arm, avoiding his eyes. "Did you find shoes to fit you?"

"Thank you, yes. These boots you wear are unfamiliar to me, but there was a large enough pair at the back of the cupboard."

I had hold of the sleeve of my coat, but Shinobu was still hanging onto it. I blinked groggily at it, and then at him.

He hesitated, and I saw his muscles shift as he took a deep breath. Then he tugged the sleeve of the coat away from me and moved forward, carefully draping the garment over my shoulders, holding it so that I could slip my arms inside. The tip of my nose brushed his cotton-covered chest, just for a split second. I caught the smell of my own sport shower gel and the distinctive smoke and pine scent I had noticed earlier. Unthinkingly I grabbed a handful of the soft, old T-shirt, pulling him closer.

"Mio." His voice had lowered an octave.

He knelt before me again, utterly still, hands hovering in the air. He was holding his breath. I wanted … oh, the hard lines of his body, the long silkiness of his hair, the smell of him, his deep, beautiful voice. The depth of my longing frightened me. It was as if he was already mine. As if he had always been mine.

I had to hang onto him. I had to hold on tight…

There was a sound in the kitchen, and I jumped, meeting Shinobu's eyes with a shock. *Jack*. I'd forgotten all about Jack.

Shinobu shook his head as if he was waking up. I released my hold on his T-shirt, and he got to his feet. He stepped back and wordlessly offered me his hand. I took it, savouring the warmth of his grip, and let him pull me to my feet.

We both let go at the same time.

I turned away and picked up my shinai carrier from where I'd left it by the sofa. I slid the katana carefully inside and looped the strap of the bag over my head, wriggling until it fitted comfortably over the top of my coat. The flap of the carrier had been ripped off, so I could touch the sword hilt at any time – and draw it fast if I needed to. I cleared my throat, trying to make my voice businesslike. "Come on. I don't want to leave Jack on her own."

The kitchen was shadowy and dim, and our feet kicked through chunks of wood and pieces of broken ceramic with eerie skittering noises. I didn't turn on the lights. The sight of the destruction was pretty much engraved on my brain anyway. Jack had opened the back door and was fidgeting restlessly on the threshold as she stared into the quiet, dark space of the garden.

"Where is he?" she said, more to herself than to us. "He promised he'd be here. If he's flaked out on us, I'm going to hunt his foxy ass down and—"

"Look," Shinobu said softly.

I crowded into the doorway next to Jack. A tiny, copper star was glowing among the leaves of the myrtle bush. As soon as I noticed it, another one winked to life. Then another. Dozens of sparks began to light up behind the foliage, shafts of sunset-coloured light piercing the shadows. The leaves stirred and rustled.

Hikaru appeared.

The white kimono was gone, replaced with skin-tight, white leather trousers and a nearly floor-length white leather coat. Like Shinobu, Hikaru had tied back his hair and his expression was serious and strained. Two white sword hilts, held in a twin scabbard on his back, poked up over his left shoulder. There was another sheath, holding a trio of small, gleaming daggers, strapped to his thigh. The light from the bush made his pale figure glow. If Neo from *The Matrix* had had a red-headed, more stylish younger brother, he would have looked like Hikaru.

"Whoa," Jack said.

Hikaru bowed to us formally, then rolled his shoulders back, rotating his neck to the accompaniment of loud popping sounds.

"Well, that wasn't the most fun afternoon I've ever spent," he said. "But the king'll see you. You guys had better behave yourselves, because I've stuck my neck out to set this up, and if you piss someone off, it's probably going to get wrung."

"Behave how?" Jack asked. To my surprise, she sounded serious rather than sarcastic.

"Don't speak to anyone unless they speak to you first, and bow before you speak. When you approach the king, you need to kneel, put your hands flat on the floor in front of you, and press your forehead against them, and you don't sit up or look at him until he gives you permission. Don't turn your back on the king. Don't interrupt him when he's speaking, and when you do speak, address him as Your Majesty. Got it?"

Jack nodded, her face earnest. Somehow, in the

absence of her normal snark, I felt it was my job to mutter, "Geez. Even the queen of England only expects a curtsey."

Hikaru didn't laugh. His eyes fixed on my face like green lasers. "When the queen of England has been on the throne for four hundred years and can fry you where you sit, then I think you'll do whatever she says. The rules you've lived by all your life don't apply any more. You're going to an entirely different plane. You mess up there, and you won't get the chance to mess up again. So if you're not down with that? Stay here."

Is this how a sausage feels right before it leaps out of the frying pan and into the fire?

Jack gave me a pleading look.

I was the one who had started this, and it wasn't my sister's life that was on the line. I needed to suck it up.

I bowed. "Sorry. Thank you for your instruction." The words and gesture were borrowed from dojo etiquette, but Hikaru seemed to relax a little. "Right. Through the looking glass we go."

CHAPTER 15

TRANSFORMATIONS

The myrtle bush flared with new light. Hikaru sucked in an audible breath. "Someone's getting impatient."

Jack stepped over the threshold onto the greyish-brown winter grass of the garden and strode towards Hikaru and the bush. I quickly hopped down after her, looking around warily. The small, shadowy space of the garden, echoing with the distant noises of traffic, felt exposed and dangerous. Shinobu's solid presence behind me, sticking close, was incredibly reassuring.

"I'll go first and hold the rupture open for you to pass," Hikaru said to Jack.

"Rupture?" I repeated.

"In order to allow you to move on to our plane, we have pierced the veil that separates our worlds, creating a rupture which we will travel through," Hikaru said, faintly lecturing.

The dream image of my reflection's hands straining against the surface of the mirror flashed before my eyes. A hole in the veil? Did that mean that things could cross from both directions? Involuntarily my hand went back to check the grip of the katana.

I told myself to relax as Hikaru knelt by the blazing, orange glow of the bush and shoved the branches up with both hands, making a gap large enough for him to crawl through.

"I hate doing this in human form," Hikaru grumbled, spitting out an errant leaf. His tail, sticking incongruously out of the split in the back of his coat, made jerky, whipping movements. I half expected him to get stuck, but after a moment he managed to cram himself into the foliage, and the white gleam of his coat and the red of his tail disappeared.

"I've got it! Come on through!" His voice drifted back to us, sounding a lot further away than the wall at the back of the garden.

"Here goes nothing," Jack said.

She got down on her hands and knees and squeezed into the gap Hikaru had left. Her progress sent leaves, bits of bark and lacy scraps of cobwebs flying up behind her. The debris spun and sparked in the orange light, making weird patterns that my eye struggled to follow.

The bush rattled violently, and I could hear Jack's muffled swearing. Then the sound and movement stopped, as abruptly as if someone had pressed the off switch. The quiet within the garden seemed twice as ominous as before.

"You go next," Shinobu said, his eyes scanning the gathering darkness. "I'll guard your retreat."

I hesitated. Clearly we were only going to be able to go through there one at a time – but leaving him alone like this felt wrong. He didn't even have a sword. I grabbed hold of the sleeve of his leather coat and gave it a hard tug. "You'll come straight after me," I said firmly. "No hanging about, no heroics. Got it?"

The corners of his lips twitched up. "On my honour, Mio-dono."

I turned away quickly, bent and then ducked into the dark space within the bush. The knees of my jeans were instantly soaked. Branches caught at my hair and dragged along the back of my coat. The bush stank of wet mud and cat pee. I crawled forward, trying not to squeak like a boy as something – I didn't want to know what – scurried onto the back of my hand with tickly feet.

I shook it off and lifted my hand, palm outwards, so that I wouldn't end up bashing my head into the wall. I kept shuffling further into the bush on my knees, waiting for my fingers to touch bricks. The pee smell was getting stronger, although I wasn't sure if it was cats' any more. It was a deeper, muskier stink. And I was still crawling, and my hand still hadn't bumped into the wall.

The wall isn't there...

"Jack? Hikaru?"

Silence. I couldn't even hear the traffic.

The ground under my knees disappeared. A shrill scream ripped out of my throat as I fell, clawing helplessly at the air.

I landed hard, and felt someone go down underneath me.

"Ow!" Jack's voice and mine blended together.

"Jack?"

"Who do you think? Get off me – I think you cracked my rib!"

"Sorry, sorry!" I rolled sideways and hit something else. Not a person this time. My groping fingers found dirt, packed hard and covered in hairy tendrils that I thought were tree roots. I hoped they were anyway. I snatched my hands back just as someone's elbow connected solidly with the back of my head.

"Ow!" I said again. "Watch out!"

"Sorry." That was Hikaru. "I was trying to help."

"Does it really need to be pitch black in here?" Jack said.

"Everyone back up slowly until you've got a wall behind you," Hikaru said, ignoring the question. "Your other friend is going to arrive in a minute and he'll take up all the space that's left."

Arms outstretched, I got cautiously to my feet,

pressing my back against the curved soil wall behind me. "Where are we?"

"Between." The way he said the word gave it some deeper meaning. "Opening the veil here instead of directly into the spirit realm prevents things from either side crossing into places they shouldn't by accident."

"Like an airlock?" *I'm not the only one worried about wandering monsters.*

"Pretty much. Once we're all in here, I can close the rupture in the veil and open the entrance to my plane."

"Clever," Jack said. "But I still don't see why it has to be so dark."

Hikaru let out a low laugh. "It's only dark to human eyes. I can see you just fine."

There was a tiny, gulping noise from Jack. If Hikaru was trying to be sexy, he'd picked the wrong angle. Jack had always been scared of the dark, and knowing that he could see her when she couldn't see him probably made her want to punch him, not get cosy.

There was a rush of cool, damp air that made my hair flitter around my face, and then a thud and a muffled grunt.

Jack asked nervously, "Shinobu? Is that you?"

I didn't dare reach out in case I ended up hitting him the same way Hikaru had hit me. "Are you all right?"

"I am fine." The already familiar voice came out of the darkness. "Although a warning about the drop might have been helpful."

"Sorry, dude," Hikaru said. "I had no idea. It's different every time. Trust me, it could have been a lot worse."

"Well, we're all in. What happens now?" Jack asked.

As if in answer, the earthen walls around us began to shake with a deep, grinding noise that reminded me of the problems we'd had on the Tube the night before. A rain of soil and pebbles pattered down. I squeaked as a rock bounced off my bad shoulder. The next second I was in Shinobu's arms, his large body sheltering me from the debris. I buried my face in his T-shirt.

"Just a minute, folks," Hikaru said, his voice rough with strain.

Light burst into the space. I squeezed my eyes shut for a second, then blinked rapidly. A hole had appeared in the wall, a perfect circle, about six feet in diameter. Hikaru was silhouetted in the centre of it in a cloud of dust and falling earth, his hands and feet braced against the sides as if he was holding it open with his own body. Maybe he was. Slowly the rumbling and shaking stopped, and Hikaru dropped his arms wearily.

"Wow, you all look terrified," he said, glancing over his shoulder. "Guess I should have warned you about that part too?"

I nodded wordlessly. Jack, who was plastered against the wall next to me and Shinobu, face-palmed. I felt the tension in Shinobu's body relax fractionally. He let me go and I stepped away, hoping my face wasn't bright red.

"This is probably why there's a rule against bring-ing humans home," Hikaru said, thoughtfully. Then he flashed Jack a brilliant, reckless smile. "Oh, well. Welcome to the spirit realm, ladies and gentleman."

He stepped through the opening. The light set fire to his hair and tail as he stretched his arms above his head. This was not the stressed, neck-popping movement I had seen in my garden but a smooth, almost catlike unfolding of muscles. The white tip of his tail flipped lazily. It made him seem disturbingly inhuman.

That's because he's not human, genius. Bear it in mind.

Jack unpeeled herself from the wall, and I stepped up to stand beside her. The two of us paused in the circular opening, shoulder to shoulder, and stared out at the spirit realm.

It was the opposite of everything we had left behind. Home was wintry cold, dark, brick and glass. This place was bathed in warm sunshine, and everywhere was green. I could hear birds: beautiful, liquid trills and low, mournful calls, like something from a rainforest. The wind rushed around us, scented with water and pollen.

This world was different … and yet the same.

It took me a moment to realize what I was looking at. The shape of the garden, the skyline of the neighbouring buildings. It was all there, completely familiar, and com-pletely alien. A mirror image of my parents' house.

The flat, triangle-shaped lawn that had been covered

in greyish turf all my life now rippled with waist-high, green-gold grasses. Their feathery fronds drifted gently in the breeze. The walls that enclosed the garden were covered so thickly in brilliantly shaded mosses and lichens that they looked soft and rounded like cushions. The neighbouring houses were buried under saplings and ferns and climbing vines that concealed any hint of brick or render. On the back wall of the house dozens of thin waterfalls cascaded down the sheer surface, splashing musically into silver pools at the base. Flat, glittering planes of mica took the place of the windows and glass extension. On top, where the roof tiles had sloped down, there were huge trees. Their bent, gnarled trunks were almost hidden under heavy, drooping canopies of crimson flowers.

"God…" Jack breathed.

I squared my shoulders. "Come on."

Together, we stepped over the threshold to another world.

As my foot touched down, a high, singing note filled the air. My fingers and toes tingled. For a moment it was almost pleasant – like being welcomed. Then the tingling became an angry buzz, spreading through my body. The singing note became piercing. I could literally feel my eardrums vibrating.

Beside me, Jack's hands flew up to cover her ears. "Mimi, I feel…"

Suddenly I was unsteady, my legs spindly and weak underneath me. I bent over, hands slapping onto the ground. But they weren't my hands any more. They were changing.

I tried to shout for help. What came out was a high-pitched bark, not quite a dog's.

Ohshitohshitohshitoh…

Shinobu yelled my name. I saw Hikaru whip round, his lips forming a curse as he ran back towards us.

Then everything went fuzzy and grey, but too bright at the same time. I whined. I felt as if someone had smacked me sharply in the nose. Hundreds – thousands – of scents assaulted my nostrils. I could smell rotting wood and the tasty grubs that wormed beneath it, the day-old trail of a rabbit passing under my snout, the marker that another of my kind, a healthy male, had left on the stones near by.

I bent my face towards the ground, scrubbing at my watering nose with both front paws. My ears flicked back and forth, absorbing the strange, lowing sounds of humans near by. Some part of me knew that humans weren't a threat, not to me. I ignored them, rubbing my muzzle against the soft fur of my foreleg.

A big shape, a human shape, moved slowly towards me. It was bright white with red patches. Distantly, I remembered it. *Friend*.

The friend smelled funny. Like my kind, and like a

human, and like something else ... something hot and irritating that made my nose water more. I sneezed and rubbed my snout again. The friend made more of the lowing noises as it got closer. The irritating smell got stronger. My fur puffed up around me. The burning smell was bad. Dangerous.

I stood upright and made noise, a high-pitched scream-bark, warning the friend back. He had something I didn't like on him, in his front paws. And it was getting stronger the closer he got to me.

Magic. Magic in his hands. Magic bad.

The friend dived at me suddenly.

No. Bad.

I skittered sideways. The nasty, burning smell wafted around me, and he grabbed at me again with his big white paws.

Bad friend.

I plunged away from him into the towering grasses, ears pinning back with effort as I wove between the shifting fronds. I could hear pursuit behind me. *Up. Go up. Away.*

There were rocks piled ahead, rocks with green shelter. *Hide.* I leapt – and jerked to a stop as a pair of human paws closed around my ribcage, catching me in midair. I snapped and struggled ferociously, then went still as I recognized the smell of the human holding me. It was familiar and good. *Safe.*

I relaxed, drawing my paws and tail up over my

vulnerable belly as the human lifted me in his arms. I found a patch of human skin and snuffled it, sighing contentedly. *Good friend.*

A human hand stroked down my back gently. The bad smell burned my nose once more, stronger than ever. I sneezed, but I didn't try to run this time. I knew the good friend would protect me.

There was a loud human noise. "Got it!"

I blinked – and found myself back in human form, cradled in Shinobu's arms as if I weighed nothing. He made a pained noise and clutched me to him, burying his face in my hair. "Thank the gods."

"I'm all right. It's OK." My voice came out weak and trembling, and I wasn't sure that I was telling the truth. I helplessly patted whatever bits of him I could reach.

Deep shudders worked through his body as he rocked me. I remembered what he'd said before – that me getting hurt caused him pain too. He'd been telling the truth. Despite the warning ache from my shoulder, I put my arms around his neck and hugged him tightly. I needed the comfort as much as he did.

"I'm OK," I repeated. "It's all good. But I just need to know, was I a—?"

"Fox," Hikaru said, moving into view behind Shinobu's shoulder. "Yes."

Shinobu's arms tightened until I wheezed. Slowly, he let me slide down to stand on my own two feet. For a minute more we clutched at each other, unwilling to let go.

"I'm fine. Shinobu, I'm all right."

"This time," he said, voice flat. I felt his hands curl into fists against my back.

I twisted my head to meet his gaze – but he wasn't looking at me. His furious eyes were fixed on Hikaru.

I shifted back and, reluctantly, Shinobu let go. Immediately I stepped in front of Hikaru, shielding him from Shinobu's wrath. But not from mine. "Explain."

"Look, I know you must have a lot of questions. But we need to get going."

"Why?" I asked. The word came out like a fox's bark, and I coughed.

"Um, take a look around. Where's your friend?" Hikaru said.

I turned in a circle, searching for Jack in the green landscape. There was no sign of her. "Oh my *God*! Jack's a fox too! Where is she? Why didn't you say before?"

"I've been trying to," he snapped. "She's bolted, and we have to find her before somebody else does."

CHAPTER 16

SPIRIT
LONDON

Close to, the wall of rock wasn't nearly as flat and featureless as the brick walls of my parents' house. It was more like a cliff, riddled with crevices and cracks. Which was a good thing because I'd only ever been rock-climbing once, and I had about twenty pounds of ropes and safety harnesses attached to me at the time. Right now, I had nothing.

Shinobu had discarded my dad's leather coat for the climb and I could see the muscles standing out on his arms and legs as he climbed ahead of me, apparently without effort. I made a grab for a handhold, dug the toe of my boot in and pulled myself up. My good arm was trembling and my bad arm was sending shards of pain shooting up and down my spine. I was puffing like a steam train, my face felt like it was glowing, and sweat was sticking my hair to my cheeks and forehead. *Attractive.*

"Hikaru, how did this happen?" I demanded between pants.

"The transformation ward is a protective mechanism, like Between," Hikaru called down. He was about six feet above me and wasn't even breathing hard.

I gritted my teeth. Ignoring the rock scraping my knuckles, the pain in my shoulders, my injury, and the sweat trickling down my skin, I climbed faster. "Go on."

"Anyone who, by accident or design, stumbles through one of our portals ends up in fox form. That way we can safely round them up and shove them back where they belong without worrying that they'll learn or steal anything or manage to convince anyone that what they experienced was real. Normally it's easy. But normal humans don't run from the smell of magic. They don't know what it is. And when you panicked, Jack bolted too."

"And you didn't warn us about this?" Shinobu's voice was icy.

"Dude, do you think I'd bring a bunch of humans here if the ward was operational? The king disabled it before I left. It shouldn't have been an issue!"

Shinobu heaved himself up onto the roof slope beneath the trees. He crouched down to give Hikaru his hand. Hikaru clasped it and sprang lightly up to stand on the narrow ledge which, in the real world, would have been the guttering above Jack's bedroom window.

I gritted my teeth harder. I wasn't going to be

springing anywhere. Every muscle I had was twitching with the strain of clinging to the rock. Clearly PE three times a week wasn't doing as much for my upper body strength as I might have hoped. I found another hand-hold and pulled myself up, swallowing a groan of effort.

Shinobu reached down towards me just as my fingers slipped off a slimy chunk of moss. Both he and Hikaru yelled in panic. Desperate hands seized me before I could fall. For a minute I was dangling in midair, with Hikaru clinging to my left wrist and Shinobu gripping my right elbow. My bad arm didn't like that at all. Grey things nibbled at the edges of my vision.

Between them they hauled me over the edge of the wall. I sat down with a bump and put my head between my knees, taking deep, slow breaths and waiting for the grey nibblers to fade.

"Would the king change his mind?" Shinobu asked. His hand found its way to the centre of my back between my shoulder blades, long fingers sliding under my shinai carrier and spreading out there. I sighed, my tension easing a little.

"Not a chance. He gave you the right of safe passage, and that stands until he's spoken to you himself."

I lifted my head. I was so dirty that if I decided to lie down flat here I'd be perfectly camouflaged. There wasn't a green smudge or a fleck of dirt on Hikaru's white leather coat, and his hair was still perfectly braided, but that neatness just served to emphasize the suppressed fury glittering in his green eyes. For the first time, I thought he looked like he might be capable of using the weapons that littered his outfit.

"Can you explain that safe passage thing to the noobs, please?" I asked.

"It means he gave you his word that you could travel here unharmed. And he doesn't go back on his word. Ever."

"Apparently *someone* doesn't know that," Shinobu said.

Hikaru flashed his fangs. "Are you trying to suggest something?"

"Would you like me to suggest something?"

They stared at each other.

Warning: Testosterone levels reaching critical.

I held up my hand. "What did you mean about getting to Jack before something else does? Isn't this Kitsune territory?"

Hikaru shook his head. "The Kingdom of the Kitsune is underground. We're on common land now, which means anything could be drifting around here looking for lunch."

Oh, lovely.

"Well, then let's find her quickly, OK?"

"Fine." He got to his feet. "Follow me. And if you hear the trees whispering to you, ignore them."

The trees ... what?

He strode away through the gnarled trunks, his

white leather coat snapping out behind him. I glanced at Shinobu. He gestured for me to go ahead of him, casting a wary look around us. Guarding my retreat again. I nodded and went after Hikaru.

There was no sign of any fox, let alone a Jack-ish one, among the trees. Big, waxy, red petals showered down on me as I walked, and I shook them out of my hair, noticing that none were falling on Hikaru or Shinobu. When I rested my hand on the trunk of the nearest tree, it shuddered like an animal, sending more petals spiralling into my hair. *Just when you think things can't get any weirder...* A thin, silver snake curled around a branch overhead. Its flickering tongue was black. I hurried past.

"Where is she?" Hikaru muttered. "Jack? Jack!"

"It's no good," I told him as I caught up. "She can't understand you. I don't know if you can normally understand English in fox form, but I couldn't. You just sounded like you were mooing."

"Mooing?"

I dodged round a tall, jagged rock outcropping that looked like an ancient standing stone. It corresponded to one of our chimneys. "Yep. And your magic really stinks too."

"Great," Hikaru muttered. "You know, my grandmother always warned me that my weakness for pretty faces would do me in one day. I'm really pissed off that she's going to be proved right."

We found Jack standing on the very edge of the peaked roof. Her nose was pointed at the flat roof of the building next door, which, here, was a wide, grassy area. It was as clear as day that she was thinking of jumping. The gap was about three-feet wide. The drop was thirty feet at least. Jack had been on four paws for all of twenty minutes. A quick glance at Hikaru's face told me what he thought her chances were of making it.

She was paying no attention to us at all, apparently not deeming us a threat. But I knew how quickly that could change.

"Ideas?" I asked softly.

"Try talking to her," Shinobu said in whisper. "She might not understand what you're saying, but maybe she will recognize your voice."

"Just don't make any sudden movements," Hikaru advised. "One slip, and—"

"Yes, thank you." I cut him off before he could terrify me more and crept slowly towards the fox Jack.

She was beautiful – slender, compact and muscular. Her pelt was dark red, with no white at all, and her paws, the tip of her tail and her ears shaded to chocolate brown. I thought she was bigger than a regular fox, but I wasn't an expert on the species. She still wasn't big enough to make that jump. Typical Jack, biting off more than she could chew.

"Hey," I said quietly. "You're kind of cute as a fox, you

know. You'd get such a kick if you could see yourself."

One of Jack's large ears quivered a little, but she didn't turn her head. I left the shelter of the last tree and froze, unable to force myself to walk any further. It was just too scary out there in the open. I got down on my hands and knees and crawled up to the edge of the cliff.

"I wonder what I looked like. I'll have to ask Shinobu later. This is definitely an experience, right? Maybe not one to share with the grandkids, though, unless we want them to think we've lost our marbles and ship us off to the old folks' home."

Jack tilted her head slightly. She lifted one paw, and I tensed.

Don't, don't, please, please, don't jump…

She put the paw back down.

I sighed. "Jack, you know what would be really awesome? If you'd make this easy on me and just come over here. Because I've got to tell you, I think I'm developing a bit of a thing about heights, and you aren't helping."

Lying flat, I inched my leg up and over the roof peak, sucked in a deep, calming breath and then sat upright with one leg on either side.

For the first time, I saw the landscape that Jack was gazing at.

London spread out in front of us, every bit of it green and shining and growing. Where home had skyscrapers, the spirit realm had verdant green mountains, cloaked in mist and topped by gargantuan trees that must have been taller than my house. Where home had roads, the spirit realm had white, winding paths, glinting rivers and waterfalls. Home had parks. The spirit realm had forests that stretched as far as the eye could see. A gust of warm, green-scented wind made me teeter, but I was too spellbound to care. Spirit London *moved* with the wind. The mists shifted and shredded and reformed, the waters rippled, the trees bowed. Golden pollen and leaves and petals glinted in the air.

"Mio," Shinobu said urgently.

I tore my eyes from the view and saw Shinobu crouched in the trees behind me with a white-knuckled grip on the rock in front of him, as if he was only just restraining himself from grabbing me and pulling me away from the edge.

"Sightsee later!" Hikaru hissed.

Oh, right. Rescuing Jack now. Get your head in the game, Mio.

I gave the guys an apologetic look and then eased myself a little closer to Jack. The rocky edge of the cliff was biting painfully into my rear end.

"Jack," I said gently. "Jack."

She kept ignoring me.

"Hey, Jack!" I said a little more sharply, ignoring Hikaru's frantic head shake. "Is it too much to ask for your attention for one minute, or what? Come on, snap out of it."

Both Jack's ears flicked back, and she danced in place. I held my breath. She backed up a step and turned round. Her yellow-brown eyes regarded me with a puzzled expression that looked really out of place on a fox face.

I curled the fingers of my left hand into the dirt and slowly reached out with the other.

"Thank you," I said. "Now will you please walk towards me? We've been at this for a while and we really need to go and get help for Rachel."

Jack took a hesitant step towards me, ears swivelling.

"That's right, Rachel. Remember Rachel? Ace cook, bossyboots, sort of OCD? Your one and only big sister. Rachel is counting on you right now. So get your furry butt over here."

Jack took another step forward. She was so close now that I could see her cute, little blackberry nose twitch as she scented me. One more step and I could grab her. My fingers were visibly shaking – it was an effort to keep my arm straight – but I didn't dare move it, or think about the fact that my left arm, my bad arm, was the only thing holding me on this roof.

Come on. Just one more step…

There was a low bird call from the mantle of red blossoms in the trees behind us. With a sound like thunder, a flock of long-necked, white birds took flight, passing over our heads.

Jack's muzzle jerked up and her back paws slipped

on the moist greenery. She skidded, front legs scrabbling for traction.

I lunged as Hikaru did. I managed to dig the finger-nails of one hand into the thick fur on the ruff of Jack's neck while hanging onto the roof with the other. Hikaru snagged her tail with both hands. For a blink, both of us were clinging to a panicked, snarling, wild animal.

Then suddenly Jack – human Jack – was lying there, awkwardly twisted and gasping for breath.

I had hold of her coat collar. Hikaru was lying right on top of her, his head practically on her belly button, both hands clamped on her upper thighs. He stared down at his hands for a second. I saw his Adam's apple bob. Then he carefully released her and sat up.

"All better," he said with forced cheer, dusting his hands together.

"What – I was – was I—?" Jack spluttered.

"Yep," I said, unclenching my fingers from her coat with an effort. "A fox. So was I, for a little bit. And you had great fur, in case you were wondering."

Shinobu had appeared behind me in one of those silent, lightning-fast moves of his. He took hold of my shoulders and carefully guided me off my precarious perch. Shaky with all the adrenaline and panic, I let myself lean on him for a second.

Jack was gasping. Her wide, incredulous eyes trav-elled over all of us. "The hell? Someone explain this!"

"It was a spell," Hikaru said, wearily. "A defensive spell on the entrance to this world. It should have been uninvoked – it *was* uninvoked – I watched it happen."

Jack sat up slowly, running her fingers through her hair. I decided now was not the time to point out that she was leaving mushy, green streaks in her white-blonde do. "Dude. I don't think you watched closely enough."

If the Kitsune had been in fox form, his ears would have been drooping.

I took pity on him. "Hikaru says he saw the spell closed down, and I believe him. Someone else must have reactivated it later, without the king knowing. Who would want to do that? And why?"

"It could be anyone," Hikaru admitted, crossing his arms across his chest. His voice was even, but the anger was still burning in his eyes. "There was a lot of resistance to my request – but there's always resistance to anything new. Going behind the king's back this way is something else. Whoever did it could be charged with treason, if what they did was proved, and that means they're dead serious about getting rid of you. The fact that they were able to reactivate the ward themselves means they also have a lot of power."

He looked down, seeming to struggle with himself. Grudgingly, as if the words cost him serious effort, he said, "I'll do my best to protect you, but … as far as Kitsune go, I'm pretty much the bottom of the ladder.

The safest thing – for all of you – might be to go home."

"No way!" Jack cried out. "Rachel needs us. You guys don't want to give up, do you?"

I shook my head. "Hikaru, getting your people on our side might be the only chance we have of getting Rachel back safely. How would you feel if it was your sister? As long as Jack is willing to risk it, I think we have to go on. Shinobu? What do you think?"

"I will follow wherever you lead," he said. The words were a vow.

Hikaru regarded all of us for a minute. Gradually, a new emotion filled his eyes. Respect. "All right. I'm in."

"Great," said Jack. "Now let's get down off this fricking roof and go see ourselves a king."

CHAPTER 17

THE
UNDERGROUND

I t took us nearly forty minutes to get off the cliff that looked like my house. I was, frankly, knackered as well as being in pain, and Jack was having trouble adjusting to two legs – which made no sense, since she'd had paws for less than half an hour. But it was hardly the strangest thing that had happened in the last couple of days. If it hadn't been for Shinobu I'd have been a Mio-pancake three times. I resolved to start doing Ojiichan's strength-training exercises again as soon as I got back home, and maybe get some weights too.

If I got back home.

"This has sucked up too much time," Hikaru fretted as I collapsed at the base of the cliff to catch my breath. "His Majesty doesn't like being kept waiting."

"It's not like it was our fault," Jack said, leaning her

hands on her knees. "He can't blame us for getting turned into foxes."

"Again, I think you're forgetting the 'can fry you to a crisp from a hundred yards away' aspect of this situation."

"Is this guy really *that* bad?" Jack asked, straightening up.

Hikaru winced. "Please, whatever you do, don't refer to His Majesty as 'a guy' within anyone else's hearing."

"We'd better take that as a yes," I said, rotating my neck carefully. The series of crunches from my vertebrae weren't encouraging. *Strength training and a chiropractor's appointment.* "We should probably get going."

The alley Hikaru lead us to was filled with huge swathes of yellow-green vines, and there wasn't enough room for all of us to walk together. Jack ended up in front with Hikaru, while I walked behind with Shinobu.

"You're different than I pegged you when you first turned up," Jack was saying to the fox spirit. I thought she was trying to make peace after the way she'd snapped at him up on the cliff-roof. "You seemed like one of those guys who flies by the seat of his pants and causes trouble for fun. But now here you are, looking after us all."

"When I first turned up, I didn't know you," Hikaru said dryly. "It's easy to treat everything as an adventure if you don't give a crap. The minute you actually start caring, it stops being fun."

"Ooh, does that mean you *like* us?" Jack asked teasingly.

Hikaru cleared his throat, turning his face away. "You're growing on me."

We emerged from the alley into a cathedral-like space where dangling vines entwined in a thick canopy overhead, turning daylight to a sort of emerald twilight. A dusty trail took the place of the road I knew in my world. Hikaru's head snapped up and he inhaled deeply through his nose. He gestured for us to stop, putting a finger on his lips.

Something's up. None of us said it, but I think the sentiment was pretty universal. I hooked the back of Jack's coat and pulled her over to stand with me at the same time that Shinobu stepped forward, putting himself in front of us.

Three foxes trotted into view on the trail. They walked in a triangle formation, their legs moving in perfect synchronization, as if they were marching. The trio caught sight of us and came to a perfectly timed halt. Each of them plonked their behinds down on the dust at the same moment.

The air around them shivered, and then there were three people standing in the road. The lead fox had become a woman, tall enough that she could look over Hikaru's head with ease. Her long, dark hair was streaked with grey and bound back neatly from her pointed face.

She wore a grey hakama – a short kimono and pleated split pants, a bit like a kendogi – and the traditional wrist guard and three-fingered glove of an archer. A quiver on her back was filled with grey arrows, and the top of a bow nearly as tall as she was protruded over her left shoulder.

She had four tails.

The two people behind her – one male, one female – seemed a lot younger. The girl looked a few years older than us. She was extremely pretty and was dressed in a red-and-gold kimono with a gold comb twisted into her elaborate hairdo. She had two tails. The male next to her could have been a kid from my school; he looked around fifteen, wore a grey hoodie and a pair of jeans, and had short hair gelled into a spiky quiff. Only the three tails poking out of a hole cut into the seat of his trousers gave away the fact that he was an ancient, powerful fox spirit.

The woman's face was neutral, and the boy looked at us with interest. But the girl's face was marred with a look of disgust and – yes – shock.

She expected to find foxes here, not humans.

The girl Kitsune only had two tails, and from what Hikaru had said, that meant she was too lowly to have rigged the trap with the transformation ward herself. But I was sure she alone, out of these three who'd come to greet us, had known about it. I glanced at Jack and saw that her hands were flexing, a sign she was itching to punch someone. I shook my head at her. She gave me a *duh* look that made me smile. *Aw. My little girl is growing up.*

"You're late," the woman said brusquely to Hikaru. "He's annoyed."

"We had some trouble with the wards."

"Trouble?" The woman's eyebrows drew together. "What kind of trouble?"

"The kind where two of my friends turned into foxes the moment their feet hit our soil," Hikaru said, folding his arms.

The woman opened her mouth, then shut it and pursed her lips together. "Interesting." Her surprise looked real to me. If she was faking, she was a very good actress.

"It certainly explains a few things," said the boy fox, grinning to himself.

"Like what?" Hikaru asked.

"I think you'll see for yourself when you get to court," the woman said, giving the boy fox a repressive look. "Come on now. Best not to keep him waiting any longer."

The three Kitsune turned and marched away. Hikaru motioned for us to follow. His expression wasn't particularly reassuring.

As Shinobu fell back to flank me again, I raised my eyebrows at Hikaru and flicked my eyes towards the three foxes. He shook his head and put one finger over his lips again; a warning that it was not a good idea to talk in front of them.

Hills shaped like buildings rose up on either side of us as we followed the foxes down the trail. Bird calls and unfamiliar animal noises echoed around us, mixing with the wind to make nature's version of muzak in the greenery, but it still felt uncomfortably quiet as we reached a dip where wide steps had been cut in the earth, leading down to a dark cave entrance. I blinked at it, confused because it seemed familiar. *Oh, right!* It was the entrance to the Tube that Jack and I took to school every day. The entrance to the Underground.

Kitsune territory.

As the foxes started down, Jack took a step back, shaking her head. "No. Not again."

Hikaru touched her arm. "What's the problem?"

"The dark. I can't. I'm sorry, I just can't. Isn't there another way?"

Hikaru called out. "Araki-san, Hiro-san, it's a little dark down there for our human guests. How about some fox lights?"

The older woman – Araki – was poised to disappear into the cave, but she stopped and looked up at us. "Of course. Thank you for reminding me, Hikaru-san."

Her tails whipped at the air, then straightened, each of them pointing out at a different angle, like the spokes on a wheel. There was a faint crack and a whiff of ozone. A bluish globe of light, around the size of a tennis ball, appeared at the tip of each tail. She flicked them upwards and they sailed through the air to bob about a foot over her head. She nodded at the male fox. "Hiro-san."

He sent three balls of light – not as bright and with a faint golden tinge – up to join them.

There was a pause.

"Miyako-san?" Araki said sternly. "You will not wish to be rude."

The younger Kitsune sniffed and whipped her tails together. Two crackling spheres of greenish electricity, bigger than footballs, surged up past her head. But instead of stopping there, the energy shot higher, stretching thin as it flew. I flinched and saw green zigzags on the back of my eyelids. There was a fierce sizzling noise.

Greyish ash drifted down. A massive hole gaped in the thick carpet of vines overhead, singed black chunks hanging sadly from its edges.

Miyako smiled sweetly. "Oops."

I hoped she couldn't hear the sound of me gulping.

"Never mind, dear." Araki's voice was velvety. "Lots of young ones have trouble controlling their lightning. I'm sure you'll improve as you mature."

The boy fox sniggered while Miyako's smile soured and dripped off her face. Her tails twitched and the smell of ozone got stronger. The hairs on the back of my neck stood up. Shinobu shifted forward, subtly getting between us. My hand lifted involuntarily, ready to grab Jack again.

"Miyako-san!" Araki tapped her foot. "I think *you* should lead the way."

Miyako turned her back on us with a flounce and marched past the other two Kitsune into the darkness. Hiro winked at us and followed her, with Araki close behind him. I blew out a deep breath.

We trooped through the cave entrance after them. The floating fox lights revealed a wide circular tunnel, lined with thick, dark-green moss. The vegetation made faint squelching noises underfoot, and the air smelled damp.

"So … you guys can make lights whenever you want?" Jack asked Hikaru. She sounded faintly reproachful. Probably thinking about our uncomfortable experience in the blackness of Between.

"I'm not old enough to do that," Hikaru said tonelessly. "Kitsune generally only develop the control necessary to form their lightning into fox lights some time during their second century."

"How old are you then?"

Hikaru cleared his throat and mumbled something. It sounded like "plenty".

Twenty? *Twenty?* These guys lived for *hundreds* of years. Twenty would make him practically a toddler!

"Hikaru-san is the only Kitsune born to King Takahiro's people in the last century, and the only Kitsune born in the new country." Araki's voice drifted back to us. "His birth was a cause of great celebration and joy. We are all expecting wonderful things from him."

The light in the tunnel was uneven, but I was pretty sure that Hikaru was turning an unattractive shade of brick red.

The tunnel opened up ahead of us, leading into a cavernous space where the ceiling disappeared into impenetrable shadows above the fox lights. The sounds of water dripping and rustles of movement echoed in the darkness. Bats? Rats? Or something worse?

"This is the station, isn't it?" I said quickly, trying to distract myself from thoughts of what might be lurking up there. "I don't understand why the spirit realm is so exactly like the human realm in so many ways. Or is it the other way round?"

To my surprise, Araki answered, dropping back to walk beside us. "No – you are correct. It is our world that echoes yours. The planes lie directly on top of each other, like, ah…"

"Like the layers in a sandwich," Hikaru put in helpfully.

"I suppose that is an adequate analogy. Now, imagine that I take, say, a pen, and I press it up into the bottom layer of bread. The filling of the sandwich and the top layer of bread would be forced into a new shape by the presence of that pen on the bottom layer, even though it is not touching them. Do you see? That is why your buildings and roads change the shape of the spirit realm."

"Then the buildings and roads we see here are, like, scars," Jack said thoughtfully. "Are there scars in our world too? From changes you've made on your side?"

There was a bitter laugh in the darkness ahead of us. "We do not make changes to our world, human girl." Miyako's voice drifted back. "We do not crush and smash and burn and destroy as your kind do. Humanity warps the world to suit itself. We adapt ourselves to fit our world. That is why—" Her voice was cut off with a small gasp. I had a vision of Hiro kicking her in the ankle.

There was a short silence.

"No wonder Kitsune don't like humans much," I said self-consciously.

"Please do not believe that," Araki said, clicking her tongue. "In general, Kitsune have always been quite fond of humanity. It is in your nature to be short-lived, full of brilliance and passion and progress. You cannot help that any more than Kitsune can help being long-lived, cautious, cunning and resistant to change. In my opinion, those who profess to dislike humans do so more from envy than anything else. Your unique human change-ability and creativity would make our long lives much more interesting. But those traits are not for us."

I glanced sideways at Hikaru. Cautious and resistant to change? Maybe the Kitsune weren't giving themselves enough credit.

We left the large chamber and Araki moved ahead of us again as we climbed down roughly hewn rock steps into another tunnel. This one was much roomier, with an even more echoey quality. I suspected that it was one of the Tube tunnels. We carried on walking.

"Please tell me we're running on Narnia time here," Jack muttered to me after another ten minutes.

Hikaru let out a crack of laughter. Araki frowned at us over her shoulder, an arrested expression on her face. She clearly didn't get it.

"You know C.S. Lewis?" Jack asked him incredulously.

He shrugged. "Why not? You heard Araki-san. There aren't many people my age hanging around the Kitsune Kingdom. I've spent a lot of time in the mortal realm. There's plenty of stuff to do there – shops, cinemas, libraries. It's cool."

Sounds surprisingly like a human childhood. And surprisingly … lonely.

"Anyway," Hikaru said, "the days and nights and the seasons might be reversed, but time passes at the same rate in both planes." He hesitated, and then said in a slightly softer voice, "Don't worry. There are hours left before dawn."

"Besides, we are almost there," Araki said. "Has Hikaru warned you of the proper etiquette in court?"

"Er, mostly," I said.

"Then brace yourselves," Araki said. She stopped

abruptly and placed her hand on one curving wall.

The tunnel shook and rumbled as a circular section of the wall began to roll back. Light spilled into the gloom. Jack grabbed Hikaru for balance. I planted my feet firmly, grateful for Shinobu's steadying hand on my shoulder.

The opening became perfectly circular. The rumbling stopped, but the tunnel was no longer quiet. A rushing, rustling noise filled the space. At first I thought it was wind moving through leaves again, like above ground. Then my eyes adjusted to the brightness and saw what awaited us on the other side of the wall.

"Holy shit," Hikaru whispered.

CHAPTER 18

THE COURT
OF THE KITSUNE

A vast space – big enough to dwarf the cavernous station we had just walked through – lay before us. I couldn't even see the walls. Maybe there weren't any. The only visible boundary was a circle of green-gold tree trunks, each of them wider than any tree I had ever seen in my life. If Jack, Hikaru, Shinobu and I had all joined hands, I doubted that we would have been able to encircle even the thinnest one. The trees curved outwards like ribs, their branches meeting at least fifty feet overhead in a lush, silver-leafed ceiling, utterly still.

I could see lights glinting between the leaves, and for a moment I thought they were stars. But they were moving. Fox lights, clouds and clouds of them, danced among the trees. The ground at the base of the trees sloped into a steep bowl shape, its sides terraced into broad steps, with a low, round hill at the very bottom, acting as a centre point. It reminded me of an amphitheatre.

Everywhere – on the hill, on the terraced sides of the bowl and along the top, among the trees – there were foxes. Foxes with multiple tails. Foxes as tiny as house cats. Foxes as big as wolves. White foxes, black foxes, grey foxes, red foxes. Foxes with giant, tufted ears, foxes with narrow, cruel-looking muzzles that reminded me of dingoes. There must have been a thousand Kitsune here, so many that even this giant place felt crammed.

And every one of them was staring at us. Their whispers echoed through the space under the trees like the sound of the tide rushing in.

"Good luck," Araki said.

She stepped through the round entrance, with Miyako and Hiro close behind her, and began the walk down the side of the bowl. Before they had taken two steps into the giant space all three were back in fox form.

"This is why someone, whoever it was, triggered the transformation ward," Hikaru muttered, his breath quick and harsh. "They needed to delay us so they could arrange all this."

"What's going on?" Jack demanded.

"We were supposed to have an audience with His Majesty. Just His Majesty. Maybe a few advisors. This – this is a full gathering of the British Kitsune."

"And that's a bad thing?" Shinobu asked, low-voiced.

"It means nothing that happens here is about us any

more. Everyone is watching. Whatever the king says will become law. He has no wriggle room. If any of us, including me, put a single paw wrong, he'll have no choice but to annihilate us. He can't afford to show a hint of weakness or favouritism, or they'll turn on him. It was dangerous enough before, but now..." His voice trailed off as if even he couldn't think of words to describe the utter suckiness of the situation.

Jack looked at me, her face stricken. I could see the thought running through her mind before she even opened her mouth. "I'm sorry. I made you all come here—"

"Don't." I cut her off. "You didn't make us do any-thing. We're all in this together. Right, guys?"

Shinobu nodded, face grave. "Of course. We have each made our own choices, Jack-san."

"And it's too late to turn back now anyway," Hikaru said. "Listen, Mio, you have one shot to convince him of your worthiness. You have to get him to treat you as an equal, to agree that you have the right to speak to him and petition for his aid in saving Rachel. If you don't, he'll be forced to rule that letting you come here was a mistake. And then things will get bad. Very bad."

"How do I do that?" I asked, my voice going squeaky at the end despite my best efforts. I cleared my throat. "Don't I have to bow and scrape?"

"Yes, but you have to do it in the right way. You can't

show fear. Act as if you're just as powerful as him, like you're only bowing and scraping because you're polite. Can you do that?"

He looked me up and down, taking in my diminutive stature, ruined clothes and the layers of dirt. His brow wrinkled in despair.

Shinobu folded his arms menacingly. "Mio-dono is the equal of anyone here. She is special."

"I am?"

Jack nodded at me, her normally golden skin looking yellow with fear. But her eyes were determined. "He's right. Don't let these guys freak you out."

Don't let the *foxes* freak me out? Right now my friends were doing a great job of that themselves. Because if we were going to get technical about it, all of this was *my* *fault.*

I'd mucked things up right from the beginning. Ojiichan had trusted me with the sword and practically destroyed his relationship with his son to get me the training and information I needed to handle it. In return, I'd abandoned my kendo, forgotten all Ojiichan's stories and treated the katana like a toy. I'd put my best friend and her sister – not to mention the entire population of London – in terrible danger. And I had no idea what to do about any of it.

Special? Specially useless, more like.

But Hikaru was right. It was too late to turn back

now. We were already through the looking glass. The sword, whatever it was, was *mine* to bear. I'd done a terrible job so far, but if any of us were going to get out of this, I had to suck it up and start acting like I knew what I was doing.

"Stand back," I said quietly. I gave them all a moment to shuffle away before I drew the katana from its carrier. My bad arm twinged sharply with the movement.

I sighed as I took the weight of the sword between my hands, closing my fingers tightly around the saya and hilt, and felt the familiar buzz of energy against my skin.

Below us, Araki had reached the low hill at the centre of the amphitheatre. A small group of foxes sat there, and Araki trotted up to one of them – a medium-sized fox with colouring very similar to Hikaru in his fox form. His tails, spread out like a peacock fan, waved gently in the air behind him. Tiny, blue sparks of lightning crackled constantly between the white tips, as if he was so powerful that he generated electricity without even being aware of it.

I counted the tails and gulped. Nine.

He had to be the king.

Below the king, two more foxes sat on the hill. The one on the left was startling white, with no trace of colour in its fur at all. The one on the right was a deep, bluish-grey, darkening to black at the extremities of tail and paws. Each of them had eight tails. As I watched, Araki bowed low before the king and spoke to him. Meanwhile, Miyako seated herself neatly behind the white fox and Hiro took up position behind the grey one.

So each of the most powerful foxes here had sent someone to look for us when we were late – and the lovely Miyako was the white fox's contribution. *Interesting*.

Araki finished speaking to the king. He nodded at her. She lay down behind him, lifting her muzzle to the sky and booming: "His Majesty bids the visitors approach!"

Hikaru drew in a deep breath. "I'll go first. Mio, you're the petitioner, so you walk right behind me. Shinobu and Jack, bring up the rear. Remember, don't look at the king directly or address him until he gives permission."

He hesitated for a second, then turned swiftly to Jack and laid a kiss right on her lips.

She started back in shock, two spots of bright colour lighting up her cheeks. Hikaru cleared his throat, nodded to me, and then stepped through the gateway.

"Geronimo," I muttered, jumping through after him.

I heard Shinobu and Jack follow, but I didn't look back as we began the long walk down the rows of steep terraces. The amphitheatre had clearly been designed for people with four legs, not two. I had to keep my eyes fixed firmly on my feet to avoid taking a humiliating tumble down the too-smooth grass. I just hoped that I wasn't breaking protocol by refusing to meet anyone's eyes for long.

The space grew gradually silent as we descended, the last whispers lingering chillingly in the air. Every time I risked a glance up, a pair of cold, foxy eyes would be there, fixed on me. It was hard to read human expressions on a fox's face, but I would have bet good money that none of them were broadcasting warmth and welcome. Had Araki been joking when she said that the Kitsune were fond of humans? These guys looked like they wanted to eat us for breakfast. Possibly without bothering to kill us first.

The katana's energy buzzed hard against my palm. I switched my grip, bringing the saya diagonally across my body so that my left hand held the sheath and my right could clasp the hilt. Hopefully it made me look confident and warlike, not nervous and injured. Hopefully.

It seemed to take for ever to reach the bottom of the slope, so long that by the time we got there I was wondering if Hikaru had been a bit skimpy with the truth on the Narnia-time thing. Then someone seemed to hit the fast-forward button and suddenly we were across the bottom of the amphitheatre and a few feet away from the base of the low hill. I felt the gazes of the foxes there like drops of heated lead landing on my face. In spite of Hikaru's warning, it was excruciatingly hard not to sneak a peek at the king's expression, just to gauge his mood.

Curiosity killed the girl, Mio. Eyes down!

A step in front of me, Hikaru came to a halt and gracefully folded himself into a kneeling position. I followed his example, trying not to let on how grateful my wobbly knees were for the chance to give up the ghost. The telltale rustles of fabric behind me let me know that Jack and Shinobu were doing the same.

I dropped my forehead down to rest on the back of my hands, making sure to keep my katana firmly under my palms. The silence stretched on. I closed my eyes as the urge to glance up at the king started to plague me again. What was he *doing* up there? Playing Parcheesi?

"Rise, Grandchild."

It was a soft, young-sounding voice, but the power in it sent shivers of fear prickling down my spine. I'd have been an idiot to believe I was hearing anyone but the King of the Kitsune speaking. In a weird way it reminded me of the Harbinger's voice. They didn't really sound anything alike, but they both carried those uncanny, almost painful echoes of power that made me feel as if I needed to fall down and beg. Lucky for me I was already as close to the floor as I could get.

I squeezed my eyes shut tighter – then snapped them open as I heard Hikaru move.

He was on his feet. My brain executed a full stop as I realized what that meant. The king had been talking to Hikaru.

Hikaru was the king's grandchild?

When had he been planning on sharing that little gem of info?

"You may address me," the king said gravely.

"Thank you, Grandfather," Hikaru said. "And thank you again for agreeing to see me and my friends with such little notice. The bearer of the meitou, Yamato Mio-dono, wishes me to convey her gratitude."

"Oh, does she?" the powerful voice said softly. "And does she also have an explanation for her presumption in keeping me waiting in my own court?"

Hell. Am I supposed to look up now, or speak into the grass, or what?

Hikaru answered before I could make up my mind. "I am afraid the responsibility for the delay lies with me. I apologize deeply. I would not insult you for anything, Grandfather."

"Explain." There was a hint of a growl underlying the soft voice.

"I believed that the transformation ward had been uninvoked, and so I failed to protect my friends from it when they stepped onto our soil. This caused an unavoidable delay."

Ominous silence purred against my skin.

"The ward was uninvoked." The growl was more obvious now. "I did it myself."

"I know. I watched you. And yet when I returned, the spell was active. I have no explanation for this – but if you wish to check it, you will find it to be so."

There was a tiny hissing noise to my left. From the white fox? Had he or she been stupid enough to leave the ward in place? Or maybe just not powerful enough to close it again after forcing it open against the king's wishes?

"Araki-san!" the king barked.

"Hikaru-san is correct," Araki said respectfully. "I checked after hearing his story, since we were in the area. The ward is active."

The purr against my skin became a rumble. Oh, the king was seriously annoyed now. The question was with whom? *Don't look up, don't look up…*

"Such a breach of the right of safe passage is unacceptable, regardless of the circumstances," the king said finally. His voice was smooth again, all traces of annoyance gone. "The Court of the Kitsune apologizes to the sword-bearer and her retinue for this error."

A gasp or a sigh went round the amphitheatre, disturbing the fine hairs on the back of my neck. Some of the tension drained out of the atmosphere, and the trembling muscles in my shoulders unknotted. But only a little. We'd dodged the first bullet. There was no telling how many more might be aimed at us.

"I should have known that you would not keep me waiting without good cause, Hikaru," the king went on, a trace of warmth in his tone now. "You have done well to deal with such a challenge alone. I commend you. You may return to your family now."

"Grandfather, if it pleases you, I wish to remain with my friends."

Another gasp – of shock this time, I was sure – filled the space around me.

"As you wish," the king said, amused.

The gasp transmuted into a rush of excited whispers that covered Hikaru's retreat. He knelt down next to me this time, but I saw from the corner of my eye that he remained upright rather than bowing his head.

"Grandson?" Jack hissed behind me.

"Great-great-great-grandson," Hikaru mumbled. "One of a dozen. And he doesn't play favourites, believe me."

Hmm. Obviously Hikaru knew his grandfather better than I did, but it had sounded to me as if the king liked Hikaru and had been relieved to have an excuse not to punish him.

"Quiet!" Araki snapped.

I jumped. The Kitsune in the bowl went silent instantly.

"The sword-bearer may rise and address the king," Araki said.

That was my cue. *Don't mess this up, Mio. For the love of God, do* not *mess this up.*

Twitchingly conscious of the eyes fastened on my every movement, I sat, eased back onto my heels, and rose, bringing my katana to my right side in the same movement. I fixed my gaze on the neat, red set of paws directly ahead of me on the jade-green hill, and took one step forwards. *That's close enough for me.*

"Greetings, sword-bearer," the king said.

He'd switched the power up again. It took everything I had not to buckle to my knees. My fingers tightened on the sword sheath so much that my knuckles cracked audibly.

Show no fear, show no fear, show no fear...

"Greetings, Your Majesty." The words came out high and breathless, like a kid answering a teacher on the first day of school.

"My grandson has told me of your quest to save your friend's sister from the Nekomata which has been unleashed on London. He vouches that you are a valiant warrior with whom it would be prudent to ally our-selves." The king paused. "He also speaks of the meitou you carry, a sword of mysterious origin and great power. Before we discuss the business that brings you here, I would hear some information which Hikaru was unable to share with me. Tell me how you came to wield such a weapon and call yourself its guardian."

With extreme reluctance I opened my mouth – and snapped it shut again as the white fox stirred, sat upright, and spoke. The fox's voice was deep and musical, fem-inine, with a strong Japanese accent. Her eyes, resting on me, were wide and golden. "I hesitate to interrupt, Grandfather, but I would like to say something before the petitioner begins her little story."

Little story? Hikaru hadn't said anything about not looking this one in the face. I gave her my best blank look. She tossed her head, unimpressed.

"Since you have already spoken without my leave, Midori-san, you may as well go on," the king said, without warmth. Grandfather or not, it looked like he wasn't fond of this one.

"My humble apologies, Your Majesty," the female fox said. There was a slight bite in her tone. "But I dislike seeing our time squandered. My grandnephew has told you an affecting tale in which he alleges that this scrap of a mortal girl is the rightful owner of that sword. A sword which, even from here, I can sense is not of mortal creation. She claims to be its guardian. Such a claim is preposterous. Her tale is a fabrication, and her purpose is to deceive us into endangering our people."

Any doubt about the white fox's involvement in the fox trap was gone now. She was definitely our enemy. But why?

"You speak very decidedly," the king said. His voice was neutral, and I couldn't tell if he was being swayed by her argument or not. "Do you dismiss Hikaru's words as easily as that?"

The white fox's ears twitched a little. "Your love for

your newest descendant is well known, Sire – but even you must admit that one who has not yet reached his first century, one born here in this country of concrete and glass, is hardly the best judge in matters magical or political. Hika-chan is soft-hearted and inexperienced. His testimony is not to be relied on."

There were more murmurs from the gathered foxes. Shock, annoyance and maybe ... speculation? I still didn't dare to look at the king directly, but the brightening flashes of light coming from his direction told me that his power was ramping up in response. Midori was challenging the king with all the subtlety of a sledgehammer to the face. And she was using us to do it.

She might or might not believe what she was saying, but either way she didn't care that if she kept talking, all of us, and Rachel, and probably other innocent people in London, would most likely die under the Nekomata's claws.

"May I speak now?"

The hard, determined voice cut through the soft whispering of the foxes. I almost didn't recognize it as mine.

The white fox bared her pearly fangs at me. A crackle of greenish electricity arced between the furthest of her fanned tails. "Keep your silence until you are commanded to speak, human."

"I'm sorry, what did you say? The king just commanded me to speak. You're the one who interrupted. Or do you think your orders take precedence now?"

Behind me I heard Jack's awed whisper. "Oh no she *didn't*."

Hikaru made a choked noise. Shinobu was silent. That probably wasn't good.

The king laughed, but the sound had an edge like a razor. "Peace, sword-bearer. Midori-san, if you are so convinced that the meitou cannot belong rightfully to this mortal, perhaps you will tell us where and how you believe she came by it?"

The white fox's muzzle smoothed back into place over her fangs. Dread made my stomach twist.

"It is perfectly simple, Grandfather," she said sweetly. "The sword was stolen from the Nekomata."

CHAPTER 19

TRUTH

This time the foxes didn't bother to keep their reaction down to a whisper. The amphitheatre erupted with shouting voices, as the foxes came to their feet in a wave of lashing tails and flashing teeth. As far as I could make out, they were roughly divided between those who were outraged over the very idea of the katana ever belonging to a creature like a Nekomata and those who had bought Midori's words wholesale and wanted me burned at the stake, preferably in the next thirty seconds.

Midori wrapped one of her fluffy tails round her feet as neatly as a cat and sat back, apparently satisfied with the dissent she had caused. The temptation abruptly became too much and I sneaked a glance at the king's face. His eyes were burning, moss-green slits in his face, which I took to mean that he was as far from happy as a fox could get.

Hikaru stepped up beside me, and despite the fact that they were currently a different species, the resemblance between him and his many-greats-grandfather was very evident in his furiously glittering eyes.

"Silence!" Araki roared. "Control yourselves!"

No one followed Araki's orders. It took a few sizzles of lightning from one of the king's tails to get everyone's attention.

"You wish to address us again, Hikaru?" the king said into the ensuing quiet. His voice was calm, but the constant flash of energy around his tails was a giveaway about his real mood.

"My aunt's claims are false, and I can prove it," Hikaru said tightly. "We have a witness here who is known to you personally, Sire. It is a provable fact that this witness is over five hundred years old. He will vouch for the sword-bearer."

The king's whiskers twitched. "An excellent point, my thoughtful child. Let Shinobu, helper of foxes, rise and step forward."

Shinobu appeared beside me. Jack was right behind him. I was pretty sure that technically she should still have been lying face down on the grass, but in the middle of this mess it looked like no one was in the mood to quibble over protocol. Jack's mouth was clamped into a tight, pale line. I hoped she managed to keep it together. We were in enough trouble.

"Speak, Shinobu," the king commanded. "What have you to say about the sword?"

"Thank you, Your Majesty," Shinobu said, bowing deeply. "I can personally testify that the sword has been in the Yamato family for five hundred years. In fact, it was given to me by my adoptive father for my seventeenth birthday. In the centuries since then, the family have faithfully guarded it. It has never belonged to anyone else."

"This is fantasy!" Midori jumped in. "Anyone with eyes can tell that the sword's power far predates that. It is ancient. No mortal smith could have imbued a weapon with such energy. Do you have some convenient tale to explain how an ordinary human sword came to blaze with a light that rivals the stars?"

Shinobu's jaw clenched.

The king let out a tiny sigh. "Answer her."

"I do not," Shinobu admitted, his voice rough. "I don't remember."

The white fox snapped at the air in triumph. "You see? Humans cannot be trusted – even immortal ones. This Yamato family are thieves who have run to us to gain shelter from the consequences of their crime. We should hand the humans and the sword over to the Nekomata. It will be satisfied and leave London, and the mortals will be duly punished for having trifled with us."

"Are you mad?" someone shouted from the terraces.

"Hand over an object of power to a creature of the Underworld?"

Miyako leapt to her paws, tails whisking the air. "Do not dare to address my mistress in such terms!"

"Be quiet before you get fried!" someone else called.

Another fox cried, "Disgraceful! The humans have polluted our assembly!"

The air of calm and reverent respect which had filled the court when we had arrived was completely destroyed. The king – whom I was staring at openly now, because it hardly seemed to matter – seemed like he was about to spontaneously combust. His fur had fluffed up around his body until he looked twice his original size and tiny sparks of electricity danced among the lustrous strands.

With great deliberation, the blue-grey fox on the king's right uncurled and stretched out its front paws. As it turned its head I saw that its eyes were opaque and milky white. It was blind.

The amphitheatre instantly went quiet. A sense of expectation quivered through the foxes. The king bowed his head to look respectfully at the fox below him and Midori's green lightning blazed around her. She bared her fangs. Miyako cringed.

"Yes, Tetsuo-san?" the king said.

When the grey fox – Tetsuo – spoke his voice was low and rumbling, with an accent that sounded Russian to me. "Might I propose a solution?"

"By all means, my friend."

"The issue is that of rightful possession, correct?"

"Correct," Midori snapped.

"A meitou is a tremendously powerful weapon," Tetsuo went on, as if Midori had not spoken. "But it may indeed be stolen, and even wielded, by a thief with sufficient daring. However, such a thief could never awaken the sword's full strength, for he would not know its true name. That is a gift which the meitou would only bestow upon its true owner. Therefore, let the child attempt to speak the katana's true name and summon its power. If she is able to do so, she will be proved to be its guardian, and as such, deserving of our respect and cooperation. If not, perhaps Midori-san's suppositions have some weight."

The king nodded slowly. "You are wise as always, Tetsuo-san. I can think of no better way to settle this dispute."

True name? Awaken the sword? I cast a horrified look at Shinobu. His expression made me want to throw up. He had no idea either. Would they really hand us over to the Nekomata? Hand over the sword? What would happen to Jack and Rachel then? What would happen to Shinobu?

Dammit, Ojiichan. If you were going to give me the katana, why did you have to be so bloody mysterious about it? Would a sealed letter laying all this out have been too much to ask? A Post-it on the trunk in the attic maybe? "BTW here are some facts you need to know…" Anything! I'm flying blind here!

"Your Majesty," Shinobu said, his tone carefully blank of the desperation I could see in his eyes. "To speak the true name of the katana here in the spirit realm might have unexpected consequences. It could be extremely dangerous—"

What had my grandfather actually told me about the sword? Hardly anything really. Or had my memory just wiped it out as time had passed, like so many other things?

"Cease your lies," Midori cried. "There is no power wielded by any mortal alive that could threaten us. Get on with it. The thief and her half-breed accomplice have already trespassed here long enough."

"Half-breed?" Jack rocked back on her heels. I could almost hear the crack as her temper, held in check for so long, began to give way under the strain. "Is she talking about me?"

"Jack." Hikaru tried to grab her arm. "Calm down."

"Did she just call me a half-breed?"

Midori's tails lashed. "You are a half-breed – a graceless, impure mongrel. The worst kind of human."

"Oh, yeah?" Jack yelped. "Come down here and say that, you furry albino!"

Come on, Ojiichan. Help me out. I closed my eyes, thinking frantically and forcing myself back into my memory of that long-ago afternoon in the attic. I strained after the echoes of Ojiichan's voice.

"Careful now, Mio," he had whispered. *"He's heavy."*

So much heavier now than it had been then. I'd been too young to understand what was lying in my hands. I'd been too young to understand the weight Ojiichan had given me to carry.

"He is yours, Mio."

He'd been warm. So warm under my touch. As if he was already mine.

"Yours to guard and protect."

I was nearly there. I could feel something stirring in my memory – what had Ojiichan said next?

The stench of ozone hit the back of my throat. I choked, my eyes snapping open. I took in the scene. Shinobu and Hikaru were holding Jack back by her arms. Midori was on her feet, green lightning whirling around her tails. The king had just opened his jaws to bark an order that was going to come too late. I saw with crystal-line clearness exactly what was going to happen next.

"… the One who remembers. The One who endures. The One who is hidden."

"The Hidden One…"

But that wasn't the sword's name. It couldn't be. The sword was Japanese – not English. Ojiichan had been translating for me, telling me the *meaning* of the sword's name without actually saying it. Was there a word – a name – in Japanese that meant all those things? There had to be.

Remembrance. Endurance.

Hidden.

In one of those sudden, blinding leaps of intuition, I realized it.

Twice I had called Shinobu's name in panic and fear, and twice the sword had responded, flying into my hand just when I needed it. Shinobu was a Japanese name. It could mean many different things depending on the characters used to write it. It could mean warrior, or purity. It could mean...

Recall.

One who remembers.

Strength.

One who endures.

Stealth.

One who is hidden.

The Hidden One...

Shinobu was the name of the boy.

Shinobu was the name of the blade.

Midori snarled at Jack. "I shall deal with you myself."

Thunder boomed through the bowl as a jagged finger of lightning streaked from one of Midori's tails and reached for my best friend. The fine hairs all over my body responded to the electricity in the air, standing upright like soldiers.

I ripped the sword from the saya as I whispered: *"Shinobu."*

Yes?

The word rang through me. It came, not from any outside source, but from inside me, from the cells that made up my bones, my blood. The voice was neither male nor female, neither young nor old. It was simply *other* – chiming, musical, metallic. Inhuman.

The green lightning changed course mid-strike and came for me.

"Mio!" Shinobu let go of Jack and lunged towards me.

Jack's mouth gaped open in a gasp of horror.

Hikaru shut his eyes as if he couldn't bear to look.

The green lightning struck the tip of the katana.

This is really going to hurt—

Colourless flames exploded from the place where my fingers touched the sword's grip. They swallowed Midori's lightning and engulfed the blade. The hilt seemed to jump in my hand, trying to jerk away. Instinctively, I tightened my grasp.

Are you ready for me?

I didn't know how to answer. So I whispered, "Yes."

White energy detonated from the katana. It rushed out from the centre-point of the blade towards the green terraces. I stumbled and nearly went to my knees, digging the saya into the ground with my spare hand to stay upright.

The shock wave hit the sides of the amphitheatre with a boom. The ground leapt underfoot. Shinobu, Hikaru and Jack went down like paper dolls. Kitsune toppled. The ring of ancient trees groaned, their branches tossing, sending silvery leaves cascading down into the bowl.

The sword's grip vibrated and shook in my grasp. I dropped the saya and brought my left hand up to clasp the hilt, fighting to hang onto the sword. The wound on my shoulder burned. I didn't know what would happen if I let go, but I knew that it would not be good for any of us.

"Shinobu!" Was I calling the boy or the blade now? I wasn't even sure myself.

The white energy battered against the earthen walls, then began to flow backwards, faster and faster, slamming into the blade, coalescing around me in a white hurricane of power. A thin, blindingly bright column of light shot from the sword's tip, dragging the blade inexorably upwards until I was holding it over my head, pointing it straight up. The light pierced the canopy of leaves above me. I followed it with my eyes.

I saw a darkness beyond the light that wasn't darkness, but the shadows of galaxies forming and dying. Suns spinning and blowing out. Planets imploding and falling to dust and flaring back to life again. I saw … power. Power that could swallow the world.

Ready now?

"Not – really…" I muttered between gritted teeth.

Too late.

The column of light fell, shattering into thousands of star-bright sparks. I shrieked with pain as they set me alight. I could feel my bones crack and snap, muscles unravelling and recoiling like thread, muscles expanding and reforming under my stretching skin.

With a shrill ripping noise, my outer clothes – coat, jeans, T-shirt – shredded. My feet burst out of my boots and socks with a loud pop. I realized, in the midst of my agony, that I was growing.

"Shinobu," I whispered. "Please. Please stop."

The manic vibration of the hilt gentled in my hands. Wailing, white energy smoothed away, disappearing like mist in the wind. Shinobu's flaming blade cooled, turning blue, then dull red, and finally returning to black and silver.

Shinobu is only one of my names. You will need to learn the others before the end. But it will do for now.

My arms, abruptly too heavy for me to hold up, dropped sharply. The sword whistled through the air and buried itself in the smooth grass at my feet. My bare feet. I stood alone, clad only in a tank top, underwear, and a dusting of silver leaves.

CHAPTER 20

THE KINDNESS OF GODS

The grey squiggles were back in my eyes, and there was no chance of concealing the wobble in my legs. Everything started to slide away sideways. I was going to pass out. Again. How many times was that now in a two-day period? I was probably setting a record…

A pair of strong, familiar arms wrapped around me and held me upright, enveloping me in folds of black fabric. My father's old leather coat. An oddly comforting mixture of smells, Dad's aftershave and Shinobu's smoky piney scent, made me breathe in deeply.

"Thanks," I muttered.

My voice sounded as if I'd gargled with a pint of vodka and puffed twenty cigarettes as a chaser. I had been screaming. Only I hadn't heard myself over the sounds of the world – and my own body – breaking and reforming around me.

"You're welcome," Shinobu said, his voice rumbling through my chest. One of his hands – not feeling quite as big as it had before – cupped the back of my neck. He stroked my hair. "Mio, are you … are you all right? You were on fire."

"Backatcha, baby," I said blearily, leaning my head on his shoulder.

Shoulder? Five minutes ago I'd have been leaning on his chest. Which meant I must be, what, at least four inches taller? That realization just made me feel all the blearier. My whole body ached, ached, *ached*. The only thing that didn't ache was my injured shoulder, weirdly enough. I felt bony and fragile, like you do the first time you get out of bed after being really ill, and the grass was cold under my toes in the remains of my ruined boots and, oh, there everything went sideways again…

"Here," Shinobu said. He drew one of my hands through the arm of the coat, supporting my weight with his other arm around my shoulder. Then he pushed something into that hand. Something faintly warm and familiar. The katana's saya.

"Thank you," I said again, with more feeling this time. I let Shinobu pull my other hand through the other arm of the coat and fasten the buttons as if I were a five-year-old, waiting until he'd finished before I carefully guided the blade back into the sheath.

Immediately I felt better – physically, at least. The

silvery wriggles disappeared from my vision and my body seemed to firm up around me. I realized I was still draped against Shinobu like a fainting maiden and made an effort to straighten up as I remembered what I looked like right now. Heat flooded my face.

He saw, didn't he? Shinobu saw. Everyone saw.

Why did it have to be my Hello Kitty underwear?

It seemed safer to concentrate on the humiliation than … well, anything else. Like the enormity of what I had just witnessed. The sword's power. What it had just done to me. What it might mean for us all. There was certainly plenty of humiliation to occupy me; I was going to be embarrassed by this when I was a hundred and five. Shinobu's gaze was aimed at me like a searchlight and I didn't know where to look.

The Kitsune were starting to stir, uncurling from defensive balls and climbing to their feet. I could feel their eyes on me again, but I had no idea what they were thinking. The bowl-shaped place was almost completely silent apart from the faint, shivery noise of the leaves that were still showering down on us. A second later Jack sat up nearly at my feet.

She squinted up at us for a minute. Her face was strangely blank, and I felt a chill of worry. Had she reached the point of total freak out? *Hard to blame her…*

"I think," she said, "that I'm going to call you She-Ra from now on. Say 'By the Power of Grayskull!'"

I let out a watery laugh. *Thank God for Jack.* "Just when I thought you couldn't be a bigger geek."

"And yet I'm not the one dressed up like a refugee from *The Matrix*. A strip-o-gram refugee."

I looked down at my bare legs sticking out of the bottom of the coat, which only came to my knees now. "Touché."

I reached out my free hand at the same moment as Shinobu, and together we pulled Jack to her feet. She tottered a bit, shook her head, and blew out a breath. "Whoa. What a rush. Hey, did you grow again? You did! Look, we're the same height!"

"Congratulations," Hikaru said, from his prone position in the grass. He looked like he'd been caught in a force-ten gale, which I supposed he had. His hair was in his face, his clothes were a mess, and he had leaves poking out everywhere. "I think that pretty much settles things. Right, Granddad?"

"Don't call me that in the court," the king said absently. His ears slowly perked back up from where they had been flattened against his skull and he lifted a paw and licked it, as if to reassure himself that it was still attached. "But yes. I can't think of any more questions. Midori-san?"

We all looked at the white fox.

She was out cold, flat on her back, paws in the air. Miyako was down too, lying in a heap at the base of the hill.

"She never did like surprises," Tetsuo said, sniffing at the air as if he could smell what we were all seeing. He seemed unruffled by what had happened as did Hiro, who was calmly grooming one of his tails. "I'd guess the shock of having her lightning stopped dead like that was too much for her. She won't come around for a while."

"And when she does, she'll be miles away and out of my fur," the king said with satisfaction. "Midori attacked a guest of the court while they were under a right of safe passage, and without my leave. She's earned herself a half-millennium banishment, at the very least. Outer Hebrides, I think."

Tetsuo chuckled softly.

An unpleasant idea slithered into the back of my mind.

I'd thought Midori was using us to challenge the king's authority and he was powerless to stop events from spiralling out of control. But maybe it was the other way round. Maybe the king had allowed Midori to challenge him, allowed us to bait her, because once she went too far he would have a reason to get rid of her without admitting that she was a threat to his reign.

If it hadn't been for me figuring out the katana's true name at that exact moment, Jack might be dead.

I could feel my eyes narrowing. Involuntarily I brought the katana up, clasping the saya and hilt so that I could draw quickly. Shinobu, apparently reading my mind, placed a steadying hand on my shoulder.

"We can't prove anything," he said, the words an almost inaudible breath in my ear that made me shiver. "And even if we could..."

Who are we going to protest to?

Hikaru, who was on his knees now, frowned at us, then turned to stare at his grandfather in dawning suspicion. At that moment Jack stepped forward and offered Hikaru her hands. He hesitated for a second, then took them and let her pull him up, although it didn't look like he actually made her exert much effort. He smiled at her, squeezing her fingers in his.

The king looked quickly away from his grandson, something like shame flickering through his eyes.

I was right. The whole thing had been a set-up. The king was willing to risk all of us, even Hikaru, to achieve his own ends. That was probably the reason he'd agreed to this audience in the first place.

He really doesn't play favourites.

Ignoring Shinobu's gentle squeeze on my shoulder, I stepped forward and caught the king's eye. *You did this. You put my friends in danger. You owe me.*

The vivid, green eyes widened, sparking with anger. Then, reluctantly, he gave me a tiny, almost imperceptible nod.

"I think our new ally needs some assistance with her, ahem, apparel," he said to the assembled foxes. "And then we can discuss how to run this cursed Nekomata out of our territory."

I didn't know if the Kitsune had houses or maybe dens hidden among the trees, but a minute or two after a pair of giggling fox girls had led me into the silver-and-gold forest and then disappeared into the shadows, they came back with a set of new clothes for me. The soft, wide-legged, black trousers and short kimono top – almost exactly like a kendogi – fitted me as if they had been tailored to my newly elongated body. The white sash for my waist was just long enough, and the sturdy boots were the perfect size too (which told me that I was going to need a lot of new shoes, because I'd gone up two sizes). The Kitsune girls even had a pair of brand-new cotton socks for me to wear.

"How is your throat?" the first girl asked sweetly when I'd finished dressing. "Would you like some water?"

I gave her a confused look.

The other one added, "We thought you might be a little thirsty. You know, after all that screaming."

They both giggled.

Most superheroes got to be cool, dammit. I wanted a refund on this whole deal.

The girls carried on giggling and whispering as they led me back out of the trees. Only the sight of their tails – they both had two – poking out of their flowery little kimonos made it possible for me to believe that they were a couple of hundred years old each. My mum's voice piped up in my head: *"No one can make you feel inferior without your consent."*

I could really have done with my mum around right now.

I'd insisted on taking the katana with me into the trees. Since the fox girls were walking ahead of me and paying no attention, I pulled the sword out of my sash and tried a few passes with it, leaving the saya in place for safety.

Hmm. I kept walking, trying a couple of low front kicks and then a mid-level side kick, movements that Ojiichan had drilled into me as soon as I learned to walk. I hadn't done any of the exercises he'd taught me in a while, but my muscles still remembered.

They remembered almost too well. I was faster now. I could feel it and hear it in the way the air whistled around my skin when I shifted. My injured arm was barely aching any more either. The hilt of the sword heated in my grip, as if it approved of this new speed.

It ought to. It had given it to me.

The blade was sentient. Deep at its core was an intelligence of some kind, far more dangerous and wilful than any of us had realized. It had decided I needed to be taller, faster – maybe stronger too, but there was no way to test that now – and just like that, I was. The sword was already changing me. At the moment it was only my body, but what might come next?

As I grappled with that thought, we emerged from the trees. Below me the terraces had emptied, but the bottom of the bowl around the central mound was filling up with Kitsune in human form. Some of the fox spirits were in modern clothes, others in traditional Japanese garb. Some were dressed in armour from a time and place completely unfamiliar to me. They all had one thing in common. They were loaded with weaponry.

I don't know why I had assumed that ancient fox spirits would turn their noses up at guns. I mean, some of them were carrying swords or bows – I even saw a war-axe – but nearly every one of them had a couple of guns holstered on their hips too. Several were carrying massive pump-action shotguns and wore bandoliers of ammo slung across their chests. They looked like something out of a zombie movie.

A shiver of definitely-not-Kitsune electricity touched the back of my neck as the fox girls bowed and disappeared back into the trees. I turned to see Shinobu striding round the rim of the amphitheatre towards me.

He was wearing a new outfit – the twin of mine. A plain, black katana and shorter wakizashi blade were thrust into the red sash wrapped around his lean waist, and his liquid prowl announced to the world that he knew exactly how to wield them. He'd rebraided his hair, but long, glossy strands blew loose around his face as he moved towards us, drifting back to reveal the smoky depths of eyes that were completely focused on me.

The Kitsune who stood in his way parted before him without a murmur. The men looked impressed and the women looked flirtatious. Actually, some of the men even looked a little flirtatious. Shinobu didn't seem to notice any of them.

"Shin—" I began. Before I could string together the remaining syllables, he went down gracefully on one knee, bowing his head before me.

"All is as you commanded, Mio-dono," he announced, his deep voice pitched to carry to the foxes around us. "The Kitsune are rallying. Soon we will be ready for you to lead us into battle. Do you have any more instructions?"

"What are you—?"

"Play along," Shinobu said softly, not looking up. "We need to keep their respect now that you have won it for us."

Oh, right. We were trying to wipe the image of me and my Hello Kitty underwear out of the Kitsune's brains. I could do that. I attempted a regal expression, hoping that I didn't just look constipated, and answered: "Very good. Thank you. You may, er, rise."

He came to an upright position in one smooth movement, like a perfect soldier. Now I could see the laughter glinting in his eyes. He was enjoying himself. I guessed after the entire Kitsune Kingdom had sneered at and tried to crush us, he was entitled to feel a *little* smug that my sword had knocked them all off their feet and nearly brought the roof down.

"Well?" I said, voice pitched low. "What now? Where are Jack and Hikaru?"

"Jack-san is choosing weaponry, with Hikaru-san's expert help. I have found a place suitable for you to inspect your troops as they gather." He added more quietly: "Try to look commanding."

I suppressed a panicked cry of "How?" and nodded, letting him lead me away from the trees, down to one of the empty terraces midway up the amphitheatre. Someone had spread out a beautifully coloured patchwork quilt on the mossy grass. In the centre of the quilt there was a low, round silver table, where a large glass bowl rested. It was filled with emerald-green apples, blushing peaches, ruby-red grapes and freckled, coppery pears. There was also a glass pitcher filled with some amber liquid that steamed faintly and two glasses shaped like those horn goblets you saw Vikings quaffing out of in films.

"What is this?" I asked, confused.

"They asked if there was anything you would like." Now that we were out of everyone else's hearing, his voice was eager, slightly anxious. "Is it all right?"

He did this for me.

My heart squeezed almost painfully. "It's lovely. Thank you." I stepped carefully onto the quilt and sat down, crossing my legs neatly and laying the katana across my thighs. "Does this look commanding enough?"

"I think so," he said, smiling a little. He sat down on the other edge of the quilt and poured some of the amber-coloured liquid into one of the goblets, then pushed it across the table towards me.

"I don't want to get drunk," I protested. The only drink that colour I knew of was cider.

"It is not an intoxicating drink," he said. "I made sure. Try it."

I picked up the glass and drank cautiously. The taste of honey, and apples, and something sharp and delicious I'd never tasted before exploded on my tongue, closely followed by a fizzing sensation of warmth that flowed into me, soothing my slightly sore throat and my nervous stomach with one sip. "Wow." I blinked down at the glass. "Not intoxicating?"

"There may be a little of their magic in it," he said. "But nothing that would harm you. That is the last thing any of them would want now."

I had another mouthful and decided that, intoxicating or not, I might start giggling if I had any more. That would be bad. I put the glass down and reached hesitantly for a grape. It burst in my mouth with the sweetest, most intense flavour I'd ever experienced. God, what did they put in this stuff? It was amazing. A bite of a peach almost made me cry.

"Don't you want anything?" I asked Shinobu, noticing that he hadn't even poured himself a drink. He shook his head, apparently happy to watch me eat instead.

Something whipped past in the corner of my eye. I turned my head to see Hikaru and Jack on one of the terraces below us. Jack had a long stick in her hands and Hikaru appeared to be giving her tips on how to use it. Probably trying to persuade her that she didn't need a shotgun, which is what she would really want, if I knew her. I smiled, wondering if I should wave and call them up here to share the picnic.

My gaze wandered to the bottom of the bowl. About fifty Kistune had sorted themselves into neat rows that looked like the ranks of soldiers you saw marching on Remembrance Day. They stood to attention as the king talked; he paced back and forth among them, his tails lashing and his head held high. After a minute he bowed his head to them all. As one, they saluted sharply. Just like real soldiers.

My mouthful of sweet, golden peach was suddenly as bitter as lemons. I put the piece of fruit down slowly, wiping my fingers on the knee of my new outfit.

Calm down. Just take a deep breath. Calm down…

I sensed Shinobu turning his head to look at me, but I couldn't look at him. I couldn't look away from the soldiers who were getting ready to go into battle with us. *This is really happening. We're going to fight the Nekomata.*

Jack is going to fight. I am going to fight. And Rachel's life is at stake.

"I don't think I can do this." The words were out before I could stop them.

There was a long, singing moment of quiet, while I waited for Shinobu to say something. He didn't.

"This … this thing…" My hands tightened on the katana's saya and hilt in an agonized mixture of unwilling love and smouldering anger. "It's like my ojiichan gave me a nuclear bomb. A supernatural doomsday device. I had no idea what it could do before – and maybe I still don't. But I know it's dangerous. Midori was right in one way: this is not something any mortal is equipped to handle. I don't know how to handle it."

"Yet handle it you have," Shinobu said. His voice was quiet. "Well enough to gain the King of the Kitsune's respect. Well enough to gain his people's confidence. He is giving you these troops as a gesture of trust and friendship."

I forced myself to sit still, resisting the urge to fling the katana away at the same time as I resisted the equally strong urge to lift it up and clutch it to me. "That's the worst part, Shinobu, don't you see that? It's all fake! They're doing this because I've persuaded them that I know what I'm doing, but I don't. What happens if – if we fail?"

Shadows and blood will devour this world. That was what the Harbinger had said.

Shadows and blood…

It hadn't meant anything to me then. It was too big, too dramatic. What could the end of the world possibly have to do with me, Mio Yamato? But it had everything to do with me – because everyone I cared about lived in this world. Mum and Dad, Aunt Fumi and my cousins Chris and Sarah, the kids I went to school with, my teachers … Jack and Shinobu. And Rachel. Poor, lost Rachel. The shadows already had Rachel.

She was counting on me. Me. When this was all my fault to start with.

"The Kitsune almost destroyed the Nekomata once before," Shinobu reminded me. "In this conflict we will have numbers and strength far out-matching those of a single cat-demon. It is foolish to be overconfident in any battle, but it is equally foolish to despair when the odds are so overwhelmingly in our favour."

"But this isn't just any fight. It's not about winning. It's about getting Jack's sister out *alive*. That's my job. Jack expects me to fix everything and get Rachel back. She seems to think – everyone seems to think – I'm some sort of badass action hero. And I'm not. I don't know how to fight. I don't know how to save anyone, not even myself." I hesitated, then whispered bleakly: "I don't know what to do."

"You will do what is necessary," said Shinobu, not a trace of doubt in his voice. "You will do what must be done. And you will do what is right. You will always do what is right, Mio."

A tense breath shivered out of me, and I slumped weakly over the katana. My voice was a wobbly mumble. "Why do you think that?"

Shinobu's big, tanned hand, marked with tiny white scars, appeared in the corner of my vision. He peeled my shaking fingers from the saya of the katana and clasped them in his, not squeezing but holding firmly. "I know you."

And that was true, wasn't it? Because he had been with me for so long. Longer than Jack, even. He had been there when no one else was. If there was a single person in this world – in any world – who knew who I was ... it was Shinobu.

We sat in silence for a few moments. Gradually the paralyzing panic faded away, evaporating like a dark, wet stain off a hot paving slab in the summer. I was still tense and worried and afraid, but I could think again.

I sighed. "You – you're good."

"I am?"

"Good for me." I finally managed to look at him.

"Mio." He was gazing back at me intensely, eyes filled with that strange expression I had seen there a couple of times before. Like he was waiting for something. Shinobu lifted my hand up and pressed it to his forehead for a second, closing his eyes. "After all this is over—"

"Mio?" Jack's head popped over the edge of the terrace. Hope and determination made her eyes almost glow. "There you are! Look what Hikaru lent me!"

Shinobu kissed my knuckles gently and released me. I got up as Jack clambered onto the terrace – and jumped back just in time to avoid losing my nose as she swung a wooden staff, which turned out to be topped with a six-inch, hooked blade.

Shinobu was on his feet in an instant. "Look out!"

"Sorry. But isn't it cool? It's called a glaive. They won't let me have a gun for some reason. But they're totally gearing up for battle, Mimi! They're really going to help us get Rachel back!"

Her voice cracked a bit there at the end. I felt a sharp pang. No wonder she was excited. I thrust the katana into my sash, dodged her weapon again, and put my arm around her shoulder. It felt weird. My armpit was on the same level as the ball of her shoulder now, which meant I ended up sort of snuggling her into my body. And our faces were even. I tried not to let it put me off.

"In other words, you're ready to kick some demon-cat butt, right?" I said lightly.

"Damn straight," she said, with a sharp nod as her arm went briefly around my waist to hug me back.

We let go of each other and looked away. I blinked rapidly, carefully ignoring Jack's surreptitious sniff.

Hikaru appeared in the same place Jack had, vaulting

up to join us. "Yamato Mio-dono!"

I groaned. When Shinobu called me that, it was cute. Not so much with Hikaru. "Do I look like a lady to you?"

"More like a ninja princess," Jack soothed.

I gave her my look. "Not helping."

"Tough luck," Hikaru said. "Now you've earned the court's recognition you have to act a certain way. That means all titles all the time from here on. Get used to it."

"Fantastic. What's going on, anyway?"

"Turns out that as soon as His Majesty got Shinobu's call for help and realized there was a Nekomata on the loose, he sent spies out to track its movements in case it tried to break through into our realm. They just came back. The beast's gone to ground. They think it found a lair."

I rubbed my forehead. "Is that a good thing or a bad thing?"

"Good, because if it's picked a permanent hiding place, that's where Jack's sister will be. Bad, because they only stop hunting when... Well, when they're full."

Jack and I both cringed.

"Ick," Jack said.

"More than 'ick'. If it's managed to feed that much, its powers will be at their peak. The lair might be a bit tricky to get into. Lucky for you, we're coming along." He smiled, a bright flash of teeth that reminded me of his devil-may-care attitude when he'd first turned up in my parents' back garden. That felt like years ago.

"Are we ready to go then?" Jack asked eagerly.

"I think so. But before we go anywhere, the king begs a word with the sword-bearer."

"Lead on, She-Ra," Jack said. "We'll follow slowly, so you and His Foxy Majesty can chat."

Shinobu somehow managed to get a step ahead of me as we headed down off the terrace, and directed a fierce glare at anyone who happened to be in my path, clearing them out of my way.

"Hey, Hikaru," Jack said behind me, her tone deeply casual. "Mind telling me what that whole, er, kissing thing back there was about?"

"If you don't know, I don't think I can tell you," he replied, a little quiver of nervous laughter in his voice.

"Oh. Well. So probably there's something about me that I ought to, um, tell you then—"

I nearly slipped and plummeted down the side of the bowl on my face. *Right now? You're going to break his heart right this second?*

"Don't," he broke in hastily. "Not before we go to fight. Whatever you want to say to me, and whatever I want to say to you, should wait until your sister is safe and we're not both holding deadly weapons."

There was a little pause.

"OK."

Phew.

306

We reached the bottom of the terraces and Shinobu and I sped up, leaving the other two behind as we approached the low hill. The king, still in fox form, was back in his place on its brow. Midori and Tetsuo, on the other hand, were gone. Araki and Hiro were back in their human shapes and stood to attention at the base of the hill. They bowed deeply when they saw me coming.

The king dipped his head for half a second. I bowed back to him, but interpreted Shinobu's quick warning glance to mean that I shouldn't return bows from underlings. I'd gone up in the world. In more ways than one. *Who knew that all I had to do to get respect was blow a place up with my crazy-ass sword and grow four inches in thirty seconds?*

The katana's hilt quivered under my palm, as if it was laughing.

"Yamato Mio-dono," the king began gravely. He was firmly back in formal mode, though the power of his voice had been dialled way down. Or maybe it just affected me less now. "In answer to your request for aid, I am sending fifty of my strongest and bravest with you tonight. Your fight is a vital one. Find the Nekomata and rid London of its foulness, and you will have erased any debt incurred for the loan of my people in this battle."

He hesitated, then gave a foxy shrug. "I also send with you my most beloved grandchild, against my will, I might add. I've tried to talk him out of going but, short of confining him to his den, I don't think I can. He's as brave and pig-headed as his mother ever was. He'll put himself in danger just to prove he's strong enough to handle it. And so I ask you to take care of him for me. Make sure he comes to no harm and we shall all be indebted to you. Will you promise to do this?"

I saw Araki and Hiro's surprised looks. Clearly this was not an idle request.

No pressure then.

But we weren't going into some desperate, last-stand type of situation here. The Nekomata was a horrific, terrifying monster, and I shuddered just remembering it, but I had fifty Kitsune on my side now. Shinobu was right – anyone would lay odds on kitty getting made into fox kibble before the night was out. We ought to be able to keep Hikaru from doing anything stupid while we were at it.

I bowed again. "I will do my absolute best, Your Majesty."

The king showed his fangs in a small, sharp smile. "Having seen a sample of your power, I am content with that."

"We move out on your command, Mio-dono," Araki said.

I quickly checked to make sure Jack and Hikaru were ready and then nodded to Araki in what I hoped was a businesslike manner. "Then move out!" I said.

Araki let out a high, ululating cry. The Kitsune stamped in unison and turned to face the king, forming two, long ranks.

At the king's feet, a string of electricity sizzled up out of the grass. Then came another, and another. They waved in the air, unfurling and stretching like living things. They reminded me of speeded-up footage of growing plants I'd seen on nature programmes. The tendrils of lightning touched and wound together, forming a sort of wreath on the side of the hill. A wreath of elephantine proportions.

The grass framed by the circle of electricity shimmered and faded away, leaving a gaping black hole, wide enough for several people to walk through side by side. Araki lifted her arm and shouted again. The soldier Kitsune repeated her shout and marched forward.

"You might want to close your mouth," Hikaru whispered directly behind me.

"You might want to stop sneaking up on me before I put a bell on you," I retorted, pressing a hand to my heart.

"Careful. He'll get all excited," Jack said dryly.

I appreciated the effort she was making and awarded her a laugh, albeit an unconvincing one.

Shinobu sighed in mock exasperation. "Children, please. Must I separate you?"

Hikaru grinned a sharp grin. "No way. In it together, Mio said. Where you go, we go."

"All must obey the ninja princess." Jack spun the glaive in her hands, watching the last pair of Kitsune disappear into the shadowy gateway. We moved forward as one. Jack and Shinobu fell in behind me, with Hikaru bringing up the rear.

"Farewell." The king's voice drifted after me as I stepped through the opening. "And may the gods show you kindness. Whatever kindness they have…"

CHAPTER 21

UNSEEN ARMY

It was a tight fit Between, and the light from the amphitheatre disappeared behind us as soon as we were through the gateway. There was a moment of utter blackness. I could hear Jack grinding her teeth and the breathing of dozens of people packed in all around me. Then a circle of light bloomed ahead. In a tight, organized formation, with no pushing or scrambling, the Kitsune moved through the gateway.

I emerged onto a wide road, with the blocky white shapes of warehouses and tall, barbed metal fences shielding industrial yards on either side. Yellow sodium streetlamps illuminated the gleaming metal spires of cranes poking up above the street. Beyond them, the moon was nearly full and painted a rusty off-white by light pollution. The shadowy ranks of Kitsune were neatly arranged by one of the fences.

Hiro detached himself from the back, bowed to me, then focused on something above my left shoulder. I turned just in time to see a dark circle snap shut, revealing a mound of construction debris.

"Where are we?" I asked.

"As close to the Nekomata's lair as we could get," Hiro said, looking around with his usual bright, interested expression. "The rupture beneath the king's throne is the most versatile one we have, but it still needs a certain amount of green matter to anchor to." He gestured to tufts of sickly looking grass and weedy flowers that poked out from among the wreckage of bricks and broken chunks of concrete and sand.

A car turned onto the road and drove towards us. My hand crept to the hilt of the katana as I watched it approach. The car's headlights blinded me for a second, then it was gone. I blinked and let my hand fall away from the sword. The warmth of the hilt lingered on my palm.

"Chill, my lady," Hiro said. "They can't see you when you're with us."

"No one could see us earlier either – when we were running from those cats. It's freaky," Jack said.

"No, it's normal," Hikaru corrected her. "We're only half here now. One foot in this world, one in the next. That's part of using spirit magic in the human realm. People – people who've never been exposed to our magic, I mean – find it nearly impossible to notice us or process what they've seen if they do. It's the same with any creature not indigenous to this realm. We're veiled from mortal eyes. We can break through it if we really want to, by touching a human skin to skin or getting in their face and looking right into their eyes. But most of the time it's better not to be seen. Having your police after us is the last thing we need."

"All right, fine. Let's just get going," I said. The sword, its saya pushed through my white sash, was humming faintly. It was eager.

The Kitsune army reformed around us, and we moved down the street at its head, with Araki and Hiro prowling ahead of me, and Shinobu, Jack and Hikaru behind. I looked around as we walked, trying to work out where in London we were. It was completely unfamiliar. If I had ever been here before it would have been in daylight, when everything was different.

Traffic roared in the distance. Another car passed us without slowing. A barge hooted somewhere out on the invisible River Thames. The steady stomp of our feet made those other sounds, those familiar London sounds, seem unreal. This city, with its bright lights and busy people, clubs and hotels and roads, well lit and wide awake even at this time of night, seemed unreal. It had nothing to do with us, with the unseen army that marched grimly towards a battle with a monster no living person but us had seen in five hundred years.

We were of another time and place. A hidden London of shadows, and silence, and sword points.

Hiro and Araki turned left. I stopped dead, and the army came to a halt behind me. Directly ahead, illuminated by floodlights, was a massive, brick structure with four circular, white towers that glowed in the darkness.

Jack let out a huff of surprise. "Is that…"

"Battersea Power Station?" I finished.

"It is the fortress that the beast has commandeered for itself," Araki confirmed.

Jack muttered, "Crap."

Which just about summed it up.

When they said "lair" I had a mental image of, say, an abandoned house or a creepy alleyway. Those would have been bad enough – but at least they would have been easy to get into, and no one would be watching or getting in the way. All right, Battersea wasn't actually a working power station any more, and all the dangerous bits of machinery had been cleared out years ago. But it was a London landmark, a tourist attraction, surrounded by walls and checkpoints and with regular patrols of security guards.

"Cat-breath *commandeered* this place?" Jack asked. "We had to sign a book and wear badges just to get in!"

"You've visited the lair before?" Araki asked, surprised.

"It was a school day trip," I said absently. "Some arty people had set up a gallery in the main hall. Jack's right

314

– I mean, how did the Nekomata get past the guards?"

There was a short, uncomfortable silence. I looked around to see everyone giving me pitying looks. A couple of brain cells fired up and supplied the answer to my question.

They only stop hunting when they're full.

"Those poor men," I whispered. Their families probably wouldn't even realize they were missing until tomorrow. After that, it would be a lifetime of missing them.

All my fault.

Shinobu found my fingers where they were clenched on the sword hilt. I let my eyes fall closed for a heartbeat as he briefly clasped my hand, soaking in the tingling warmth of his wordless touch. Gratitude – and something else, something I didn't want to try to name right now – flooded through me. It straightened my back and lifted my chin. *OK. OK, I can do this.*

I opened my eyes and looked at the place again.

In most places the beige brick wall that surrounded the old power station was topped by a steel mesh that took the barrier to nearly twelve-feet high, but here on the road there was a lower section of metal fencing, including the security gate, all covered in warning notices and health-and-safety signs. It was just a bit higher than my head. It made me dizzy to realize that meant it was probably about six feet.

"How are we getting in?" I asked.

In answer, Hiro and Araki stepped forward and knelt down, each of them cupping their hands for me to use as a step. I forced myself to ungrit my teeth because clearly I was expected to set an example for the troops here – but I was never going to get used to using people's hands for a step.

I put one booted foot gingerly into Hiro's palm. He supported my weight easily. I reached up and caught the crossbar about six inches below the spiked points of the fence shafts and lifted my other leg. Araki supported it and boosted me up. For an instant I was paralyzed with panic: *spikes, spikes, spikes, oh heeeelp…*

But then I realized that my upper body was already past the spikes and my arms weren't trembling under the strain of holding me up. It seemed like the easiest thing in the world to lift my boot out of Araki's grip, lodge my heel on the crossbar between my hands, balance there in a crouch, and then drop down to land lightly in the concrete yard.

I looked around. Beyond the old power station, the river stretched out, glossy black and streaked with white-and-orange reflections, topped by a slightly unfamiliar view of the familiar city skyline. There it was. The real world.

A world that Battersea was no longer part of.

I had seen this place before. I'd seen pictures of it

taken at night. But it had never looked like this. I would bet my entire savings account that any normal humans who came this way tonight would find their eyes passing right over it, their attention wandering, until they forgot they'd ever glanced at the old power station in the first place. Its outline wavered as if I was staring at it through cloudy water filmed with oil. Nothing – not the lines of bricks and windows or the shapes of the towers, things that should have been straight and reliable – would stay still to be looked at. Everything here was changing. *Receding.* The stink of the beast breathed off it.

The old power station was like us now. Halfway in the next world. But the next world for the Nekomata wasn't the spirit realm.

It was the Underworld.

My muscles tensed, ready for battle. I turned round, impatient for the others to arrive. Then I blinked. I'd climbed over that fence? With just a leg-up?

Holy crap, I am a ninja.

Jack's face appeared behind the spikes. She wore a grimace of effort as she dropped her glaive over the top, then scrambled after it. Shinobu came next. No surprise that he vaulted over with one hand and landed with a mere bend of his knees. A wave of Kitsune warriors swarmed after him, making the human defence seem about as insurmountable as a steep kerb.

"With these guys helping, taking the Nekomata out

is going to be a piece of cake," Jack said as she walked up next to me, looking back at the fox spirits admiringly.

"Bloody, screamy, stabby cake," I agreed.

It took about thirty seconds for that idea to go right out of the window.

Hikaru dropped down casually and trotted towards us … and staggered. He caught himself straight away, but the movement was so uncharacteristic that I looked at the ground to see what had tripped him. There was nothing there.

"Huh. I thought… What?" Hikaru put his hand to his head.

Behind him another Kitsune tripped, but this one hit the concrete and didn't get back up. Araki, who had nearly reached us, suddenly slumped to her knees, shudders wracking her body. Hiro weaved sideways. The charge of fox spirits crumpled as if they had been clotheslined.

"Mio!" Jack cried, grabbing Hikaru as he wobbled. Shinobu went to help her.

I swore. "Back! Get back over the wall!" What was the word I was looking for here? *Oh, right.* "Retreat!"

Shoving, dragging and even in some cases lifting bodily – which answered the strength question, because, yes, I was definitely stronger – we managed to get the Kitsune back over the fence. Araki was so out of it that it took me, Shinobu and Jack working together to bundle her across the spikes.

As soon as we were back on the other side, most of the Kitsune began to perk up again. They stood around looking indignant, grumbling and swearing as they got their balance back and the colour returned to their faces.

"At ease," Hiro mumbled from where he sat in the middle of the road, his head between his legs.

Hikaru, apparently none the worse for wear, took off his long, white coat and wrapped it around Araki, who definitely was. We eased her down to sit on the pavement next to the giant NO PARKING sign. She was grey-faced and clammy looking, fine trembles making her fingers slip as she tried to pull the coat closer around her.

"Araki, what's the matter?" I asked, kneeling next to her. "Tell me how to help you."

"Can't," she gasped out between chattering teeth.

Hiro crawled towards us to sit cross-legged on Araki's other side. His tails were twitching and his brows were a straight, angry line, but his hands were careful as he tested Araki's pulse and peered into her eyes.

"I think she will be all right in a few moments," he said. I noticed that he looked older suddenly, and his speech patterns had turned formal. He must make an effort to seem so young; stress had made him revert to a more natural way of expressing himself. "The Nekomata is more powerful than we thought. It laid a trap for us in the ground. The moment we breached its barrier it began to sap our magic. The oldest were the most badly affected. I've never felt anything like it. It must be incredibly ancient."

"I don't get it," I said as I absently rubbed Araki's back. "The thing only has nine tails, like your king."

"His Majesty is nine hundred years old. Spirit animals stop growing tails when they reach one thousand years old," Hikaru said. "Most don't reach that age – we may not die of natural causes, but there are plenty of other hazards to take us out. Once you pass a millennium your power goes up exponentially."

"So you're saying that thing could be thousands of years old?"

"That is how it felt to me," Hiro confirmed.

"No," Shinobu said decisively, and we all turned to look at him. "I have fought this creature three times now. It is a terrible beast, yes, but there is no way any of us could have won, even once, against a creature as ancient as you say. It would have swept us aside like dust."

"Yeah, he's right," Jack said. "Mio and Shinobu sliced the thing up, like, a few hours ago. And it ran from your fox fire then too."

"Perhaps some other force – some other being – is lending it strength," Hiro said slowly, troubled. "But what that may be, I cannot say."

My Mistress, the Nekomata's voice crooned in my head.

I forced myself to speak up, pushing the unsettling

memory away. "These protections. They didn't seem to get to me. Jack, what about you?"

She nodded. "Didn't feel a thing."

"I was also unaffected," Shinobu said.

"So then the trap is like the mirror image of the one that caught us when we passed into the spirit realm," I said, working it out as I went. "It's keyed to react to magical creatures, but not humans. Which makes sense, since … well, humans are the Nekomata's prey. Most of us aren't a threat to it, and it wouldn't want to keep free food from wandering in."

"It makes little difference," Shinobu pointed out. "The thing is sure to have placed more magical protections on the building itself. If the Kitsune are unable to breach the walls, then none of us will be able to get in."

"Calm yourselves," Araki said, lifting her hand. The grey tinge was beginning to leave her face, though she still looked pale. "The creature may have the aid of some unknown ally, but we are not powerless either. Our lack of knowledge merely made us incautious. We can break through this trap if we join together. And even if we are unable to enter the lair ourselves, I am sure we can make it possible for Mio-dono and her companions to do so."

"What? We can't send them in there on their own!" Hikaru burst out. "They need us! That thing is a nine-tails. That's why they came to us in the first place. We should go back and get more help."

"We don't have time for that," Jack said firmly. "My sister is in there and that thing is going to kill her at dawn. I'm getting her out, even if I have to claw the walls down with my fingernails."

Hiro stood and laid his hand on Hikaru's shoulder. "This enemy must be faced and defeated. We cannot keep our allies from the battle which is theirs merely because we are unable to fight alongside them."

I looked away from the expression on Hikaru's face. It was too painful.

"We'd better hurry it up then," he said after a second, shrugging away Hiro's hand. "Dawn isn't far off."

The words acted on the Kitsune like a war cry. Even the ones who still looked weak and tottery got up and joined hands, making a neat, square block of bodies in front of the gate. Hiro ushered us to the back and then went to the front to help Araki up with an arm around her shoulder. Hikaru hesitated, clearly torn.

"Brace yourselves," he warned. "This could get a bit – showy."

Then he followed Hiro and put his arm around Araki's waist to steady her.

I stood on my tiptoes between Shinobu and Jack and watched Araki take a few deep breaths. She lifted her face to the sky and began to sing.

It was a strange sound, low and wavering, but beautiful. Fox tails waved gently, hypnotically, in the air behind them. As the other fox spirits joined their voices to Araki's, the small hairs on my body once again began to stir. Their eerie song gradually gained strength, vibrating through my teeth, my bones, through the katana. The sword rattled against my ribs, and I pressed it tightly into my side with my arm to keep it still.

"Mio," Jack whispered on my left side. "You still remember, right?"

"Remember what?" I whispered back reluctantly, not wanting to disturb the delicate magic of the foxes' song.

"What we said about Rachel and the sword. If it comes down to a choice, you put Rachel first."

Lightning began to spark on the wall and fence ahead of us, flickering and dancing along the lines of the mortar and twining around the vertical metal struts of the gate. I stared at the gathering electricity and remembered the white fire that had burst from the katana and swallowed Midori's lightning. I remembered an amphitheatre full of immortals blown right off their feet by the power of the explosion. I remembered the fox king's parting smile that had held both anger and respect, and a tinge – just a tinge – of fear.

I remembered watching suns die in the shadow of the sword's column of blinding light.

Shadows and blood will devour this world...

It had seemed simple before, at the house. Not even a choice, but a certainty. I knew now that, no matter what,

I couldn't let my friend, my friend's sister, die. I would fight for Jack and Rachel. I would kill to keep them safe. I would die if I had to.

But would I give up the sword?

Even if I knew that Rachel would be safe, that Jack and Shinobu and I would be safe, even if I knew that by doing it I would buy everyone I cared about some temporary safety … what then? What about the future? The rest of the world? I had seen what the katana could do. The Nekomata was a creature of complete evil. It would be the equivalent of handing over a nuclear bomb that could kill millions to save a single person.

Blood and shadows… Shadows and blood…

Horror made cold sweat break out on my face as I realized that Jack was asking me for the one thing that I didn't think I could do for her.

"You know I'll do the right thing," I said, through numb lips.

Jack gave me a sheepish, sidelong look. "Yeah, I know. Sorry."

I'm the one who's sorry. So, so sorry…

A glance at Shinobu, standing solidly on my right, told me that he understood exactly what the exchange had been about. I wanted to demand reassurance. I wanted to ask him if the sword had already changed me, or if I had always been this cold and ruthless, underneath. But I couldn't say a word. Not in front of Jack. And

I wasn't sure if I wanted to know the answer anyway.

Shinobu leaned towards me, his voice nothing more than a brush of warm breath against my ear, a comforting rumble low in his chest. "You are Yamato Mio-dono. You are the sword-bearer. You *will* do what is right. What is necessary to keep us all safe."

For the second time his hand brushed over mine on my sword hilt, and then fell away.

But what was right? What was necessary? Would I really care about the world if the people I loved – Jack, and Rachel, and my parents – weren't in it? Could I make that choice?

What would I be if I couldn't?

What am I if I can?

Thunder boomed, and I jerked violently. The security gates flew open with a crash, health-and-safety signs dashed to shards against the bricks. The Kitsune's lightning swept down and hit the ground inside the wall with a sizzle like ice cubes falling into a deep-fat fryer.

"One step forward!" Araki yelled hoarsely.

We advanced. The wave of lightning pushed ahead of us. When I squinted I could see something like smoke – heavy, oily coils – burning off the ground where the lightning crackled.

"One step forward!" Araki called again, more strongly this time. She had pulled free of Hikaru and Hiro's supporting arms.

We passed through the gate. The electricity flared up ahead, standing nearly a foot high in some places. There was another crack of thunder. The black smoke was a thick cloud now, boiling in the air above the flicker of the Kitsune's energy.

"More power!" yelled Araki.

Several Kitsune whipped their tails. Balls of lightning – red, bluish, golden – sailed up over the line to smash into the lightning wall, and were consumed by it. The lightning roared higher.

"Two steps forward!"

It was working. *Working!* We were only a hundred yards away from the cat's lair now. We wouldn't have to go in there alone. I wouldn't have to make that terrible, desperate choice between my friend's life and the rest of the world—

I heard glass breaking.

Above the lightning and the black smoke, the tall windows of the power station were bulging out, shattering under the pressure of what pressed against them. A dark mass burst through and spilled down the walls, seething across the concrete towards us. It wasn't until the first sleek bodies leapt over the lightning wall and hit the Kitsune like a battering ram that I realized what I was looking at.

It was just too crazy.

"Not again!" Jack said, bringing her glaive down.

Cats. Thousands of them. Thousands upon thousands.

The organized lines of the Kitsune army dissolved into chaos as the fox spirits were forced to let go of one another to defend themselves. Swords flashed. Guns barked, muzzle flares reflecting from the dull maroon bricks of the power station. I saw the shapes of larger animals among the sea of cats, snarling and sending bolts of lightning flying, and realized that some of the Kitsune had lost it completely and reassumed fox form. Screams and yelps filled the air.

The cats broke through the last Kitsune line and leapt at me, Jack and Shinobu, clawing and spitting. I abandoned any thoughts of fluffy kittens, drew my sword and fought back. It was that or go down under the weight of them. I saw a Kitsune near by get swallowed up under a pile of least thirty felines and leapt towards him, slashing and stamping, using every bit of my new strength to haul him out. He emerged covered in blood, panting, his eyes wild, and transformed under my hand, turning into a black-and-white, double-tailed fox, the size of a Doberman Pinscher. With a bloodcurdling growl, he turned on the cats, ripping through them with teeth and lightning balls. The scent of charred meat made me gag. I backed away.

The Kitsune's wall of lightning was dying down, flickering and fading away without the foxes' joined power to feed it. Black smoke surged through the gaps.

Araki appeared beside me, a modern composite crossbow in one hand. Blood dripped down the side of her face. I didn't know if it was hers.

"Follow me!" She turned and charged directly at the power station, loading and shooting the crossbow like a machine, streaks of lightning shooting from her tails and clearing a path through the black smoke before us. Shinobu and Jack flanked me as I chased after her. Hiro shot out of nowhere, a gun in each hand, and fell in beside her, adding his lightning to hers and his bullets to her arrows. A second later Hikaru was there too, bringing up the rear, dispatching pursuing cats with his swords.

The six of us hit the wall with a clash. Araki and Hiro leapt towards the nearest door – a large, rusted metal thing that looked like it had been used for heavy goods – and started trying to force it open. Their combined blue-and-gold lightning flashed and crackled around the doorway with the Nekomata's magical protections. Hikaru planted himself behind us to fend off the tide of cats that was flowing back towards the power station. With showers of rust and a deep, protesting groan, the metal door began to rise up. An inch. Two.

Hiro's eyes rolled back in their sockets. He collapsed against the wall, black smoke wreathing his ankles. The golden lightning on the door suddenly flickered and died.

Araki yelled his name, but her voice was drowned

out by a crash from above. Broken glass pinged off the concrete, and then a new wave of cats fell down on us. I grabbed Jack with my free hand and dragged her into the shelter of the doorway just in time. Shinobu whirled in after us. Araki fell under the onslaught, swearing and fighting, her electricity crackling all around her.

Before I could go to her aid, Hikaru shoved past us, dropped his swords, and slammed both his hands onto the door.

The impact rang through the rusted metal with a hollow boom. Thunder cracked deafeningly. Sizzling, white energy detonated around the entrance, and the door shot up with a protesting shriek, sticking at the level of my hip.

"Go, end this!" Hikaru shouted. "And don't die!"

I ducked and rolled under the door. Jack and Shinobu followed me.

The door fell closed behind us with an earth-shuddering clang.

We were in the Nekomata's lair.

And there was no way out.

CHAPTER 22

THE FORTRESS
OF THE CAT

I froze where I was, still crouched, katana drawn. My eyes, scorched by the lightning outside, were almost blind. The sudden quiet after the sounds of battle made my ears hum. Behind me, I heard Shinobu ease to his feet. Jack wheezed softly. None of us spoke.

What now?

What now?

Gradually my breathing slowed. My shoulders slumped. I put one hand on my knee and pushed myself up, still holding the blade defensively. Jack blew out a relieved breath. There was a soft, metallic whisper as Shinobu stepped forward, having sheathed his wakizashi. The katana he had borrowed from the Kitsune was in his right hand. The three of us stood abreast.

We looked around.

It was a tall, narrow space, about as long as a football

pitch but a quarter as wide. The ceiling was held up by columns of dingy, cracked tiles, white at the top, with a wide strip of darker tiles halfway down, and then painted white concrete below. In the roof, a long strip of broken glass, marked with metal rods, ran the length of the chamber, letting in a blaze of brilliant, white light that seemed far too bright to come from the moon. The light fell in jagged fragments, highlighting a patch of weeds in the cracked cement floor here, a pile of crumpled papers there, but failing to break through the deepest darkness. Wonky metal safety barricades, slumping and bent, sectioned some parts of the space off. An abandoned hard hat gleamed in one corner, vivid yellow, like a baby duck about to be swallowed by the shark shadows around it.

"This isn't where we came on our school trip. The place is huge. I think the main part is probably ahead," I whispered.

Shinobu began: "We need to be cautious—"

"We need to find Rachel," Jack broke in. Her voice was edgy and insistent, as if she thought I might have forgotten why we were here.

Her instincts are good. Guilt stabbed at me. I clamped my teeth together.

"I know," Shinobu told her. "But like all cats, Nekomata are territorial. Now that it has claimed this place, it will have started to build a nest somewhere. That is where we will find your sister."

And the Nekomata, I finished silently.

Jack took a step away from me, her glaive at the ready. I reached out to grab the back of her coat.

"No," I hissed. "We have to stick together. Together we have a chance. Alone, it can pick us off and eat us like chicken nuggets."

"Look, I might have bleached hair, but I'm not actually a blonde," Jack said impatiently. "And I'm not, like, three either. You can let go of me. I won't wander away, for Christ's sake."

I released her, flexing my fingers. The katana vibrated gently in my other hand. I lifted the sword, trying to make out the flame-shaped ripples in the silver cutting edge. It was too dim. But I could still feel the energy moving under the surface of the metal. Every moment that I carried the sword, I became more attuned to it. This was not a great time to have doubts, but it was suddenly very clear to me that bringing the katana anywhere near this battle was a huge risk. Voluntarily carrying it right into the Nekomata's nest was probably insanity.

But without the sword's power, none of us were getting out of here alive.

"Um, hello?" Jack said. "Are we searching or what?"

I met Shinobu's eyes over the edge of the blade. I knew that he would walk out of here with me right now if I asked him to – if we could find a way out. But Jack wouldn't. And neither would Rachel.

I nodded.

He drew his second blade again and moved into the lead. Jack and I fell in behind him, wordlessly recreating the arrow-head formation we had seen the foxes use earlier today. We moved slowly through the space, skirting the light coming in through the ceiling.

Shinobu and I both jerked at a scraping sound to our left. Jack lifted her hand apologetically, gesturing downwards. She had stepped on a crushed drink can. As we watched, she warily used the blade of the glaive to poke through the heap of rubbish near her, then shook her head. Nothing.

I jumped again as something uncoiled in the corner of my eye. My head snapped round. Just an empty patch of concrete. A moment later I caught a fleeting glimpse of darkness unfolding above me, but when my gaze darted up, there wasn't even a shadow to explain what I'd seen.

It would have been comforting to think I was imagining stuff, but I'd learned by now that when I saw something, no matter how freaky, it was a bad idea to ignore it. I had the impression that the shapes of the tiled columns, the height of the ceiling, the cracks in the cement floor, were warping around us, ever so slightly. The Nekomata's magic, or the magic of its Mistress, was rippling through this place like radiation, affecting everything it touched. I could feel it slithering around me. I shuddered.

The katana's blade caught a ray of light and flashed. The slithering sensation faded a little. I squeezed the silk-wrapped hilt in thanks.

"You all right?" Jack asked.

I nodded. "You?"

She shrugged. The movement was jerky. Her mood worried me, but there was nothing I could do to help her. The only thing that would fix Jack was getting Rachel back safe and sound. If we didn't manage that, she would never be right again.

Don't make me choose. Oh God, don't make me choose...

The chamber was big, but it was echoingly empty. It didn't take long to search it, and even before we had checked the last pile of rubbish, I knew that the Nekomata was not here. The space was too open and accessible, too close to the edge of the compound. The Nekomata would have picked a better place for its nest. Somewhere it could easily trap and dispatch intruders.

We had to go deeper into its lair.

There was a tall, arched opening in the wall between two of the pillars. Shinobu eased through it first. He hesitated, a tiny puff of air leaving his lips. As soon as I crossed the threshold, I understood why. A soft, ghostly sensation – like hair or feathers, or some other thing I didn't want to think about – trailed across my skin. The sense of unseen things moving all around me intensified.

I tried to ignore the disturbing feeling and assess

the space we were in. This chamber was at least three times as large as the last one, but it was built on the same lines – long and narrow. If it had ever had a roof, there was no trace of it now. Holes gaped in the brickwork beside the glassless windows. Battersea's four famous white towers loomed, one at each corner, above walls that climbed at least a hundred feet above us into a mishmash of scaffolding, catwalks and metal caging. Beyond the nearest tower, the moon blazed in a black, starless sky.

It wasn't the same moon I had seen as I'd approached this place. Or the same sky. The light was too bright and the blackness too black. In one of those strange jumps of intuition, I knew: this was the sky of Yomi.

Despite the brilliance of the moonlight, stark, impenetrable shadows lurked everywhere, beneath the metal platforms and on the huge heaps of rubbish – discarded papers, rags, plastic bags and dry leaves – that stood nearly as high as my head.

I became aware of my breath, and Jack's and Shinobu's, clouding in the air before us. It hadn't been that cold a second before. Maybe the lack of ceiling had something to do with the sudden dip in temperature.

Or maybe not.

"It's here," I whispered.

A low, shuddering moan of wind moved through the chamber. Crumpled papers and leaves rattled on the concrete floor as a cloud drifted across the moon, plunging us into sudden, total darkness.

We waited, stock-still but shivering, in the black. The wind moaned again. Rubbish stirred as if it was alive, and I had the helpless feeling that reality was rearranging itself around us while we stood frozen at the epicentre. My skin prickled with goose flesh.

A ray of moonlight broke through the cloud, falling on something tossed carelessly into the heap of debris beneath a metal platform near by. Something that hadn't been there a moment before.

A human body.

"Rachel!"

Jack's scream shattered the unnatural silence. I heard her feet scrape on the cement as she ran forward.

The cloud shredded fully away from the moon, revealing the dark shape of the Nekomata clinging to the underside of the platform above Rachel.

My voice and Shinobu's blurred into one shout of fear as we charged after Jack. She reached the platform a couple of steps ahead of us and skidded underneath, throwing her body protectively over Rachel's. The Nekomata's face, split in two by a row of needlelike fangs, dropped down into her view.

Jack bared her own teeth.

"Get away from my sister!"

The glaive flashed, and the Nekomata yelped –

I thought more in surprise than pain – as a trickle of black liquid dripped down its cheek.

Shinobu ducked under the platform, blades slicing the air around him like a silver halo. The demon flicked its head away from his weapons, neck elongating until it was as thin and flexible as a swan's. The movement put it right into the path of my katana. I lunged. The Nekomata flinched at the last second, and what should have been a killing strike only grazed it.

The monster howled. Tentacles shot over the sides of the platform, and the beast heaved itself up and away. Its spreading shadow fled into the complex network of scaffolding and cages on the wall.

"Stay with Rachel!" I shouted at Jack.

I sheathed my sword, grabbed a scaffolding pole and began to climb. My weight made the whole jerry-rigged mess jerk and wobble. Above me, there were rusty metal bars – the rungs of a ladder welded to the wall. I transferred my grip to one and jumped across.

The scaffolding kept shuddering. I looked down before I could think better of it and saw Shinobu coming after me.

"Rachel is alive," he called up to me. "Unconscious, but alive."

I let out a shuddering sigh. "Oh, thank you. Thank you."

I wasn't sure if I was talking to him, or God, or what.

It didn't matter right then. Rachel was safe and Jack was with her.

I waited as Shinobu leapt onto the ladder beneath me. My last sight of his face showed that it was filled with the same determination I felt. Hikaru had summed it up perfectly. *End this. And don't die.*

It was now or never.

The Nekomata, perfectly camouflaged in this landscape of black and silver, had disappeared somewhere above us. All we could do was climb. The tinny sound of our feet on the metal rungs made it hard to listen for sounds that might give the demon's location away. *Where is it?*

The ladder passed into a section of criss-crossed metal reinforcements, like cages, that spread out on either side of us, bisecting the wall. Rickety-looking scaffolding was attached in the gaps, as if someone had started, but not bothered to complete, maintenance work. A wide, metal walkway was bolted on above that, obscuring my view of what was beyond.

A black talon the size of a bowie knife lashed at my face.

I didn't draw the katana. At least, I don't remember doing it. It was just in my hand, and my hand was moving.

The Nekomata's claw hit the flat of the sword. I reversed the blade and sliced sideways, biting into flesh.

A high squeal of pain echoed out of the shadowy scaffolding a few feet away, to the right. It had been waiting for us.

Shinobu surged up behind me, his body caging mine as he caught the rung above my head with his left hand. The borrowed katana was in his right. Two more claws slashed at us. Shinobu deflected one. I let myself drop a rung and thrust my katana out into the space under Shinobu's arm. The blade sliced the top five inches of the Nekomata's second claw neatly off.

Something coiled around my ankle over my boot.

Shit.

I grabbed hold of a rung, the hilt of the katana clanging into the side of the ladder.

The tentacle on my leg *pulled*.

A grunt of pain burst out of my lips as I clung to the rusted metal. The rivets securing the ladder to the wall groaned. My hip, knee and ankle felt as if they were popping out of their joints.

Shinobu swung away from me, then grabbed a scaffolding pole to the left with his free hand, and launched himself over it in a move I'd only seen watching the Olympics. At the height of the swing he let go. He flashed past me, sword extended, and sliced through the tentacle holding my ankle. As I snapped into the wall with the release of tension, he caught a pole to my right. Safe.

Another claw whipped by me, heading for Shinobu's

unprotected neck. It ripped the tie from his braid before I brought my boot back and stomped on it with all my might, crushing it into the wall. Once it was trapped, I slashed it to shreds.

It was too much for the Nekomata. With a furious hiss, it rushed out of the scaffolding and scuttled up the wall, disappearing over the side of the walkway above us.

Shinobu swung himself back one-handed to land on the ladder below me again.

"Thanks!" I puffed between my teeth as I carefully resheathed the katana and started climbing.

I caught a glimpse of his heartbreaking smile "Thank *you*, Mio-dono."

I reached the metal platform and climbed through the hatch, with Shinobu half a second behind me. We both drew our swords.

The walkway ran the entire length of the wall. It was about six-feet wide in most places, with a safety rail mostly intact along its edge. We were nearly half-way up the wall here. Through the broken windows and gaps in the brickwork, the city's lights twinkled. The Nekomata was nowhere to be seen. I craned my neck warily upwards.

"Where did it go?" I muttered.

The platform shook, sending me to my knees. With an eye-watering shriek of rending metal, the section of the catwalk behind us – the hatch we had just climbed through, along with a chunk of the welded metal ladder below – ripped away. I flung my arm up to shelter my face as brick dust and sharp scraps of metal the size of coins rained down over us.

"Goodie, goodie. Now I have you just where I want you."

The platform shook again as the demon landed in front of us. Through the haze of dust, I saw its terrifying, smug grin. All nine tentacles were back in place and waving vigorously.

Shinobu stepped forward, flanking me where I knelt. We exchanged glances. I could see he was thinking the same thing as me: *All that running away was a blind. It lured us up here.*

"My Mistress scolds me for playing with my food," the demon said. "But I think playing is what makes life worthwhile, and I can't help my nature." Its voice was smoother, richer now, more like a purr. And it was bigger. Much bigger.

Hikaru had been right; the thing had gorged itself. But it was more than that. The Nekomata was drawing on its Mistress's powers – whatever they were – and turning the old power station into a portal to the Underworld. It had created a rupture here that would probably only close with its death. We weren't in the mortal realms any more.

The monster was in its element.

I climbed warily to my feet, keeping the sword at the ready.

"Tsk." It shook its head at me with mock sadness. "Nothing to say? So disappointing."

My hands clenched around the grip of the sword and I willed the blade not to waver. "If you're waiting for me to start crying and quivering with fear, you'll have a long wait, Tibbles."

"So you are not frightened at all?" it asked. "Not even a little? Not even for your precious friend?"

"What?" I snapped suspiciously.

"In a few moments, the illusion that I made for her will fade away, and then she will come looking for you and for her sister," the demon said dreamily. Its pale, pink tongue ran over its fangs. "All of this exercise has made me hungry again. Perhaps I should have a little nibble…"

One of its tentacles wormed up to point at a section of the wall above its head. At first I saw only a patch of shadow. As I blinked, the shadow faded, and I let out a tiny, involuntary gasp. The Nekomata's deep, gloating chuckle rolled through the air.

Rachel hung helplessly from the wall above the ripped-out section of the platform, wrapped round and round with thick, sticky black strands that stretched away from her body like a spider's web. The only parts exposed were her upper face and dangling feet in their pink slippers. Her eyes were huge, staring and blank with horror.

"It has been many long years since I had a pair of sisters," the Nekomata said. "No, I do not think I shall eat her just yet. She and your friend will be a special treat for me. Once you are dead."

The tip of my sword was making juddery figures of eight in the air. I couldn't speak. Jack was down there, desperately trying to wake an illusion that would disappear and leave her grieving and alone in the shadows. The Nekomata had set that up on purpose just to torture us. To torture her.

"You – you—" Hatred strangled my voice.

Shinobu stepped forward, dragging the Nekomata's attention to him with a slash of his wakizashi. "Enough talk. If you want the katana so badly, come and take it."

"So kind of you," the monster purred. "I do like an invitation."

Tentacles unfurled, blurring through the air. A wall of deadly, black daggers. I hurdled one that shot at my feet, sliced through one that came at my face, ducked, rolled and came up behind the monster. I brought my blade round in a whistling, two-handed overhead strike, aiming at what I hoped was the thing's heart.

Three tentacles jumped out at me, forcing me back. The Nekomata's head spun 180 degrees to grin at me. "Try again!"

On the demon's other side, Shinobu let out a shattering battle roar. The flash, flash, flash of his swords was like distant lightning – he cleared a path through the tentacles and arrived at my side just in time for a deadly new tangle of black talons to shoot at us. It was as if neither of us had bothered to lift a blade at all.

I spun away, jumped, struck, and cried out as one of the claws sliced across my collarbone. The long, deep cut welled with blood and the demon laughed. I threw myself into the fight again, fury rising up inside, hot and dark, trying to take over. I fought it down as I fought the monster. I had to use my head here if I wanted to win. I had to *think*.

Shinobu and I whirled and slashed, cutting through tentacle after tentacle, deflecting attack after attack. The Nekomata opened more cuts on my arms, stomach, upper legs. Shinobu took a blow to the head and blood splattered down his eyebrow and flew out, streaking the side of my face. Slowly, the Nekomata forced us back, back, until we were defending the jagged, ripped-off edge of the platform, with the rail to our right and a fifty-foot drop at our backs.

I had tamped the anger down, but now despair began to seep into its place. No matter how many tentacles we cut off, no matter how many slices we managed to open on the vast mantle of the demon's body, it simply regenerated. It was holding us off almost lazily, playing with us, just letting us tire ourselves out. We weren't doing enough damage.

It was too strong.

A high-pitched, terrified wail echoed off the walls. I jerked away from the Nekomata, my back hitting the broken safety rail as I looked up.

The black, gummy substance was peeling away from Rachel in thick hanks. Her upper body and arms were already free. She was struggling desperately, tearing at the web wherever she could reach it, uncaring of the fact that it was the only thing preventing her from falling off the wall to her death.

"Rachel, stop!" I shouted. "Stop! We're coming to get you – you have to stop struggling!"

It was as if she couldn't hear me. Her eyes were rolling in their sockets, her body convulsing with terror.

"Oh, she will not listen to you, dear," the Nekomata said. It drew back a little, to enjoy the scene. "I've told her all about my plans for her, you see. She would rather break her neck."

A choked sound of rage echoed from my throat. I couldn't find any words that would express the fury I felt.

"Awful, isn't it?" the demon said in a tone of mock sympathy. "You cannot win, you know. You never could. Simply give me the sword and I will fix her there, safe and sound. It would only take a moment…"

"It lies," Shinobu warned softly.

Rachel screamed again, struggling harder than ever.

This is it.

It was here. The moment when I was supposed to prove myself. But prove myself to be what? A hero? Or a human being?

In a split second of forever, the future unspooled in my mind, and I saw my choices, all the actions that I could take, the endless possibilities, spinning out from this instant.

I could keep my promise to Jack. I could dive forward and try to catch Rachel.

But the katana was in my hand. If I caught her, I would spear her through and kill her.

I could drop the sword.

But the Nekomata would snatch it up the moment it left my grasp.

And then we would all die.

First me and Shinobu, probably quickly, under the monster's talons.

Rachel and Jack, slowly and horribly.

The Kitsune, our allies who fought for us beyond these walls, who had followed me in trust with no idea of the terrible battle they would face.

Then a wave of others, innocent people who had no idea this battle was being waged, who had never even heard of a Nekomata. Anyone, everyone, who came the monster's way.

And once the demon was sated, it would hand over the sword to its Mistress.

Shadows and blood.

The end of the world. The end of everything.

All my fault.

With a sharp snap, the last thread holding Rachel in place gave way. Rachel plunged downwards, towards the gap in the platform...

Shinobu dropped his swords and threw himself into her path.

He sailed over the gap in the walkway, his arms closing around Rachel's small form in a perfect rugby tackle. The pair of them landed on the other side of the walkway with a crash that made the entire structure shudder. The broken sheet of metal tilted, and they skidded, sliding inexorably towards the edge.

One of Shinobu's hands shot out and caught the safety rail, jerking them to a stop just as their feet zoomed off the metal platform.

The Nekomata and I both stood frozen, staring in disbelief.

Shinobu turned his head towards me. "Help?"

Relief and exhilaration set my body on fire. *He did it.*

I began to run towards them, intending to make a flying leap over the gap, force the tilted section of walkway back down, and then haul them away from the edge. With my body's new strength, reflexes and instincts, I knew I could make it.

But I wasn't fast enough.

One of the Nekomata's tentacles whipped past me. It caught the broken section of safety rail that Shinobu hung from and snapped it off as easily as I would snap a plastic school ruler.

My own scream deafened me, enveloping me in roaring silence.

I saw Shinobu fling Rachel away from him as he plummeted from the walkway, his long hair and torn clothes flying around him. I saw Rachel land in a mound of rubbish, bounce, and roll safely to the floor. I saw Shinobu land in the tangle of metal wreckage below, mouth opening in a shout of agony as the scaffolding pole broke through his chest, blood bursting out around the wound like a red flower. I saw his eyes search for me. I saw them go dull. I saw his body slump and his head fall back.

I watched him die again.

Again.

Peaceful eyes, full of the sky, not afraid…

It should have been me. I should have tried to save her. It should have been me.

Laughter, rumbling and beautiful, and a crooked smile…

I didn't hold onto him.

Arms around me, sheltering me, the smell of smoke and pine…

I let him go.

A green blade flashes down in the red light…

I should never have let go.

The shadows writhed around me. Darkness crept up the walls as the wind moaned through the power station again. The clouds slowly swallowed the moon. Below, everything was silent except for Rachel's ragged sobs.

"All alone with the big, bad cat. Poor thing, so sad," the Nekomata purred mockingly in the black. Its voice took on a falsetto, singsong note. *"Oh, who will save me now?"*

"No one," I forced the words out between my lips like shards of broken glass. "No one can save you from me now."

The katana burst into flames.

Light bounced from the walls, showering rainbow-white sparks like an arc welder. Brilliance flooded the derelict building as cold rage flooded me. I let the anger take over without a fight, let it surge through every fibre of my body and soul, banishing the howling pain that I didn't dare examine, banishing fear and doubt, everything. It no longer mattered if I lost control. Shinobu was dead and I didn't care any more.

I didn't care.

Not about right or wrong, or what would be left of me when this was done, or even saving the big, stupid, clueless world. Nothing mattered. Nothing except *killing this thing.*

I disappeared in flame and fury.

Now... the katana whispered, its metallic voice gentle in my mind. Now, you are ready for me.

CHAPTER 23

THE NIGHT ITSELF

The Nekomata's smile widened as I walked towards it. Its eyes were fixed on the sword. "Oooh. Pretty, pretty."

Tentacles shot from the demon's mantle, surrounding me with vicious, black talons.

I went from walking to leaping in a breath. As my feet left the walkway, I spun, blade flashing and blurring faster than I could follow with my own eyes – a whirlwind of white fire setting everything near me alight. A moment later I landed in a crouch, arm fully extended to the right. In my hand, the katana's flames spat and fizzled as they ate the black substance coating the blade.

The Nekomata drifted backwards, surprise and the beginnings of pain distorting its face. Then it cried out.

Blood spurted everywhere, spraying the pitted walkway. Nine tentacles dropped away and landed with a drumroll of meaty thuds.

I had disarmed it.

The Nekomata fell, thrashing and screaming.

The heavy mass of its mantle twisted in on itself, struggling to regenerate from such a massive amount of damage inflicted in such a short space of time. The wounds, which had been cauterized by the katana's supernatural fire, smoked and bubbled like slugs sprinkled with salt.

Slowly I straightened up, bringing the blade forward. The monster whined, its shadowy flesh slithering away from the pale flames. I took a step towards it.

"No! Wait!" it cried.

Another step forward as I located the centre of the mantle – and the demon's heart – in my mind's eye. I lifted the katana.

A thin tentacle ripped itself free of the Nekomata's creeping blackness and wrapped around my forearm. It wrenched me from my feet, shook me like a ragdoll, and flung me away with all the strength the monster had left.

I went flying, hurtling towards the wall. In one second I would be a smear on the brickwork.

Not a chance.

I snapped my arms out to slow my flight and, with an effort that made every muscle scream, forced my body to twist, and flipped head over heels in midair.

My feet hit the wall with an impact that made the bricks buckle.

I pushed off.

The katana's pearly flames streamed around me, propelling me down towards the walkway like a shooting star. My body burned with the furious cold of its energy. I no longer knew if I wielded the blade or it wielded me. We were one form, one will, one desire with a single cutting edge.

We were death. Vengeance. Power.

We were the night itself.

An uncanny, high-pitched cackle, like a hyena's laugh, burst from my throat as I plunged into the centre of the Nekomata's mantle.

My blade penetrated the demon's heart with a wet pop and punched straight through the metal platform beneath. The Nekomata convulsed, contracted; its shriek of pain filled the chamber.

I knelt on the beast's congealing body, feeling its death throes tremble through the hilt of the sword into my arm.

"She is coming," it gurgled. The needlelike fangs were bathed in blood again. Its own blood this time. "My Mistress. She will take – the sword. Kill you. Kill everyone."

I eased to my feet, planting one foot on the walkway and the other firmly on the Nekomata's chest, and pulled my sword free. It screamed again. I watched dispassionately, unable to summon up the slightest tinge of pity or remorse, as the mantle knotted up on itself, its glossy surface turning dull and hard, like rock. Its shape was changing, becoming smaller, more catlike.

"She will – kill you – all," it hissed.

I reached down and grabbed a handful of the lank, black fur on its head, putting myself nose to nose with the monster. I waited for its eyes to focus on me. "Not if I kill her first."

With one stroke, I cut off its head.

Under my foot, the demon's body solidified, cracked and crumbled into a thick heap of something like ashes. My arm sagged a little as the head I held hardened to stone. I stared into the dead eyes of the monster. Then I dropped the head and let it roll away.

The katana's flames flared up with new brilliance, rolling down the hilt of the sword to engulf my arm. They tickled faintly as they sank under my skin.

I have decided I like you. We're a good team, you and I, it sang in my mind. Let's make a little deal. You give me what I want, and I will give you power. Limitless power. The kind of strength that mortals have dreamed of since the dawn of time. I will tell you all of my true names. All you have to do is help me.

"What do you want?" I asked dully.

What all sentient beings want, my beautiful, simple child, it breathed softly. Freedom...

I nodded. Then I rammed the blade, fire and all, straight into the saya. The flames snuffed out as if I'd dumped water over them. "Piss off."

The moon burst through the clouds in long fingers

of silver. I staggered and crumpled bonelessly onto the blood-splattered metal, clinging to the safety rail as the walkway seemed to quake beneath me. Sharp bubbles of rust nipped at my skin, reminding me that I was, most unfortunately, still alive.

A few minutes later, I heard movement below, and then voices.

"Mio?" Rachel called unsteadily. "Mio, are you – are you all right?"

"Stay still, Rachel. Mimi! Do you need me to climb up to you? Mimi?" That was Jack.

I took a couple of deep, shuddering breaths.

"Mimi! Say something! Are you OK?"

"I'm fine. Just give me a minute." My voice came out flat and dead. It was the best I could do.

I forced myself back up onto my feet. The demon's head was a dull, grey lump against the safety railing. If I wanted to take it down with me – and instinct said that it would be a dick move to leave it rolling around here for anyone to find – then I was going to have to tuck it into the front of my kendogi and tie it in place with the sash. And that meant carrying the katana and climbing one-handed.

Because the world just hasn't screwed with me enough today.

Making sure to touch only the saya of the sword, and with the demon's head crushing my chest painfully,

I located a section of intact scaffolding and climbed, very, very slowly, down the wall of the power station. Jack and Rachel watched nervously, shouting out encouragements and advice. They weren't helping, so I ignored them.

My muscles twitched and spasmed. My joints clicked. My head pounded, and the vertebrae of my back ground against one another with each movement. I felt a hundred years old and I decided that being ancient was not as easy as the Kitsune made it look.

When I reached the ground, a tear-stained Jack and a pale, tottery Rachel were waiting. They enveloped me in hugs, stroking my hair, patting my back, whispering thanks and comforting words.

After I'd waited long enough to let them feel better, I shrugged them off and dropped the demon's head and the katana into a pile of rubbish. Then I went to Shinobu.

It was just like my dream. The dream that had shown me his face for the first time.

Blood on his chest. Arms lying outstretched, hands palm up, as if he was waiting for someone to take them. But his eyes no longer reflected the sky. His lips no longer framed my name. He was gone.

I didn't hold on tight enough. I let him go.

Gently, gently, *gently*, I eased him off the pole that had gone through his body, wanting him away from the ugly pile of metal wreckage. I fumbled as I tried to lift him. He flopped to the ground and I fell with him, unable to let go.

I clutched his face to my shoulder, burying my nose in his soft, smoke- and pine-scented hair. My body locked into silent, shaking sobs. Tears poured down my face. They made tiny, pattering noises as they landed in his hair and on his neck.

Shinobu. Shinobu. My Shinobu.

The grief was too intense. Too extreme. I knew that. In many ways Shinobu was still a stranger. I had met this man, this boy, less than twenty-four hours ago.

But I had always known him. I had been waiting for him every day of my life. That was why I had dreamed about him before I even realized who he was. Why I had been compelled to take the sword. I had needed to find him and set him free. That was what I had been born to do.

For five hundred years he had been trapped, waiting for me. Now, before he had tasted freedom for a single day, he was dead. He had died saving Rachel, a girl he had never even met. He died because he didn't want me to have to make that choice, the choice that would have broken my heart.

He died for me.

I would never know how it felt to kiss him. I would never get to work out all the strange, conflicted, frightening things he made me think and imagine and feel. Never hear about his family and help him grieve; never help him build a new life. I had let him slip through my fingers. He was lost in the darkness again. This time for ever.

I didn't hold on tight enough. I should never have let him go.

Jack and Rachel sat one on either side of me, shocked and upset. I had to move. They needed me. I couldn't sit like this all night, mourning for this boy, this beautiful boy I'd barely begun to know. Dawn was coming. People would be coming.

I breathed in Shinobu's smell, rubbed my wet cheek against his hair. *Just a moment more. One moment more.*

"Mio," Jack said softly. "Mio, please…"

A tiny, hurt whimper choked from my mouth as I forced myself to loosen my grip on his body. He slumped over my arm. I kept our chests pressed together, hiding the wound that had killed him.

My hand slid round to cup his neck under the heavy fall of his hair. The skin of his nape was soft and vulnerable. My other hand crept up to cover his eyes. I was sure if I tried to close them, they would snap open again on their own. I couldn't bear to see that.

I pressed my lips gently against Shinobu's. I was shivering with cold, my mouth wet with tears – but his skin still felt faintly warm. I could imagine, almost, that he was only sleeping. That I could feel breath heaving in his chest. That the thick lashes brushing my palm fluttered.

Fingers stroked gently across my cheek, tucking my hair back behind my ear. Warm, long fingers. Too long, far too long, to belong to Rachel or Jack, who would never have touched me that way anyhow.

Shinobu's lips opened under mine.

"Is this the afterlife?" he whispered.

I let my hand fall from his face and stared down into his deep, smoky eyes.

This isn't real.

"No…" I managed to say, my voice breaking. "This isn't heaven."

He smiled up at me, a crooked smile of shock and joy and disbelief. There was no filter there, nothing between me and his feelings as he said, "I beg to differ."

His arms lifted and wrapped around me, clutching me as tightly as I'd held him moments before. He brought our mouths together again. My sobs shook him.

His lips were so warm – *so warm* as they parted mine. His breath set my cold cheek on fire. Trails of sparks flowed gently down my back in the wake of his hands as they moved to clasp my waist.

Sobs turned into gasps. He drank them from my mouth.

"Shinobu."

"Don't cry," he whispered against my lips. "Don't cry, my love. My Mio. Always mine…"

He'd never called me that before. Oh God, it was real. It was real.

He was alive.

He was mine.

"I don't understand."

Rachel's bewildered voice broke in like a hammer

shattering a window pane. I jolted, and Shinobu reluctantly let me ease back as we both remembered that we weren't alone. Jack, speechless for once, stared at us in wonder and disbelief. Rachel was so pale that the bruise-like shadows under her eyes looked black.

"I don't understand," she repeated. "He died. He was dead. It went right through him."

It went right through him.

I reached apprehensively for the front of Shinobu's kendogi. It was soaked with blood with a great ragged hole in the centre, just under his breastbone. But the skin beneath it was smooth and golden, without a scratch.

Something flickered in Shinobu's eyes and was gone before I could make sense of it. "Well," he said dryly. "It seems I am not quite human after all."

Shuffling and stumbling, we made our way out of the central chamber of the old power station and through the tiled outer room. By the time we reached the loading door where we had come in, a soft radiance, completely different from the blazing, unnatural glow of the moon, was beginning to filter in through the skylights. It made the metal barrier look extremely solid.

"Er. Any ideas?" I asked.

I was leaning on Shinobu heavily. At this point he was the fittest of us all. I was too grateful to point out the irony, especially since he was carrying the stone remnant of the Nekomata under his right arm and holding me up with the other. I had the sash back around my waist and the katana shoved firmly into it.

"I suppose I could try to climb up to one of the windows and see what's going on out there," Jack volunteered.

"No!" Rachel clutched at her sister's arm. She hadn't let go of Jack since we'd started moving.

If the pale light of approaching dawn made the door look solid and intimidating, it made Rachel look practically transparent. I couldn't even imagine what she must have been through in the time that the monster had her all to itself. She had excellent reasons to want us all to stick together. But Jack was biting her lip, clearly torn.

I was torn too. I wanted out of here. Even more than that, I wanted – needed – to know what had happened to the Kitsune army who had risked their lives to help us.

"I'll—" Shinobu began.

A deep, rumbling groan of metal cut him off.

The loading door was winching up, dust and dirt spiralling off it and turning to gold as the sunlight spilled into the opening. A slender form ducked under the barrier, a long, white sword in each hand.

Hikaru.

He stared at us all for a second, speechless. Then he grinned.

"Hello, honey," he sang, putting the swords away. "Did you miss me?"

Jack let out a wobbly laugh. "Not in a million years, hairball."

"Aw. You're so mean to me. Did you turn the kitty into roadkill all by yourselves?"

"Mio did," Jack said. "The rest of us just enjoyed the show."

Rachel, her wide eyes taking in the white, leather outfit, the swords, guns, and most of all the tail, opened her mouth. But instead of the big-sisterly demand for information that I was expecting, all that came out was a little sigh. She let go of Jack's arm and dropped like a stone.

Hikaru darted forward and caught her before she hit the ground, swinging her up into his arms. That was the second time a hunky guy had grabbed her in a matter of hours and she hadn't been able to enjoy it either time. Her life really sucked.

"Thanks," Jack said.

"All in a day's work."

The door finally finished lurching upwards. On the other side, fifty bruised, bloodied and extremely worn-out-looking Kitsune peered anxiously in at us. At the front, Hiro and Araki – both of whom were sporting brightly coloured bandages which looked like they had come from someone's fancy kimono – stepped forward into the opening and bowed.

"You have succeeded, Mio-dono. Our people are in your debt," Araki said. "Name the favour you would ask of us."

It took me a moment to remember what she was talking about. *The king's promise.*

"Can I – um – think about that for a while? If that's OK? There's ... something I really need to do right now."

With Shinobu beside me, I picked my way stiffly outside, across the desolate, windswept plain that used to be Battersea's car park, down to where the land dipped and the river lapped at the concrete barrier.

Wordlessly, Shinobu held out the demon's head.

It felt a lot heavier now than it had up on the platform. I backed up a bit, took a run and threw the remains of the Nekomata as far out into the water as I could.

It was enough. With a huge splash – bigger than it should have been, really – the head sank.

I stared at the ripples it had left behind.

"And don't come back."

The foxes swiftly hustled us away from the site of the battle. In front of the Kitsune, I was determined to support myself on my own two feet, so Shinobu made do with holding my hand tightly. Every time I flicked a glance at him, I could see that beautiful, crooked little smile tugging at his mouth. That, and the occasional casual bump of our shoulders, was enough to keep me walking, despite aching muscles, bruised bones and muzzy head. We didn't talk much, though.

I had a lot of thinking to do. Like ... what was I

going to wear? After everything we'd just been through it seemed a strange thing to worry about, but the fact was that I no longer owned any clothes or shoes that would fit me. That was going to be awkward to explain to my parents. And I had to come up with an explanation for the wreckage the Nekomata had made of our kitchen too. One they'd buy without grounding me for the rest of my natural days. Or at least until I was thirty.

Then there was Shinobu himself: a five-hundred-year-old warrior boy who had been plonked down here in twenty-first-century London just in time to save me. He was invisible to most people. He might even be immortal. And I'd fallen head over heels in love with him, and he with me, in less than twenty-four hours.

Finally – most worrying of all – there was this gnawing, bone-deep certainty which echoed through me with every step I took away from the scene of our bloody victory. The knowledge that the fight to keep the katana safe was definitely.

Not.

Over.

Luckily, once I'd laid out each of these unanswerable problems in my head, I realized I was too exhausted to do anything about any of it. So I just smiled back at Shinobu, and swung our joined hands between us, and marched beside him through the sleeping streets of London in the light of the rising sun.

ACKNOWLEDGEMENTS

Usually when I get around to writing my acknowl-
edgements I indulge myself with at least one
paragraph in which I complain about everything. How
long the book took to write, how the characters never
listened to me, and how, yet again, I nearly gave up halfway through and went off to herd yaks instead.

But this time around, I'm stunned to realize that I
have nothing to whine about. Despite the fact that this
was my first urban fantasy and my first exercise in writing a non-standalone book, *The Night Itself* was probably
the most pure fun I've had writing since I left school.
I've loved every minute of it. It feels like this story and
these characters were a gift that the universe lobbed at
me, and I was so lucky that my hands happened to be
outstretched at the right moment, ready to catch them.

In order to encourage the universe to make a habit of

random gift-lobbing, I feel honour bound now to mention all the people who lent their time and talents to unwrapping the present and making sure it got to you readers as swiftly and efficiently as it did.

First, a special thank-you to Nancy Miles, my wonderful agent, who has made being a writer – and making a living from being a writer – easier and less stressful in every way since I had the amazing good fortune to snare her for my own. I can't imagine what I ever did without her.

Further thanks are owed to:

Annalie Grainger, Wonder Editor, who loved this project from the first, and as usual helped to improve everything I came up with in so many amazing ways that I would have to write another book in order to thank her adequately.

Dr Tina Rath, for quoting the poem *The Bedpost* by Robert Graves, which was the original spark of inspiration for The Name of the Blade, and Rachel Carthy, whose considerable expertise in Japanese myth and folklore helped me fill in all the puzzling blanks in my knowledge of Kami, Yokai and their mysterious ways. These ladies are both owed additional gratitude for putting up with all the questions from a non-Londoner on the nooks and crannies of their city. Any mistakes or inaccuracies or liberties I have taken with geography are my responsibility alone!

The Furtive Scribblers Club as a whole, who (as always) lent me their simply astonishing cumulative powers of mental acuity and allowed me to bounce ideas off them until they must have felt completely battered. I'm not going to name names this time because I always leave someone out! You know who you are.

The wonderful, wonderful team at Walker Books, including (but not limited to!) the delightful Hannah Love and Paul Black for their PR mojo, Maria Soler Canton for the spectacular cover of *The Night Itself* – and for putting up with me being a Nightmare Author from Hell throughout the whole process – and, of course, fiction publisher Gill Evans. It's been an exciting year, hasn't it?

My Twitter and blogging pals, who responded to the news of this trilogy with such excitement and offered me bags of encouragement, including sternly ordering me off Twitter and back to writing a time or two: Liz D. J., Emma D., Viv D., Lynsey, Sarah, Enna, Jenni, Laura H., Elizabeth May, Daph, Misty, Ashley, Kaz Mahoney, Lauren, Sophie R., Keris Stainton, Keren David, Rebecca J. Anderson, Jackie Dolamore, Lee Weatherly, Sarah Rees Brennan and many more! I wish there was room to list everyone, but even if you're not named here, I hope you know how thankful I am. Special thanks to the Dear Readers of my blog, the most faithful and intelligent fans a writer could ever have.

Bel Downing, who generously bid in the Authors for

Japan charity auction and won the right for her name-sake to die horribly at the claws of one of the most evil villains I've ever dreamed up. I hope your demise was as satisfying for you to read as it was for me to write!

And, finally, to my own family, most especially my parents. Always, in every book, whether I say it or not.

Love *The Night Itself?*
Love Zoë Marriott's other books!

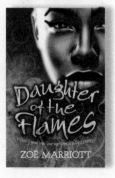

The Name of the Blade, Book Two:
Darkness Hidden is coming summer 2014

Visit Zoë online at **www.zoemarriott.com**
and **thezoe-trope.blogspot.com**
Follow her on Twitter, **@ZMarriott**